23 AND You AND Me

23 AND YOU AND ME

MICHELLE McCRAW

CITY OWL
PRESS

23 AND YOU AND ME
Forza Family, Book One

CITY OWL PRESS
www.cityowlpress.com

Cover Design by MiblArt. All stock photos licensed appropriately.

Edited by Tee Tate.

For information on subsidiary rights, please contact the publisher at info@cityowlpress.com.

Print Edition ISBN: 978-1-64898-478-5

Digital Edition ISBN: 978-1-64898-479-2

Printed in the United States of America

 CITY OWL PRESS
Escape Your World ◆ Get Lost in Ours

To my cousins Mary and Ralph, who helped plant the seed that bloomed into this story.

Prologue

SEPTEMBER, NEW YORK CITY

"Walking on Sunshine" played on Sunny's mental soundtrack like she was the heroine in one of her mother's rom-coms. It didn't matter that rain pattered against her umbrella and splashed against the tan brick building, making it even drearier inside. Or that the puddle she'd stepped in on her way there from the subway had soaked through her brand-new boots. Sunny was at the studio to make magic.

Not movie magic like her parents. But television was still acting, and this season her name appeared in the opening credits. Someday she'd make the leap to movies, and they'd be proud of her. They'd be one of those families that showed up for each other. Who hugged in public, not for the cameras, but because they loved each other.

Cue the soundtrack.

Odile met her in the lobby with a Dior J'adore–scented kiss on the cheek. She'd worn it ever since those Charlize Theron commercials and even dyed her long hair the same golden color, trying to look timeless. Too bad *New York Bomb Squad's* blue-tinted lighting turned it greenish. "Should be an exciting week."

As they walked through the security turnstile, Sunny waved at

Guillermo, the security guard. "You mean painful. Why didn't they hand out the scripts last week?" She could memorize song lyrics on the first try, but the technical lines she had to say as a forensic analyst wouldn't stick. "Want to run lines tonight?"

"Sure. I guess it's a good thing we lowly analysts won't have too many." Odile nudged her as they stepped into the elevator. "Though maybe you'll get another sexy scene with Curt."

Sunny cocked a hip. "Think I can convince him to pop a breath mint this time?"

Odile's hazel eyes gleamed greenish, though it might've been the weak elevator lights. "Ingrate. I'd give my left boob to be promoted to the star's girlfriend."

"I know. I'm grateful. Really." It had been a dream to land the role as Curt Suede's TV paramour. She'd watched him drive fast cars, seduce women, and walk away from explosions since she was a preteen.

"You should be," Odile said as the doors opened onto the studio. "Remember how quickly it can all go to shit."

The hum of the room stopped. All eyes, cast and crew, landed on Sunny and Odile. But there were no smiles, not like at the table read for her first screen kiss with Curt.

Their somber faces made her itch. "Happy Monday, everyone," she called. Odile went left, toward one end of the U-shaped table, and Sunny walked to the center, next to Curt.

"Morning, Curt." She set her water bottle next to her copy of the script.

Curt grumbled and guzzled his coffee. He was shit before nine a.m.

Sunny persisted. "What's going on? Why is everyone being so weird?"

Curt grunted and raised his cup. An intern scurried over and replaced it with a full one.

"Thank you." Sunny smiled at the intern since Curt never did.

He sipped, then said, "Big scene this week. You've got a lot of lines."

"I do?" She flipped open the script and scanned the pages. She had a lot of lines with Odile's character this week, digging into their friendship. She glanced up at Odile and smiled, but Odile hunched over her script, the fluorescent lights sparkling on her blond hair. Sunny scanned ahead until the word *explosion* leaped off the page. Odile's character had snipped the wrong wire.

Cold prickles washed over Sunny's skin. She knew they were approaching mid-season and needed to amp up the drama, but she hadn't expected this. The show often killed off its guest stars—in a fan-favorite drinking game, viewers drank every time a guest star appeared and then tossed back the rest of the drink when they died —but never a recurring character like Odile's.

The unfairness of it all bubbled into Sunny's midsection. Odile was doing good work on the show. She didn't deserve to have her part—her job—cut. And unlike Curt Suede, who'd be doing action shows until the day he died, Odile was approaching the dead zone of her career, where she'd be too old to play the sexy love interest but too young to play the wise mother. She'd be back out there auditioning, and why? For a pop in the ratings after the promos teased a very special episode?

Ed, the director, clapped his hands. "All right, everyone. Take your seats. Let's begin."

While she followed along in the script, Sunny glanced at Odile. Her back straight and her skin pale as marble, she looked more like a statue than the vivacious woman Sunny knew. The pages fluttered as she turned them.

When she read her final line, "Boss, we're out of time. I'm cutting it," her voice trembled. Then Ed read out the stage direction about the explosion, and silence descended over the U-shaped table.

"No!" Sunny rocketed to her feet. Under the force of everyone's stares, she repeated it. "No."

Ed raised his bushy gray eyebrows. "Is there a problem, Ms. Lafortune?"

Oh, shit. Ed is looking at me.

Her mouth moved before her brain engaged, following the

familiar pattern. "It's wrong. This is wrong." Odile was part of her family, the one she'd built in New York that was better than the real one she had in Los Angeles. Sunny would fight for her friend. "She doesn't have to die."

Ed's brows crashed down. "But it's the emotional punch we need."

"No," Sunny said. "We can find another way."

Curt's mouth gaped, and his coffee breath choked her. She could sit back down, meekly agree with Ed, and save her career.

No, she couldn't.

She laid her hand over the word *explosion*. "Having her recover from her injuries would be more emotionally satisfying."

"Her body parts are scattered across a city block," Ed said. "This isn't a Gwen Lafortune rom-com. Our audience of twenty-five-to-forty-year-old men want gore, tragedy, and revenge. Not happily ever after."

No happily ever afters. The story of Sunny's life. But she could try. For Odile. "Can't we give them both?"

"No, Ms. Lafortune. We can't." Ed's voice carried the flatness of finality. Like the flattened building the carpenters would be constructing for that scene.

"Then I can't, either." Tipping up her chin, Sunny walked out of the room.

Like the scene in that week's episode of *New York Bomb Squad*, she'd just made her career go BOOM.

Chapter One

JANUARY, SUBURBAN COLUMBUS, OHIO

This is it. After everything that happened, I'm going to die in a freaking golf cart.

Gabe gripped the steering wheel, his normally tan fingers turning frost-white, all his focus on keeping the vehicle from slipping on the icy curve and spilling out his family.

"I could walk faster than this," Uncle Bobby grumbled from the back.

"I couldn't." In the front passenger seat, Grandpa massaged his knee. "That's why we're riding."

"Leave Gabe alone." From the soft *oof* behind him, Gabe figured Aunt Pat had elbowed her brother. "You know he has—" Her voice faded to a whisper too low for Gabe to hear.

He didn't want to hear it. After five years of therapy, he was well aware of his own issues. He braked—slowly—and brought the cart to a skidding stop in front of the kiddie coaster. Clenching his jaw, he glanced at the low, snow-crusted lift hill, just to show he could. Then he turned his back to the sinuous steel structure and faced the Beach Island Board of Directors, also known as his family.

"We determined this one's in pretty good shape," he said. "The maintenance crew is checking each car and performing minor repairs on the track as the weather allows. Ramirez says they'll be done in about two weeks."

"Kiddie rides," Uncle Bobby snorted. His smooth cheeks were red from the cold. "I want to see the moneymakers. Twister of Terror. The Basilisk."

"Bobby." This time, Gabe witnessed Aunt Pat's elbow. For a woman who had to wear thick-soled sneakers to reach the you-must-be-this-tall-to-ride lines, she had a vicious swing. "We asked Gabe to give us a tour of the winter projects. Let him direct it."

Uncle Bobby muttered something under his breath and crossed his arms over the Beach Island Amusements logo on his fleece jacket.

"Guests under forty-eight inches should enjoy the park, too," Gabe said. Though he wished the kids would stay at home. He wished everyone would stay at home. Then Gabe wouldn't have to worry all the time about someone getting hurt. And maybe he could do what he wanted for a change.

"Right you are," Grandpa said. "Kids who ride this one grow up to ride Twister of Terror."

Gabe shuddered inside his extra-large down coat.

"Plus, they buy plenty of snacks," Aunt Pat said. When she nodded, the flower on her knit hat bounced. "Gabe's a smart boy. He's always done what's best for the park."

Gabe blew out a frustrated breath, which clouded in the icy air. At thirty, he hadn't been a boy for a long time, not since the board had asked him to shoulder the massive responsibility of the park nine years ago.

"Fine, fine." Uncle Bobby pointed over the trees to the wooden curve of Mystery Mountain. "But show us that one next."

Gabe narrowed his eyes at him. "Seat belt."

After Uncle Bobby refastened his belt, Gabe drove carefully along the blessedly straight path to Mystery Mountain. He fixed his eyes on the empty queuing area to avoid the towering hill.

"The team is checking the chain lift, same as every winter. Taking it apart, cleaning it, reassembling it. The cars, too."

"I'm glad we kept this one," Grandpa said. "Not too many wooden coasters left."

"'Cause they suck," Uncle Bobby grumbled.

Gabe silently agreed. The wood warped in the rain and again in the sun. Left unchecked, the coaster would become rough over time, leading to injured passengers. Ramirez griped about it constantly. Year-round, his maintenance chief dedicated a small crew to assessing and repairing this ride. Grandpa probably had no idea how much it cost to keep his pet coaster's ride smooth, even though Gabe called it out every quarter in the financial reports.

His phone buzzed, and while Grandpa and Bobby argued the merits of wooden versus steel coasters, he checked it. Another call from DN-YAY. He hit the Ignore button. He'd deal with that annoyance later. For now, he had a bigger concern: the hill to Twister of Terror.

He cast a glance at his passengers to ensure their lap belts were buckled—too bad golf carts didn't come with beefier restraints—and hit the accelerator. He hoped someone from Ramirez's crew had laid down some ice melt. Despite the cold, his palms started to sweat.

"Gabe, you going to take a vacation this year?" Grandpa asked.

"What?" Was the incline just wet, or was that a thin layer of ice?

"A vacation. You know, sunshine, sand, umbrella drinks?"

"No time," Gabe said through gritted teeth. "Less than four months to opening day." He gambled and accelerated to build momentum to climb the hill.

"It's your turn to go to the Expo this year," Aunt Pat said. "You can get your umbrella drink on in Orlando."

Crap. They'd skipped his turn last time. He'd hoped to pass on the Expo again this year. How was he going to get to Florida? He'd never survive a fourteen-hour drive. He pressed harder on the accelerator, making the tiny engine whine. "Why don't you go, Aunt Pat? I'm more of a beer guy."

"They have beer in Florida. Besides, you know I prefer the snow. I've already got my trip to Whistler planned."

If Gabe hadn't been steering the cart up the hill, he'd have shivered. He'd spent all his life in Ohio, but, unlike the rest of his family, he dreaded every winter. Why would anyone go somewhere even colder and snowier on vacation?

The cart's back half fishtailed, arrowing his attention back to the road. His pulse roared in his ears. *Straighten out. Don't tip.* The adrenaline pumping through him urged him to yank the wheel. Instead, he held it firm, steering gradually in the direction of the skid. At last, the cart leveled out, finally gaining purchase at the top of the hill in front of Twister of Terror. A shuddering cloud of his breath gusted out as he peeled his fingers off the steering wheel. He should've predicted that Aunt Pat and Uncle Bobby didn't weigh enough to counterbalance his mass in the front.

Uncle Bobby chuckled. "Way to give us a little excitement, Gabe." He stepped out of the cart. Gabe did, too, though his legs trembled. He wiped the slick of sweat from his brow.

"Yo, Gabe!" The safety gate clanged shut, and Tony Ramirez jogged out from the maintenance area.

Relief mingled with the dissipating adrenaline. The board would listen to Ramirez. Safety was his job. Gabe's jaw unclenched. "Ramirez. I didn't expect to see you out here today."

"I thought I'd show the board what we're working on here. Give you a break."

Gabe was still too tight-strung to smile at his friend, but he nodded. "Thanks."

Uncle Bobby and Aunt Pat followed Ramirez toward the blue steel monstrosity. Grandpa clutched Gabe's arm, bending him down closer to the old man's height. "I'll drive the cart back with your aunt and uncle. Why don't you head over"—he tipped his chin —"and pay your respects."

The warmth that rushed through Gabe's veins had nothing to do with the weak winter sunshine. Still, he checked his watch, his father's battered old Omega.

Grandpa said, "Don't worry. We'll meet you back in the office in half an hour. Take your time."

"Thanks, Grandpa." Gabe might not have looked much like the short, slender old man, but Grandpa always seemed to know what he was thinking. "See you later."

He meandered toward the circle of trees Grandpa had indicated. Stepping between them into Founders' Park always calmed him, even in winter with ice coating the young trees' branches and the flowers—yellow tulips for his mother—still resting underground.

He avoided the plaque and lowered himself onto his favorite bench, the one that faced away from Twister of Terror's steel corkscrew. He traced the round watch face on his wrist, the smooth, cool glass settling his nerves. He'd never looked much like his dad— too tall, too broad, too dark—so, instead of looking in a mirror to remember him, he came here and dug through his memories for images of Dad's hand clutching his smaller one as they walked through the park, of Dad's almost hairless arm with this watch on it. The watch he'd handed to Ramirez before— Before.

His phone buzzed again in his pocket. Again, he pulled it out. Dismissed another call from DN-YAY. A few minutes of peace was what he needed. No phone calls, no ice, no board of directors. No Theme Park Expo in flipping Florida.

A crack rang out, making Gabe duck his head. When an ice-coated tree limb clattered onto the next bench over, Gabe shut his eyes. Breathed deep to slow his racing heartbeat.

Pushing his hands onto his knees, he stood. He hefted the limb onto his shoulder and headed toward the park's landscaping shed. CEO or not, when there was work to be done, Gabe did it. He might not have his parents' light builds or their cold tolerance, but he'd learned that lesson from them.

If only they'd taught him how to enjoy their legacy, the park, without them.

"Gabe, what are you doing?"

Quickly, he straightened, tucking the snow shovel behind his back. He shouldn't feel guilty. He was watching out for his employee. Employees. "Clearing this ice."

Darlene crossed her arms and shivered. "The maintenance crew's on the way."

"They have important work to do. I've got this." He chipped at a hunk of ice on the sidewalk in front of the administrative office building. What if Darlene had slipped on her way in this morning? Or Grandpa? He'd never forgive himself.

She leaned on the doorjamb. "Tough meeting with the board?"

"No!" But his voice rose in that petulant way he hated. He cleared his throat. "It was fine. They're pleased with the work we're doing. You should go back inside. You're not wearing a coat."

"Neither are you. Come in here. You have real work to do." Carefully, she turned and walked into the Beach Island administrative office building.

Real work. That's what it was. When he was a kid, working at Beach Island, even when he'd been on vomit clean-up duty under Twister of Terror, had been fun. Now, it held nothing but bad memories. And spreadsheets.

Gabe leaned the snow shovel against the side of the building. He sprinkled a last trowelful of ice melt over the sidewalk and followed his assistant.

Darlene leaned on her desk. "You have a call with a new paper goods supplier at one. At two, you're interviewing a candidate for the entertainment director position. In the meantime, you need to review these." She picked up a stack of papers. "Applications for summer jobs. I've already screened them."

Gabe paused before he took the stack. Sure enough, the papers fluttered in her hand.

"You all right?" He scanned her face. She was a few years older than him, in her mid-thirties. Her skin was winter-pale, but it wasn't drawn with fatigue like it sometimes was.

"Course I am." She stared right back. "Are you?"

Shoving the papers under his arm, he looked toward his office door and its brass nameplate that read, *Gabe Armstrong, Chief Executive Officer.* "Of course. Why wouldn't I be?"

"Oh, I don't know. Bobby irritating you again about the safety improvements. Or...Riley."

"Who?" If she could pretend she wasn't having a flare-up, Gabe could pretend, too.

"You might think—"

His phone rang, interrupting her. Gabe pulled it out of his pocket. DN-YAY again. For a second, he weighed his options: another conversation about his ex-girlfriend, or a hassle with the sketchy DNA testing company that'd screwed up his results? "Sorry, I'm going to take this. I'll come check on you after."

"Don't bother. I'm fine." She circled the desk, lowered herself into her chair, and swiveled until her back was toward him.

Shaking his head, he walked into his office and closed the door before swiping to accept the call. "Gabe Armstrong."

"Mr. Armstrong, this is Sunny from DN-YAY. I'm calling about your test results."

Sunny? Was this company for real? Of course not. They'd already screwed up his results, telling him he was seventy-five percent Italian. The Armstrongs were originally from Scotland, and his mother's family was Danish. Who confused northern Europe with Italy? A company that employed *Sunny,* that's who. He should've known a DNA testing firm that advertised nonstop on Riley's favorite fake-reality dating show would be more sparkle than science. Their jingle—*DN-YAY, find out who you are to-DAY!* —tinkled through his mind.

"Did you run the test again?" After he'd gotten his results, he'd emailed Customer Service to demand a retest. Clearly, they'd mixed up his results with someone else's.

"We did, and we confirmed the results. You have two brothers and a sister, all still living."

"That's impossible. I was an only child." He snapped the blinds shut, blocking out the view of the nearby arcade and behind it, Twister of Terror.

"Mr. Armstrong." The woman's voice gentled, like she was talking to a small child. "Have you talked to your parents about the results?"

Kind of hard to talk to someone who'd been dead nine years. His blood went hot, and the peace he'd felt at Founders' Park evaporated.

"Why would I talk to anyone about it?" he snapped. "The results are wrong. You know what? Forget about it. Take me off—"

She spoke over him. "Mr. Armstrong, listen to me." Her voice dropped lower, like she didn't want to be overheard. "I've talked to a lot of people about their families, and things can get...complicated. We found the parents you listed on your information sheet in our database. We have their test results too. I'm sorry, but it's impossible for them to be your biological parents."

Not his parents? And when had they taken DNA tests? And why? His knees wobbled. He flung out his hand for balance and hit the back of the armchair by the window. Gripping the fabric, he eased himself into the seat. "What?"

Her voice went even softer. "You really should ask your parents about the test results."

"They're dead." The words cracked out of him like that snapping tree branch. He straightened in the chair, squaring his back to the window and the view of the roller coaster hidden by the blinds.

"Holy shit! Oh, I mean, I'm very sorry about that." He could almost hear her cringe over the phone line. "Do you want to talk to a genetic counselor?"

"Not unless they're going to rerun the test and explain what the hell happened the first two times."

"Look," she half-whispered, "DN-YAY has some issues, I'll admit it, but they ran your results three times. Your biological siblings are living in Las Vegas."

"Las Vegas?" That broke something inside him. He was from

Ohio, the Midwest. He'd never been to Vegas. He slumped in the chair. "I didn't want to take the test. It was all Riley's idea."

"Who?"

"Riley. We had the couple's version. Two tests. A Christmas gift."

"Oh!" When excitement bubbled in her voice, a spark of hope flared in his chest. "Maybe your tests got mixed up," she said. "Is Riley from Las Vegas? It could be his siblings we found."

"His?"

"Shit, I'm sorry. I'm new, and I'm screwing this up so bad." He heard skin slapping on skin like she'd covered her mouth. "I wish I could tell you what you want to hear. DN-YAY has its problems, but it's unlikely they'd mix up a man's test results with a woman's."

The hope fizzled out like the last mortar in Beach Island's Saturday-night Firework Extravaganza.

"We didn't even take them together. She saw all those damned ads. She said it'd be fun." Riley had wrapped the test packages in shiny silver paper with white polar bears wearing red scarves. The bears were doing un-bearlike things like sledding and holding candy canes in their paws.

Gabe didn't have a Christmas tree at his townhouse, but when he'd come home after work a few days after their breakup, Riley had left his kit sitting on the kitchen counter, next to her key to his place. The bears mocked him with their joyful Christmas grins.

"After she—after she left, I, ah, I took the test. Does alcohol affect the results?" When he'd swabbed his cheek on Christmas Eve, his saliva had to have been fifty percent Maker's Mark.

"No." She paused. "I'm sorry she left you." Her voice was so soothing, he almost believed she cared. "Especially at Christmas."

"Doesn't matter. It's a Hallmark holiday, anyway."

"Christmas isn't a Hallmark holiday!"

Who was this woman? She didn't sound like a customer service representative.

"Sure it is," Gabe grumbled. "Cards, wrapping paper, Black Friday. It's all about buying stuff." He'd fallen into that trap. That night at the restaurant, he'd had the black velvet box in his coat pocket. He hadn't had a chance to offer it to Riley before she'd stood up from the table and walked out.

"No, it's not. It's supposed to be about friends and together-ness. Family." Her voice took a wistful turn on the last word. "Oh."

Yeah. Oh.

"No one should be alone at Christmas." Her voice had lost all its former effervescence. "I should know."

In the beat of silence that followed, Gabe heard other, more stri-dent voices over the line. She was in a call center. He didn't know this person, and he shouldn't have been sharing his feelings with her.

"I wasn't alone." Somehow, it was important that she not feel sorry for him. On Christmas Day, he'd dragged his hungover carcass to Aunt Pat's like he'd done as long as he could remember, even before his parents had died. She'd made the same dried-out turkey she always had. No worries about salmonella. Those suckers could've never survived the too-long roast in Aunt Pat's Viking oven.

But if what this woman said was true, Gabe hadn't belonged at Aunt Pat's. Aunt Pat wouldn't have given a Brooks Brothers tie to someone who wasn't her nephew, would she?

Sunny from DN-YAY couldn't hear all the roiling that was going on inside him. "It's good you were with friends," she said. "Are you going to be okay?"

"I'm fine," he said. It was a phrase he'd learned after his parents died. People knew not to push once he'd said that. They knew they'd done their job by asking, and he'd done his by being self-sufficient.

"Are you sure?"

She didn't know the script.

"Positive," he growled.

"On the bright side, this means you have a second chance. At family. At love."

What had this call turned into? First she told him he had family in Las Vegas he'd never known about. Now she was going off about love? Maybe monosyllables would shut her down. It used to work on Riley. "Sure," Gabe said.

"So are you going to look up your bio family?"

Who was this Sunny person? Did her supervisor know she was so...so...pushy and unprofessional? He'd have sent someone like her to remedial customer-service training. "I don't think so."

"But what if they're looking for you? They all got tested. They checked the box to be notified of relatives we find. You didn't, so we won't contact them, but you should consider reaching out. Look, I..." She lowered her voice to a whisper. "Family's important. I always wished I had siblings, didn't you? Like on that show, *The Brainiac Bunch*. Now you have a chance to meet yours. I'll email you their names. It's public information since they checked the box. You can call them. Meet them."

Meet them? "No. Thanks." He hung up. It was warm in his office, but chills raced over his skin. *Thanks for dropping this bomb on me. Thanks for making me question everything I thought I knew about myself.* Could it be true? DN-YAY's website made all sorts of claims about their accuracy. But couldn't they be wrong about this? Some sort of mix-up. Maybe he hadn't sealed the envelope properly and someone else's DNA had gotten in with his.

But...what if she was right? What if everything he thought was his—his parents, Grandpa, Aunt Pat, Uncle Bobby, his cousins, Beach Island—wasn't?

Gabe stood and shoved his phone back in his pocket. The sweat-dampened sheaf of applications crinkled under his arm. He tossed the stack onto his desk—his dad's desk—*the* desk—and didn't even worry that some of them fluttered to the floor. He flung open the door and strode past Darlene.

"Gabe, what's wrong?"

"Nothing. I'm fine."

He snatched his coat off the rack and flung it over his shoulders, not bothering to change into his boots. He stomped out into the gray January afternoon, past the back of the arcade to the corrugated metal machine shop. Ramirez looked up, but when he saw Gabe's expression, he stared back down into the guts of the Mystery Mountain car he was working on.

Gabe crossed the room to the far corner, where a heavy chain suspended one of the cars from Twister of Terror from a steel beam overhead. He grabbed a wrench from the tool chest and cranked one of the exterior bolts. He didn't need any power tools. His anger would provide the torque he needed.

But even the whine of Ramirez's drill and the hiss of the welder working on the other end of the garage couldn't drown out the doubt that roared in Gabe's ears.

If he wasn't who he thought he was, did he even belong here?

Chapter Two

"Thanks." The line went dead.

Sunny ripped off her headset and tossed it into the corner of her cube. It wasn't even a real cubicle, not like the one her character, Sadie, had on *New York Bomb Squad*. Actually, that wasn't a real cubicle, either, since it'd just been part of the show's set. But DN-YAY, the real office in Ohio where Sunny worked now, put all the customer service representatives at white laminate desks with half-walls around them that looked like the study carrels at her old high school library back in California.

Why had she mentioned *The Brainiac Bunch?* She hadn't thought about that old show in years. And a grump like Gabe Armstrong had probably never seen it. Not many people had, since it had been canceled after only one season. Even though it was all pretend, it was the closest thing to family she'd ever known.

Her phone buzzed in her pocket. It'd been doing that all day. Texts from her parents. Separately. It didn't look like an emergency though they demanded she call them. Sunny was at work. They'd taught her work was the most important thing. And she guessed it was true even if that work was for a sketchy DNA testing company and not a role in next year's blockbuster action flick or swoony rom-com.

She needed her crappy job. To pay for the repairs to her car so she could leave that crappy job behind in the dust and return to where she belonged: the stage.

Toby's voice startled her. "Sunny, I need to give you some feedback."

Slowly, she rotated in her chair to face him.

Her boss stood over her, crossing his arms over his thin chest and crumpling the front of his lab coat. He wore the coat even though, as a customer service manager, he didn't work with DNA samples.

"Did you just offer to send our client's confidential information to another client?" He also referred to their customers as *clients* like DN-YAY was a law firm instead of a bottom-tier DNA testing company.

"Well, yeah." No point in denying it. He must have been listening like a creeper. "I just told a guy his parents lied to him until they died. And that he has two brothers and a sister he's never met. Shouldn't he be allowed to reach out to his family?"

"You know we have policies and procedures for that." He gestured at the dusty copy of the handbook wedged into the corner of her cube.

Gabe Armstrong was not going to go back to DN-YAY's website and click the button to contact his relatives. To improve her craft, Sunny studied people, and what she'd heard in his voice was confusion and fear. But if the contact information was sitting in his email box, the facts would be harder to avoid. Eventually, he'd open the email, then he'd reach out to his family. Maybe they'd be better than the parents who raised him. What kind of parents lied to their kid about being adopted? Her parents had a lot of flaws, but at least they usually told the truth. Even when it hurt.

His birth family wanted to know him. Otherwise, they wouldn't have taken the tests and checked the box to be contacted. And Gabe Armstrong needed them. She'd heard the pain in his voice. He was all alone now that his parents were gone.

She knew the pain of being alone.

She sat up straighter. "I was just trying to make it easier on him. It was a lot, you know?"

Toby parked his hands on his hips. "It's not your job to make it easier on him."

She shifted in her chair so her back hid the contact sheet she'd printed out before making the call. She stared at the DN-YAY logo on the right front of his lab coat. Apparently, it *was* her job to tell Gabe Armstrong that he wasn't who he thought he was. Last week, it'd been her job to tell a woman she had a high risk for breast cancer. A couple days before that, she'd told a guy his biological mother was actually the woman he'd thought was his older sister. And when she'd seen who his biological father was, she'd transferred him to a genetic counselor. That's why they paid the counselors the big bucks. Sunny wasn't about to do it for twelve bucks an hour.

Cata, her roommate, had lured her in with stories of the fun workplace—interesting stories, casual dress, and beer on Friday afternoons. Plus, she could ride to work with Cata until she saved enough to pay for the repairs to her car, which was currently coated in ice and parked in their complex's lot, where it'd been towed after breaking down on the way to Los Angeles.

Cata, a psychology grad student, found customer-service work fascinating.

For Sunny, DN-YAY was a paycheck until she could get back on her feet. It was a good hiding place, too. She hadn't had to tell her parents about the fiasco in New York. They thought she was still working there.

Though, to her film-star parents, working in television was only slightly better than working in customer service.

"Sunny, are you even listening to me?" Toby towered over her where she sat. "I'm trying to give you feedback."

She glanced around at her coworkers in their cubes. Some of them were talking to customers, but others had given up any pretense of working and stared at her, open-mouthed, with their headset cords dangling.

Stand up for yourself. It was what Odile had told her. *No one else will do it for you.* Though, in the end, Sunny had stood up for Odile, and it had destroyed her career.

Stay cool, Sunny reminded herself. *No need to go full-on New York here. Just another month or two, and I'll have enough for the car repairs.* She held out her palms. "I was just trying to offer exceptional customer service."

Neither one of them had to look at the banner at the front of the room. Foot-high letters proclaimed that DN-YAY provided EXCEPTIONAL CUSTOMER SERVICE.

Toby's upper lip curled behind his wispy mustache. "Exceptional customer service doesn't violate the company's procedures. I'm going to have to write you up for overstepping your role."

She bolted from her chair. With her heeled Tory Burch boots, which were much better suited to the clubs of New York than to a desk job in Ohio, she was nearly as tall as Toby. Three cubes over, Cata's mouth dropped into a horrified *O.* She knew exactly what was coming.

"Isn't it my *role* to be a decent human being, Toby? Because that's all I was trying to do."

"You're paid to uphold the processes and policies of DN-YAY. Not to meddle in people's business." He wagged his finger at her. A smear of something red, ketchup, Sunny hoped, stained his sleeve. "You are an entry-level customer service representative making slightly more than minimum wage."

Cata's eyes widened so the brown irises were ringed by white. For half a second, Sunny wondered if the person on Cata's line was hearing this, too.

She breathed in through her nostrils, hoping it'd cool off her brain. She could still walk out of there with a job reference. She could even sit back down, apologize, and keep her job.

Nope. She'd stood up for Odile in New York, and now she was standing up for herself. She wasn't about to let Toby and his ridiculous lab coat fire her. Not for trying to do the right thing.

"I don't think I can support DN-YAY's procedures if they don't allow me to show a little compassion for our customers." She clasped the badge clipped to her favorite T-shirt, the vintage one with the sparkly unicorn on the front, and pulled.

She dropped the badge onto the gray industrial carpeting at his feet. "I quit."

Whirling, she grabbed the papers next to her keyboard and stuffed them into her purse. Then she shoved past Toby and stomped out of the customer service bullpen in her boots, holding her breath until she reached the street and gasped in the cold winter air.

And that's when she realized she was standing in front of her former place of employment, having thrown a bridge-burning tantrum, with no prospects for employment, no Plan B. For the second time in four months.

Plus, this time her car didn't run, she was two thousand miles from where she intended to be, and it was the middle of winter. She squeezed her eyes shut.

A chilly breeze tingled at her chest. Looking down, she saw a hole in her T-shirt, right at the base of the unicorn's flowy glitter tail. *Shit!* She'd ripped her favorite shirt, and on the way out, she'd flashed everyone with an eyeful of pink lace bra cup.

Tugging her coat over her chest, she trudged across the street to the bar—the sketchy one they always bypassed for the cleaner, brighter one a few blocks over—to wait for Cata's shift to end. She needed a drink.

Sunny plopped onto a barstool and made the mistake of looking up at the television. *Hollywood Observer* was on, showing celebrities on a red carpet. Not just any celebrities. Her parents.

Her mother, Gwen Lafortune, wore a long red silk gown. Not an ounce of fat broke the line of the unforgivingly clingy fabric. The long, fitted sleeves outlined the gym-honed musculature of her arms. Her hair, the same blond shade as Sunny's, curled around her shoulders. She posed, elbows bent, hip cocked, chin down, the way she'd coached Sunny so many times. She looked the age she'd claimed for years: thirty-five.

The bartender shuffled in front of her. "What'll it be?"

"Bud Light in a bottle. Please."

The TV screen drew Sunny's gaze again. Her dad, Gene, looked every inch the action hero he played in films. But instead of jungle fatigues or jeans and a ripped T-shirt that showed his muscled chest, he wore a tux. The camera flashes lit up the gray he'd started to allow to show at his temples.

Wait. The light was all wrong for Los Angeles. The building they stood in front of, too. There were outdoor heaters everywhere, and the photographer crouched in the corner of the screen wore a black parka. They must be... She scanned the background of the shot and spotted One World Trade Center's distinctive antenna.

Shit.

They were in New York.

That explained all the messages.

The bartender plunked down her beer. He wiped a stained rag across the sticky bar and left her alone. Slumping over the wooden surface, she tried not to touch anything but the cool glass of the bottle.

Slowly, she pulled her phone out of her back pocket. Three messages from Mom. Two texts from Dad. They never called her just to check in. They knew. Her stomach hollowed.

If she called now, while they were at the premiere, they wouldn't pick up. She'd fulfill her duty while delaying the criticism. She hit the button to dial her mother. It rang a few times, but after the fourth ring, instead of an outgoing message, her mother picked up.

"Susan, isn't it wonderful?" No hello, no how-are-you. But at least she sounded happy.

"Oh. Yeah, Mom. I saw you at the premiere. You look fantastic."

"Thank you. Did you see my shoes?"

"Sorry, I missed them. What're they like?" Good. She could distract her mother like this all day.

"They're Jimmy Choo. Nude slingbacks with rhinestones across the pointed toe. They wear like a dream."

"They sound gorgeous, Mom." Sunny swigged her beer. "Whose premiere is it?"

"It's an Oscar contender. Starring—wait. Did you listen to my messages?"

"No?" Sunny glugged down the rest of her beer and signaled for another. "I just got off work." Permanently.

"And you haven't spoken to your father?"

"Not yet."

Her mother's voice dropped. "It's the most fabulous opportunity for you."

"For me?" She hadn't called to yell at her for wasting her last fabulous opportunity? Gene wouldn't hesitate to do it. He was the one who'd gotten her the audition for *New York Bomb Squad*.

"A role. Back in LA."

"A role for me?" As her parents had told her countless times, you got only one chance to impress people. Why would Gwen offer her a role after she'd walked out on her last one?

"Of course for you. Who else?"

Who else? Sunny could name a dozen actresses about her age who were more talented, more beautiful, and less likely to walk out of a table read because of something that wasn't even her business.

"Really, Mom? That's great. What's—"

"Gwen and Susan Lafortune, together on screen. Pure magic!"

Those tingles in her belly had to be excitement. Not disappointment that her mother was more excited to be seen on screen than to have her daughter return home. Or maybe it was just all that beer. Sunny held the phone away from her ear and burped.

"—you can't be late. Understand?"

Sunny straightened on the stool. "Of course. When—"

"Your father wants to talk to you. Here he is."

"Susan." Her father's voice sounded strained. "What's this I hear about you walking off set?"

She winced. "They were about to kill off my friend's character. And I couldn't let them—"

"You couldn't *let them?* Susan, you are the talent. Not the money. Not the power. Until you're a producer, you say your lines and keep quiet. Understand?"

"Yes, Dad." Sunny's finger trembled as she lifted it to swipe away the moisture from the corner of her eye. Standing up for Odile seemed like the right thing to do, but she hated the note of stern disapproval in his voice.

"Now, for this project of your mother's. Did she give you the details?"

"No. What's—"

"Where are you?"

"In a bar."

He huffed out a long-suffering sigh. "Are you still in New York?"

If she lied and said yes, they might ask to meet her. She had to give him the humiliating truth. "No. I'm in Ohio."

"What the hell are you doing there?"

"Visiting a friend?"

"If someone had asked me yesterday, I'd have said you couldn't find Ohio on a map. We need you home next month. Shooting starts on the thirteenth of February. Understand?"

That was a little over three weeks away. She didn't have much time. "Shooting? When do I audition?"

"As soon as you can get here. Is there going to be a problem?"

Before she'd left for the audition in New York, he'd warned her to save her money. It was a bit part at the lower end of the pay scale. And she'd done what he said, as much as she could considering the sky-high rent on even a tiny apartment in Manhattan. At first. But as her role grew, when she got that opening credit and the salary bump that came with it, she caved to the expectations to wear the right clothes, eat in the right restaurants, and be seen in the right bars. Even the higher salary seemed to slip through her fingers like water. Then, when everything had gone to hell, her cash evaporated.

Just like he'd warned her, she'd exhausted her small savings during the three months she'd looked for another acting gig. Unsuccessfully. Because the *New York Bomb Squad* producers had blacklisted her from the casting list of every television show, movie set, play, and toothpaste commercial in New York.

She couldn't ask her parents for cash to come home. Not while her father still had a little faith in her.

"No. No problem." She'd figure it out. She'd get to LA despite the sad balance in her bank account and her nonfunctional vehicle. She could do it without groveling for his help and fracturing the fragile bubble of his confidence.

She couldn't let her parents see her like this. Hell, she didn't want to see herself like this. She pinched her shirt together where it had ripped.

Still, she had to remember Leslie Odom, Jr., who said, "The path to moments of greatness in your life will be paved, in part, with your spectacular failures."

Mr. Odom would've been impressed by the spectacle Sunny had made of her failure.

"Good." Her dad's voice broke her out of her wandering thoughts. "Looking forward to seeing you."

"Really?" Suddenly, she wasn't in the skeezy bar anymore. She was a little girl wearing her prettiest, ruffled dress, and the housekeeper, Nadia, had curled her hair into long, shiny ringlets. Her parents had just come home from their latest projects. Sunny thundered down the enormous staircase into the foyer, and her father bent at the waist, picked her up, and spun her around. It was the last time she could remember getting a hug from her father.

"I have to get back to the party," he said. "See you no later than the thirteenth."

"Okay, Dad." But her father had already hung up the phone.

She'd find a way. She always did. She'd be there in plenty of time to audition, even if she had to waitress in the 24-hour truck stop by the highway to do it. Even if she had to hitchhike.

If she was going home, she had to close the curtain on her life in

Ohio. She'd already quit her job. She'd try to find Cata another roommate to split the rent. She didn't have any other strings to cut.

Except one.

Before she left, she'd hand those papers to Gabe Armstrong. In LA, she'd make her parents proud. He deserved a family reunion, too.

Sunny was peeling the label on her fourth beer when Cata ducked into the bar. The dim lights shone on her dark skin, and her braids swung as she shook her head.

"I know, I know," Sunny said, sliding from the stool. After four beers, she wasn't sure if what she knew was that the bar was too skeezy to be inside or that she'd made a terrible life choice by quitting her job. The one Cata had gotten her at her lowest point. The one she needed for cash to get to LA.

Cata held out her arms. "Bring it in."

Sunny stepped into her embrace. In three months, Cata had become a good friend to her. After her ancient Mercedes sputtered to a stop on I-70 in Columbus on her way back to LA to make a fresh start, when the repair shop told her the car needed more repairs than the car was worth, she'd texted everyone she knew. One of her New York friends responded with the name of her former NYU roommate, who was in the graduate psychology program at Ohio State.

Sunny had only been looking for a safe place to tow her car and then sleep in it until she got herself together, but Cata had an extra bedroom. And a job. And the emotional support she so desperately needed. Now she'd screwed up the job her new friend had been kind enough to recommend her for.

"It's okay, honey," Cata said. "Let's get you home."

Sunny laid a couple of bills on the bar and wobbled out behind Cata.

Cata's car was still parked in the DN-YAY lot. While they scraped the crusted ice off the windows, the fresh air and movement sharpened her brain and brought with it a stab of guilt. What could she say to make it better? What could she do to ensure Cata kept the job she inexplicably loved and didn't experience any consequences from what she'd done?

Finally, when the heat blasted over her chilled cheeks inside the car, she said, "I'm sorry. I shouldn't have blown up like that. I should've waited until the end of my shift and then resigned."

Cata snorted. "Toby's an ass. Hell, sometimes I want to quit, too. I would if I wasn't so fascinated by our weird, wonderful customers and our even weirder employees."

"I hope he doesn't take it out on you."

"Don't worry about me. I can handle Toby. But," Cata tilted her head, "this makes you two for two on big, dramatic exit scenes, you know."

Sunny felt Cata's words like a knife in her chest. But she kept up the sunshiny veneer over the guilt her father had planted, which had grown into a full, leafy tree of poisonous shame. "I'm an actress. Big, dramatic scenes are what I do."

"You're not an actress right now."

"Of course I'm an actress," Sunny snapped. "Just because I don't have a role at the moment doesn't mean I'm not."

"Ah."

"No." Sunny held up a hand. "I know what that 'ah' means. No psychologist Cata."

"Hmm. Let's unpack all this at home." Cata turned the key in the ignition. "Wine, ice cream, or both?"

"Definitely both. And pizza? The greasier, the better."

It was only when they settled on Cata's blue velveteen sofa, a glistening slice of pizza in one hand and a glass of Spanish red in the other, that Cata asked, "So what are you going to do now?"

Sunny sipped the bold, fruity wine. She wished Cata had waited until they'd opened the second bottle. She set her slice on her plate and wiped her fingers on a napkin. "Actually, I'm going back to California. My parents have a role for me."

"Acting? TV or film?"

Sunny shrugged. "They were light on the details. All I know is, I have to be back in LA in three weeks."

Cata's eyebrows winged up. "And this is what you want to do?"

"Of course. I'm an actress, and they've gotten me an audition."

"Why 'of course'?" Cata tilted her head. "You walked off your last show, and you haven't looked for another acting job since."

"I just—I've been in a slump, okay? Besides." She laughed, bitter. "Where would I audition in Columbus, Ohio?"

"There are casting calls," Cata said. "I checked. And you did that weekend gig at Beach Island over the holidays."

Sunny raised her eyebrows. "I dressed in a ratty period costume and sang Christmas carols with high school choir kids."

Cata pointed at her. "And you loved it."

"The boots were a size too small." But she forgot all about the pinch in her toes when she sang in front of a live audience and conducted those high school kids.

Cata squinted one eye. "And yet, that wasn't the job you walked out of. Have you considered that you sabotage yourself when you hate what you're doing?"

"I didn't hate *New York Bomb Squad*. It was the best job I've ever had." That's what her parents would have said. Sunny almost believed it. She poured another glass of wine and topped up Cata's glass. "And now I have another fantastic opportunity. Maybe if I sell my Mercedes for parts, it'll be enough to buy a plane ticket."

"Don't you need your car in LA for auditions?"

"Crap." Though she'd rather take the bus than borrow one of her parents' flashy cars and remind everyone she was one of *those* Lafortunes. The one who wasn't box-office bank.

She knew, down to the penny, how little had accumulated in her bank account. "I have enough money saved for the starter, especially if I sweet-talk that guy at the shop. I can get to LA on what's left of the brakes."

Cata's forehead crinkled. "That doesn't sound safe."

Sunny shrugged. "She's a tough old girl. She'll make it."

"What about you?"

She wiped her face blank. "I'll be okay, too."

"Okay? After that flame-up at DN-YAY?"

Cata's straight talk called for ice cream. Sunny picked up a spoon, scooped out a giant chunk of double chocolate fudge, and shoved it into her mouth. Lafortunes didn't talk about feelings. They talked about success. She let the creamy sweetness melt on her tongue.

"Are you sure it's not your fear of failure that's leading to self-sabotage?"

"What? No! DN-YAY sucks, but *New York Bomb Squad* was a fantastic career opportunity."

"Was it, though?"

"Of course it was. I've wanted to be an actress as long as I can remember." She waved the spoon. "Quitting DN-YAY took away my last reason for not going back to acting. I'm sure it was my subconscious telling me it's time."

"Now who's the psychologist, talking about her subconscious?"

She set down the spoon. "That last call really bothered me. Gabe Armstrong." She rolled the name around on her tongue. A good name, with weight to it. "His parents lied to him all his life. They never told him he was adopted. He had no idea he had another family. And now he has a chance to meet his siblings, and he turned it down. I always wanted to have siblings." A brother or sister would have eased the loneliness of growing up as the Lafortunes' only progeny. She'd cried for weeks when they'd canceled *The Brainiac Bunch,* as if she'd lost her actual siblings and not her coworkers.

Cata's tone was gentle, but her words weren't. "You can't project your own desires on other people."

"Why wouldn't he want to meet them?"

"He must have reasons. And DN-YAY has policies. Procedures.

For everyone's protection. Besides, he could probably find them himself."

"But I have the papers that'd make it easy."

Cata gasped. "You didn't."

"What?" Sunny gave her an innocent, wide-eyed stare. "I had the papers. It'd have been a waste to leave them at DN-YAY."

"So you're going to find this guy and hand him his relatives' information? What if his biological family doesn't want to be found?"

"They want Gabe to find them. They took those DNA tests and checked the box to make their results public. I bet you anything they know he's out there and want to reunite." Just the thought of it filled her heart with warmth. "Besides, he's local, lives over by Beach Island. I probably passed his place a dozen times while I worked there in December. It's got to be some kind of destiny for me to help him."

"Destiny?" Cata narrowed her eyes. "Why are you the one to say what he needs?"

"It's obvious, isn't it? His parents are dead. And he's got this whole other family, and all I need to do—"

"All you need to do? Why is this your problem?"

"Because he's lonely. I could hear it in his voice. And I can fix it."

Cata pressed her lips into a thin line. "Maybe you should start with your own—"

"Can I borrow your car tomorrow?" Sunny wasn't about to let Cata get started on that again.

Cata flattened her lips. "You can drop me off at school and then take it. But you'll be safe, right? I mean, you're the one acting like a stalker, but you don't know this guy. Just drop the papers in his mailbox and leave."

She snorted. "I promise I won't go inside. I'll just hand him the papers. Or leave them on his doormat. I need to do this before I go home."

"Okay." Cata reached over and squeezed Sunny's shoulder. "I'll miss you."

"I'm sorry about the rent. I'll put up some flyers—"

"No." Cata held up a hand. "I don't need help finding a roommate. I mean, I'll miss *you*. My friend."

Sunny sniffed and grabbed the TV remote off the coffee table. "Movie?"

"Sure. What do you want to watch?"

"Duh. Quitting a job calls for a musical."

"No!" Cata knew what was coming.

"Karaoke-style. So do your vocal exercises or whatever."

"You know I can't sing."

"Everyone can sing. The louder the better."

Cata stood. "I'll need a lot more wine for this."

"Wine isn't good for your vocal cords." Sunny scrolled through the list of musicals.

"But it's much better for my inhibitions."

Sunny scrolled through the list. All the feelings Cata had stirred up called for bittersweet, angsty power ballads.

Cata sipped her wine and choked. "No. Not *Rent*. Too sad."

"No, it's not!" Sunny held the remote high over her head. "It's about seizing the day. Friends. Family."

"Fast-forward through the part when Angel dies."

"Deal."

"You're my family now, you know."

"I know." Sunny covered up her sniffle by hitting play.

Chapter Three

G abe opened his townhouse door Friday morning to find a woman standing there, her hand raised as if to pull the knocker.

In the nine years he'd been living there, he'd opened the door to many people. After the funeral, there'd been a procession of family members and friends with casseroles and takeout. Occasionally, there'd been dates and girlfriends. Regularly, delivery people. But not once had he opened the door to a stranger as breathtaking as this.

He stood there, blinking like he'd been hit in the face. By a fairy princess. With cascading golden hair that skewed to reddish like a winter sunrise and long-lashed sky-blue eyes, she was almost too beautiful to be real.

She blinked those big eyes twice, tangling the lashes, and then stuck out her hand. "I'm Sunny."

"Of course you are." Shit, what'd he said? He shook the loose bolts out of his sleep-deprived brain. "I mean, good morning." He shook her hand. Had he forgotten an appointment?

"You're Gabe, right?" she asked. Her hand was so small, so soft in his meaty one. He gentled his grip.

"Yes." Was she one of the Beach Island performers?

"We talked on the phone yesterday. About your family."

What the hell? He yanked his hand out of hers like she'd electrocuted him. That voice. He knew it. She was the reason he'd tossed and turned all night. That he felt like a stranger in his own skin. That he'd almost called in sick today because he was a fraud to be going to Beach Island. Like he belonged there.

"Hang on." She held her delicate hands out in front of her, palms out. "I—I know this must be weird for you."

"Weird?" His voice rose, louder than he'd intended. "You told me I wasn't who I thought I was. And now you show up on my doorstep? Am I being punked?" God, he hoped he was. That a camera crew would jump out of his bushes to tell him, *Just kidding. You really are an Armstrong and CEO of Beach Island.*

When nothing like that happened, only silence and the calm gaze of those blue eyes, he edged back toward the threshold. Those DN-YAY commercials had said nothing about doorstep service. It'd all seemed so impersonal, swabbing his cheek and tossing it into a postage-paid envelope he'd later dropped into a blue mailbox. Nothing had prepared him for this beautiful demon to flip over his equilibrium like a pretzel loop.

"No, it's just me," she said. "I wanted to give you this." She held out a couple of printed pages.

Gabe took another step back. If he took them, it'd be real. With enough work and enough bourbon, he could forget yesterday's phone call. But he couldn't ignore black-and-white facts. Proof, maybe.

"I don't want it." He put his hands up, a barrier against the papers. "I don't want anything to do with it."

"It's your family." She shook the pages. "Maybe they're looking for you."

A sharp pain erupted in his chest. "I'm thirty years old. Don't you think if they wanted to find me, they would've by now?" That was the torturous thought that'd kept him up. If what this woman said was true, there was at least one person who knew it: his biological mother. Clearly, she hadn't wanted him then. And if she'd changed her mind later, she'd have turned up by now.

"I—I don't know much about it. About adoption. But I have information now that'll help you find them. Don't you want it?"

His body was a block of ice. And not from the January cold outside. "No. I don't." He backed into his foyer and shut the door in her fairy-princess face. He strode as far away as the small place allowed, into the kitchen, where he pulled out a stool and collapsed onto it. He scrubbed his hands over his face like he could erase the imprint of Sunny and her words.

In the machine shop yesterday, with the scent of sweat and grease in the air and work that required his full attention, he'd almost forgotten the bomb she'd dropped onto his life. But when he'd come home to his solitary townhouse, her words had echoed in his brain.

You have two brothers and a sister, all still living. You can meet them.

Did he believe her? If so, did he want to meet this other family, the one who'd given him away? Brandon had been almost like a brother to him. Wasn't the family he knew enough?

But was the family he knew even his? Was what his parents had left him—Beach Island—his to inherit? His to manage? No one had ever said anything to him to hint that he wasn't really an Armstrong. Not his parents, not his aunts or uncles, not his grand-parents. Surely they'd have told him if he wasn't one of them.

He glanced at the cabinet over the fridge where he kept the whiskey. Then at the clock on the range. Eight a.m. A workday, and he was late.

If he believed he belonged with the Armstrongs, he'd go to work. Sign off on payroll. Review the summer job applications. Do the work that needed to be done to keep the family business running, to keep everyone employed, the way everyone expected him to do.

He was responsible for Beach Island and its two hundred sixteen full-time employees, plus the four thousand seasonal people he needed to hire by May first. He had to focus on that, not on DN-YAY and this person who'd inexplicably brought the world-upending news to his doorstep.

He glanced at the clock again. Seven minutes after eight. She had to have left by now. He grabbed his keys, shouldered his satchel again, and trudged back to the front door. He expanded his chest and opened the door.

To find her still standing there, shivering. "H-hi, Gabe."

Chapter Four

The mountain of a man who was Gabe Armstrong stood framed in his door again. Sunny welcomed the heat that curled out around him, brushing against her cold cheeks.

She held the papers out to him. "Changed your mind?"

He looked at the papers like they were covered in dirt and other unmentionable substances. "I'm going to work."

"Oh." He marched past her, spanning the small porch in one long-legged step. He was halfway down the sidewalk when she turned.

Sunny scurried after him. Why hadn't he taken the damned papers like a normal person would? And why couldn't she leave them on his doormat like she'd promised? She knew better, but she couldn't resist choreographing a family reunion for him. The nine months she'd spent on the set of *The Brainiac Bunch* were the best time of her life. She'd felt like part of a real family. And now Gabe was walking away from his own chance at one. The papers crinkled in her fist.

"Can I walk with you?" she asked when she caught him. If he wouldn't take the papers, she could toss them into the back seat of his car. Then she'd have made her best effort to help him. She could go to LA with a clear conscience.

He looked down at her. It wasn't quite as hostile as the glare he'd given the papers, but his deep brown eyes were colder than the dormant, snow-covered trees next to the sidewalk. He shocked her when he snorted and said, "Walk with me? Fine."

She trotted to keep up with his long steps. It was okay. A quick jog would warm up her thin Southern California blood. But he surprised her again by striding past the parking lot where she'd left Cata's car and exiting the complex to the main street. He turned toward Beach Island.

It was a familiar path. The bus stop Sunny had used during her stint as a caroler at the park was just up ahead. But she'd never walked this fast. Between the bulky petticoats of her costume and the ridiculous, too-small period boots, she'd had to watch her step on the sometimes-icy sidewalk. Maybe he rode the bus to work. His dress pants and gorgeous wool overcoat belonged to a guy who drove an Audi, not a guy who relied on the dingy bus, but who was she to judge? Her car still sat dead at her own, less nice apartment complex.

She had just a few steps to the bus stop to convince him to take the papers. But the direct approach hadn't worked before. Maybe indirect was better.

"Where do you work, Gabe?"

He didn't answer right away. Glanced at her. Continued down the sidewalk. "I work up there." He tilted his chin at the park entrance just past the bus stop.

"Really? Me, too. I mean, I did. Briefly. During the Holly Days. I was a caroler."

He shot her a sharp glance. "What's your last name?"

"Lafortune."

"Ah." But he didn't say anything more. Maybe he didn't watch *New York Bomb Squad*.

She pressed on. "What do you do?"

"I work in the office."

Of course he did, with his business apparel. "In payroll?" It was the only department she'd visited in the one-story office building.

She didn't remember seeing him when she'd picked up her paychecks. And she'd have noticed someone who looked like Gabe.

"Not exactly."

They walked down the middle of the giant, empty parking lot. "Why do you walk and not drive?" she asked.

"It's not far."

"But it's cold."

He glanced at her again, his face inscrutable. "I don't drive."

"But you own a car, right?"

"No." His jaw was granite like the Allegheny Mountains she'd driven through on her way from New York.

"You have a fancy suit and a cashmere coat but no car?"

"That's right."

As fast as he moved, it probably was easier for him to walk to work than to drive. But why didn't he drive? Unable to relinquish her wheels when she'd moved to New York, she'd ended up spending almost as much for parking as she did for rent.

"Is that why you don't want to go visit your biological family? Because you don't drive? Because there are planes, too. I'd..." Now she was barreling past the line she'd promised Cata she wouldn't cross. "I'd drive you to the airport." Though she'd have to borrow Cata's car again to do it.

"You would?" His steps faltered. "You don't even know me. Why is it so important to you that I meet them?"

Sunny tried to catch her breath. "Look, I don't know you or your family. What I know is that family is important." And when the family you were born into didn't give you what you needed, unconditional love and support, you made your own. Like she'd done with the other kids on *The Brainiac Bunch*. Hell, she still kept a framed copy of their cast photo and exchanged birthday cards with the actors who'd played her parents. But she couldn't tell him that. He'd think she was silly for imprinting on a fake family. "Sometimes you have to find your own family. And it looks like your family in Vegas wants to be found. I just want to help."

"I have a family."

"But they—they're gone now. Don't you want to meet the rest of your family?" She narrowed her eyes. She hadn't pulled the right lever yet. "They might need something from you."

When he stilled, she knew she was onto something. Still, he hesitated, glaring at the steel gate that barred the employee entrance. The blue curve of Twister of Terror was visible through the bare branches of the trees.

"I don't fly, either," he said, his voice so low she almost didn't hear him.

"You don't?"

"No." He turned to her, his arms crossed over his broad chest.

The words bubbled out of her without thought. "I'm on my way to Los Angeles. I'll drive right through Vegas. You could ride with me."

"You're going for...for work?" An adorable little crease separated his thick eyebrows.

Her face went hot. "No, I quit. I couldn't, after..."

"Oh." The crease disappeared, and his face went stony.

"I have a job opportunity. And that's where my parents live. I'm leaving as soon as my car's fixed."

His forehead creased. "You're offering to drive almost two thousand miles with a stranger?"

Sunny shrugged. "It'd be more fun than driving alone. You could pay for gas." Her mouth was making plans without even consulting her brain. Cata would kill her.

She scrabbled in her purse for a pen. On the back of the page she still clutched in her frozen fingers, she scrawled her name and phone number. "Think about it, okay?" She shoved the paper into his chest, and he grasped it.

Flashing him her brightest smile, she turned and headed back toward Cata's car. Whether or not he took her up on her offer, she'd accomplished her mission: she'd given him his brother's contact information and the DNA results. It was literally in his hands now.

Chapter Five

I n Gabe's opinion, ride-sharing apps were one of the greatest inventions ever. And Pick Up Grandma, a startup by a couple of Ohio State grads, was his favorite. He didn't have to bum rides from his cousin Brandon anymore—couldn't, anyway, since he'd moved to Chicago—and his not-driving wasn't as glaringly obvious when he rode up in a Ford Ranger driven by a sixty-something woman instead of a bright-yellow taxi. The best part was that the drivers, almost all of them women, didn't question his request to take side roads instead of the interstate out to Aunt Pat's home in the suburbs. They drove the speed limit and filled the cab with distracting chatter.

His driver pulled away with a wave, leaving Gabe standing in front of Aunt Pat's suburban mini-mansion. It was familiar and yet somehow not, considering the papers he'd hidden in his bedside table like a dirty secret. They'd left a permanent impression on his eyeballs, warping the familiar like a funhouse mirror.

Michael Forza - age 38 - Las Vegas, NV
Mary Forza - age 35 - Las Vegas, NV
Raphael Forza - age 31 - Las Vegas, NV
Somehow, the fact that his brother Raphael was only a year

older than he was made it worse. What made his birth parents keep Raphael? What had Gabe done or been to be discarded? Had he stuck out from the Forza family the way he had from the Armstrongs, a cuckoo in a crow's nest?

He curled his hand around Aunt Pat's door handle, hesitating. Should he ring the doorbell? If he did, she'd know something was wrong. And he wasn't ready to reveal what he'd learned. Not until he knew it was true.

Given the erratic behavior of DN-YAY's former employee, he wasn't a hundred percent sure he believed it. Though Sunny Lafortune herself seemed to be what she'd claimed. Yesterday in the office, he'd looked up her personnel record. She'd passed the background check they ran on all employees, including employment verification at DN-YAY. Her résumé showed a background in acting, though, not genetics or psychology, which seemed to reflect more poorly on DN-YAY for hiring her than on Sunny herself.

The skin on the back of his neck itched as he opened the door and headed to the kitchen. He'd been coming here since he was a kid and knew the rooms and hallways as well as the ones in his own townhouse. Did he still belong here? Had he ever?

"Gabe." In the cheery yellow kitchen, Aunt Pat held out her arms to him, and Gabe leaned into her embrace.

"Hi," he mumbled.

"What's wrong, sweetie? You're all stiff." Pat released him and stepped back, craning her neck at him. She always made him feel like a giant child. "You didn't take the freeway here, did you?"

"No, I'm fine. Just—just a lot going on."

"Not at the park. It's winter. You should be coasting now."

"Coasting?" He snorted. "We'll be doing maintenance right up to opening day, triple-checking the safety systems, making everything shine."

"Of course, of course. We'll talk about it in the meeting. Coffee?"

"I'll get it."

He walked to the coffeemaker and opened the cabinet above it. But today, the rows of matching mugs, all lined up, didn't welcome him to choose. Instead, they were a barrier telling him, *You don't belong here. Not your mugs. Not your family.*

An arm reached past him and grabbed a mug. "Hey, Gabe. Forgot what you were doing?"

Brandon smirked at Gabe before he poured himself a cup and set the carafe back on the warming plate. He belonged. As far as Gabe knew, he was Aunt Pat's biological son. Though, since his cousin was just a few months younger than Gabe, Gabe remembered nothing about Brandon's birth.

Gabe shut the cabinet door. "No, just changed my mind. I didn't know you were here."

"Only for the weekend." He leaned against the counter. "Hey, want to go out tonight? I could drive back to Chicago tomorrow. We'll go to O'Reilly's like we used to. It'll be like old times. Except now we're old enough to have a beer."

Gabe furrowed his brow. He wasn't in any mood to be social tonight. "No, I've got some...paperwork to deal with. And an early morning tomorrow."

Something flashed across Brandon's face. Guilt, maybe, or hurt. Gabe hadn't meant to remind him that he'd given up everything, including college, for Beach Island while Brandon went off to Chicago for business school and his fancy marketing job. Brandon looked like Chicago, from his slicked-back dark blond hair to his navy cashmere sweater. His thick stainless-steel watch glinted in the track lights when he sipped his coffee.

When he lowered the cup, the expression was gone. "Guess I'll drive home after the meeting, then."

"The meeting?"

"Yeah." Brandon waved his coffee cup, and a little sloshed out and dripped onto the tile floor. "I thought I'd sit in today."

Gabe frowned. Aunt Pat still held her board seat, so Brandon wasn't a member. He didn't attend their meetings. He never had to worry about reining in Uncle Bobby's thrill ride addiction or keeping concession costs in check. He never retrieved dropped eyeglasses from the net under Twister of Terror or cleaned up puke from the teacup ride.

But Brandon hadn't always been uninterested. A few months after Gabe had taken his dad's seat on the board, Brandon had made him an offer. His blue eyes had been kind that day, softened with sympathy, when he'd volunteered to take the burden from Gabe's shoulders.

And Gabe had wanted that so badly. He'd wanted to go back to school, finish his mechanical engineering degree, and then go far away so he never had to lay eyes on Beach Island again. But in the end, he'd stayed. Brandon had urged him to sell the park but warned him they needed to improve the numbers first. That meant cutting corners, especially on safety. Laying off their loyal employees. Gabe wouldn't do that.

Aunt Pat poked her head into the kitchen. "Bobby and Grandpa are here. We can get started."

Brandon walked out. Gabe growled and grabbed a paper towel. He bent to wipe up the hazardous splash of coffee on Aunt Pat's floor.

In the dining room, Brandon sat next to Grandpa. Brandon was taller than their grandfather, but his eyes were the same shade of pale blue. Gabe took his seat across the table beside Uncle Bobby. The chair creaked under his weight.

The board never bothered with Parliamentary procedure or, in fact, any process at all. In his early days on the board, right after Mom and Dad had died, Gabe had tried to introduce some structure and even offered to bring in Darlene to take notes, but everyone else resisted, so the board meetings continued to run more like family chats than like meetings of a multimillion-dollar private corporation.

Gabe sat back and let them talk through Grandpa's arthritis, Aunt Pat's latest Junior League function, and Brandon's advice on

Uncle Bobby's investment portfolio. As he'd done since he was a kid, Gabe stroked over the whorls in Aunt Pat's burled wood dining table. The table glowed with years of wood polish. It'd come to Aunt Pat from her grandmother, long before Gabe was born. And it would pass to Brandon or his kids, assuming he had any.

Gabe hadn't kept many of his parents' things after the accident. Their furniture had been generic modern, nothing like this table. Plus, it wouldn't have fit into his townhouse. He hadn't been able to keep their house. Like Aunt Pat's, it'd been out in the suburbs, and right after the accident, Gabe couldn't even ride in a car to work. But his parents wouldn't have cared about the house. They'd always preferred experiences to things.

A sheet of paper slid across the spot of table Gabe had been staring at. Startled, he looked up. Everyone else scanned identical papers in front of them.

"Mile of Mayhem." Bobby leaned back in his chair like he was already riding it. While he'd never had Dad's head for business, he shared his enthusiasm for thrill rides. "Bent Cuban eight. Double heartline roll. Rides smooth as silk. A theme park in Abu Dhabi is closing down, and it's going up for sale."

"What's its safety record?" Gabe asked.

"I knew you'd ask that." He chuckled. "I've asked for it, plus the maintenance logs. They should be here next week. But we need to move now before other bidders find out. I asked Brandon here to run the numbers, and on the other side of the sheet is the financial analysis."

It was just like Uncle Bobby to decide without considering the most important factor. "Wait. You expect us to vote on this without the safety records?" Gabe asked, not flipping the sheet.

"What I want to know is where it'll go," Grandpa said. "Park's full."

Bobby's cheeks reddened. "We could—"

"No." Grandpa and Gabe spoke at the same time.

Bobby waved his hand. "I wasn't going to propose that we put it over Founders' Park. Though Luke would've much rather had a roller coaster built to remember him than a pond. With *swans*." He didn't meet Gabe's gaze. The swans were for Gabe's mother, Lucy, and he knew it. "No one rides the carousel anymore. If we tear that down, plus the teacup ride, there'll be space."

Gabe didn't mind losing the teacup ride. He had to station a full-time cleaner there to deal with the vomit situation. But he had fond memories of riding the carousel, flanked by his parents. His favorite steed had been the tiger, white with black stripes. Standing on the seat of the carved bench next to the tiger, Dad could reach up and ring the brass bell as they passed.

"Gabe," Bobby barked. Startled, Gabe looked up from the table. Everyone stared at him. "What do you think?"

He pushed the paper away. "I can't vote on this until I've seen the maintenance logs. I'm not bringing an unsafe ride to Beach Island." But it was more than the missing documentation that gave him pause. Was he still a voting member of the board if he wasn't really an Armstrong? Did his vote even matter? Would he be able to vote once he saw the safety record, or would his own ambivalence freeze him?

"Once it's here, you can take it apart and put it back together again. You can install whatever safety features you want," Bobby said. "Within reason."

"Can I?" Gabe asked. "Liability's more expensive—"

Bobby interrupted, "—than prevention. We know, we know."

As always, Gabe wondered if they did know. If it'd been a park patron, rather than his parents, who'd died on Fright or Flight, the park would've been sued and probably had to close. Beach Island would be no more, and Uncle Bobby and Aunt Pat would've had to find real jobs instead of being semi-retired while Gabe ran the day-to-day operations for them. And protected the patrons from the sloppy practices—including his own—that'd killed his parents.

Aunt Pat snapped, "Bobby, you should know better than to bring us a half-cocked proposal. We'll vote when all the information's in."

Bobby hissed out a breath. "Fine. But if we wait too long, someone else'll snatch it up. That park up north," he grumbled.

"We could make the offer contingent on satisfactory maintenance logs."

Everyone whipped their heads to Brandon, who'd spoken. Who'd said *we* as if he were a member of the board.

Bobby smiled. "So we could. Anyone opposed?"

Now the heads whipped back to Gabe. And he should've opposed it. The maintenance logs were only the first step in evaluating what needed to be done to bring the ride up to his—their—standards. The modifications it required might double the price they'd pay to purchase and ship it. But even knowing all this, he hesitated. Was it his place to stand in Uncle Bobby's way? Was it his decision to make?

The words caught in his chest and died. He shook his head.

"Well, then," Uncle Bobby said. "I'll email our offer today. Our *contingent* offer."

Aunt Pat brought up the concession budget for the coming season, but Gabe couldn't pretend to be interested in that. Instead, he traced the wavy, coaster-like patterns in the dining table. Did he belong here? Was Beach Island still his legacy? What if the DNA results were wrong, and his indecision, his ambivalence, was caused by a mistake?

There was one way to confirm it: meet his siblings. If he could see a resemblance, or if they knew what'd happened, he'd know if he belonged here or there. And if it was clear that he belonged *there,* he'd offer to give up his seat here. Brandon could take over if he still wanted it.

Chairs scraped back. The meeting had ended. But before Gabe could push back from the table, Aunt Pat plopped into Uncle Bobby's seat next to him. "Gabe, what's wrong? Is it Riley? Or—or them?"

"Not Riley," he said. Aunt Pat had mothered him the entire week of Christmas after he'd called to tell her Riley wouldn't be coming to the family's party.

"Oh, honey." Aunt Pat stroked his hand. "I know it's hard getting through the holidays without them."

It had been, but dealing with this news was even harder. "Aunt Pat, do you remember when...when Mom was pregnant with me?"

She pursed her lips and twisted them to the side while she blinked, perhaps flipping through her mental photo album. Then her eyes widened. "Your mother and dad had gone on a tour of the parks out west. You know, all through Texas and California. Took them six, eight months to do them all. And when they came back, they brought you. She must not have known she was pregnant when they left." She leaned in closer. "I think they'd been trying for a while, thought a vacation might do them good. They called you their little miracle."

"Huh." He'd never asked before. He'd just assumed he'd arrived in the usual way. Though, now he thought about it, there weren't any pictures of Mom with a pregnant belly. There were plenty of him as a newborn, though, and a hospital bracelet in the baby book that used to be on Mom and Dad's bookshelf. It'd probably gone to storage with the rest of the painful memories.

"Gabe, you look pale. Are you feeling all right?" Aunt Pat rested the back of her hand against Gabe's forehead.

He leaned away. "I'm fine. Just tired."

"You should take advantage of the off season. Get away. Clear your head."

He gave her a half-smile. "Maybe I will. Though there's so much to do: hiring for next year, overseeing the maintenance. Maybe we should bring in someone to do the hiring."

"An outsider?" She looked like he'd proposed to run naked through the park on July Fourth. "Our family has run this park for forty years. And we'll run it for forty more. Darlene can cover for you while you're gone. Bobby and I'll step up. And don't worry at all about the Theme Park Expo. You don't need to go. I'll go. Or we'll send Brandon."

Which category did Gabe fall into if what DN-YAY had told him was true: family or outsider? And if he didn't chase down the lead to his siblings, wouldn't he always second-guess himself the way he had today? In a position where he made decisions that ensured patrons' safety daily, doubt was dangerous.

His aunt patted his shoulder. "Don't you worry about it. Just take some time off. Relax. Get some sun."

Gabe didn't know much about relaxation, but he knew somewhere known for its sunshine: Las Vegas.

Chapter Six

Gabe clenched his fists outside the door of Sunny's second-floor apartment. He'd walked right into the complex after Pick Up Grandma's driver had dropped him off. The tiny security hut was empty, and the barrier arm was raised. A rock propped open the door of her building. At Beach Island, leaving gates unlatched and doors propped was grounds for termination. But bursting in like an enraged bull wouldn't help his cause. Before he raised his hand to knock, he took a second to wait out the pulse pounding in his ears.

And then he heard it.

Behind the door, a female voice belted out "Don't Rain on My Parade." It didn't sound like Barbra Streisand or even the Glee cast. The voice was high and strident, and every once in a while, a raspy growl roughened it. Yet it was unvarnished, with no instrumental track. It was real, and live, and in a different league entirely from Beach Island's summer shows.

He waited, listening, until the last line rang out, leaving his ears craving more. Someone's knuckles rapped on the door. They had to be his, but he could no more control them than he could resist the siren's call from inside that apartment.

When Sunny opened the door, breathless, in a pair of yoga

pants and a ragged *Cats* sweatshirt, Gabe stepped back, over-whelmed. Her hair was tucked up in a ponytail, revealing the heart shape of her face and her ears, which were pierced but empty of earrings except for thin silver cuffs around the outer cartilage. He stood there, holding his breath and blinking, for a solid two seconds. He should've gotten used to her beauty after meeting her at his house. He hadn't.

Thankfully, he remembered how pissed off he was that she'd table-flipped his life, and that got him breathing again.

"Gabe? What're you doing here?" She wiped at a trickle of sweat at her hairline.

"I got your address from Beach Island. You know, you should really live somewhere with better security."

She tipped her head to the side and squinted. "Are you going to attack me?"

"No." He shoved his hands into his pockets.

"Then why are you here?"

"Can we talk? Inside or somewhere else?" Over her shoulder, he spotted an open suitcase and a laundry basket piled high with clothing next to a blue velveteen couch.

Wordlessly, she stepped aside, allowing him to enter.

The place smelled like lemons. And sunshine. Or maybe that was Sunny herself. He stopped himself from taking a deep breath as he passed her. A high counter separated the small living room from a galley kitchen. A short hall led from the living room to a tiny bath-room with two closed doors—bedrooms, he assumed—on either side. The living room window blinds were pulled up, letting the late afternoon winter sun pour in. Gabe felt too big, too dark, in the small, bright space.

Sunny moved a stack of folded towels onto the low coffee table and curled into one end of the couch, one foot underneath her. The only other seat was a flimsy white papasan chair, likely to collapse if he tried to sit in it, so he took the other end of the couch. Like the rest of the apartment, it was undersized, so the foot she'd propped up on the cushion was only inches away from his leg. Even her feet were beautiful, slender without being bony and ending in straight, pink toes. Her toenails were painted a sparkly purple. He wiped his hands over his pressed-together thighs as if he could compact himself further.

She stayed silent, waiting.

"I..." His voice came out full of gravel. He cleared his throat. "If you're still offering, I'd like to take you up on your offer to ride out to Las Vegas. With you."

"Oh." Something crossed her face then. Doubt, maybe. Now that he was here, taking up too much of her space, she was probably reconsidering. Trying to think of a way out of her offer.

But who else would drive him two thousand miles across the country? Pick Up Grandma would've laughed. And the thought of getting in an airplane made every internal organ squeeze tight. He held his breath again.

"My car's dead right now," she said. "It doesn't start. And it needs new brakes. You pay half of the repair cost. Up front."

"Can I look at it? The car."

Her eyebrows shot up. "You want to make sure the paint color matches your eyes?"

"No, I'm good at mechanical stuff. Let me take a look."

She scanned his wool trousers, his crisp white shirt, the cashmere coat he'd draped over the arm of the sofa. "You. Fix cars."

"It's a hobby." Gabe shrugged like it was no big deal. But it was the only thing that relaxed him these days.

"You said you don't own a car. And you don't drive."

"I don't have to drive a car to enjoy working on it. You own a car and don't know how to repair it. That seems just as wrong to me."

She stared at him for almost a full minute, her blue eyes sharp like Twister of Terror's curved steel against a summer sky. "Okay."

He snagged a towel from her stack. "Mind if I get this a little dirty?"

"I guess not."

She unfolded herself and plucked a pink puffy coat from a hook near the door. Sliding on a scruffy pair of moccasins, she led the way out of her building to a twenty-year-old light-blue Mercedes. Other than a few spots of rust on the wheel wells, the exterior looked to be in decent shape. Unblemished bumpers, intact glass. Either she'd kept up with the bodywork or she was a safe driver.

"Pop the hood," Gabe said. He shrugged out of his coat and unbuttoned his dress shirt. She stood frozen, staring, as he tugged it off to reveal his white undershirt. He looked down. It was clean. And it covered his torso. Though it was a little tight over his chest, especially with the cold making his nipples stand up.

He folded his shirt and placed it, along with his coat, on the closed trunk of the car. She licked her lower lip.

"The hood?" he repeated.

"Right." She unlocked the car and slid into the driver's seat. The latch clunked when it released.

Gabe walked to the front of the car, slid his hand under the edge until he found the latch, and unhooked it. Pushing up the hood, he peered inside. Not the cleanest engine he'd ever seen. He scooped handfuls of dried leaves out of the corners.

"Okay, start it," he shouted.

"It doesn't start," she shouted back.

"Stick the key in and turn it. I want to hear what it does."

Nothing but silence. Probably the starter. Could've been the battery, but if it were that simple, she'd have replaced it. Without even taking a screwdriver to the engine compartment, he could see a couple of worn belts and a dangerously brittle hose. He'd bet the brake pads were thin, too, but he'd need tools to check them. A repair shop would charge her thousands for the work that needed to be done.

Gabe lowered the hood and came around to the driver's side door, wiping his hands on her towel. "I'll have it towed to my garage. I can fix it. No cost, but it'll take me a few days. And I'll pay for the gas."

"You'll fix it. For free. And then buy gas for a two thousand–mile road trip?"

"Yeah."

"Why?"

He crossed his arms. "I'll fix it, you drive, no questions."

"You want me to drive your Miss Daisy ass across the country?"

"Question."

Her lips quivered but didn't turn up into a smile.

He needed to sweeten the pot. "I'll pay for the hotels, too, at night."

"Separate rooms?"

He cringed inside. Was that what she thought of him? "Of course."

"Fine, Mr. Armstrong. You just bought yourself a chauffeur."

He held out a hand for the keys. "Go back inside where it's warm. I'll call the tow truck."

"A few days, you said?"

Hell, it'd take him a couple days to locate the parts for the Mercedes. He rubbed his hands together, making a mental list of the proper order for the repairs. Much more fun than payroll. Still, he needed to wrap things up at Beach Island so Darlene could manage while he was gone for a week or two. "We can leave on Saturday."

She pulled the car key off the ring and dropped it into his palm. "Thanks, Gabe."

The way she looked up through her long eyelashes melted him. He cleared his throat. "No problem."

She turned around and sauntered back toward her building. Gabe blinked away from the lower curve of her ass in those yoga pants.

Business, Gabe. Before, when he'd been the unquestioned scion of the Armstrong family, the legitimate CEO of a multimillion-dollar theme park, he might've asked her if she wanted to go to dinner. Suggest they get to know each other better.

But now, what did he have to offer her? He didn't know who he was, and DNA results or not, neither did she. Besides, she was on her way to LA. Permanently.

They'd keep it simple, transactional. He'd fix her car; she'd drive him where he needed to go. Then she'd continue on her way while

Gabe figured out who he was, what he'd been, and what to do about it.

"Why is there a car in my shop?"

Gabe startled and slammed his head against the underside of the Mercedes's hood. He should've known he couldn't keep a whole car from Ramirez, even hidden back here with the maintenance crew's pickup trucks and golf carts.

He wiped his hands on his rag and then turned toward his friend. Ramirez's thick arms were crossed over his broad chest.

"I'm fixing it for a friend," he said. He rubbed his head where he'd bumped it. No blood. Just a lump rising from his scalp.

Ramirez grunted and turned to head back out toward the main shop. Bullet dodged. Gabe tossed the rag onto the ledge of the engine compartment and bent over the serpentine belt he'd been loosening.

"On a Tuesday?" Ramirez's voice was closer this time and accompanied by the heavy treads of his steel-toes on the concrete floor.

Pain sliced into Gabe's scalp when he bumped it again on the unyielding hood. "Would you cut that out?" he snapped. "I'm going to give myself a concussion here."

"Wouldn't be your first, probably not your last. Which friend?"

Sunny's image shoved into Gabe's brain, all thick honey hair and yoga-pants curves, accompanied by that voice. His breath caught in his chest. "You don't know her."

"Ah." Ramirez leaned a hip on the powder-blue side of the car and cast a critical gaze over the engine compartment. "You've got your work cut out for you."

He could've meant with Sunny or with the Mercedes. Gabe didn't ask. "Yeah," he said.

"What's the problem?"

Should he tell Ramirez about the DNA results? They'd been friends since they were teenagers working at the park. Ramirez knew his parents well, had been there that day, the day the joyous part of Gabe's life ended with a snap of steel. After, he'd been the clap of a firm hand on his shoulder, a stiff-jawed nod when Gabe needed reassurance, a silent presence nearby while Gabe worked out his feelings with a wrench in his hand.

But their friendship had been born and raised at Beach Island, and Gabe wasn't sure he belonged there now. Instead, he said, "Faulty starter. And I need to get it safe enough for a road trip. A long one."

Ramirez grinned. "Turning this pumpkin into Cinderella's carriage is gonna take some work. You'll have the whole thing in pieces by the end of the day."

"Probably." Gabe shrugged. "Don't want to miss anything."

Ramirez stilled. "You know I—"

"I know. Me, too." They'd been over and over what happened nine years ago. Gabe's worst mistake. No need to rehash it. He'd never let it happen again.

"But why—"

"Gabe! You here?" Darlene's voice came from the main door of the shop.

"In here," Gabe called, grateful for the interruption and glad he hadn't put his head back under the hood.

Darlene walked in, clutching a handful of papers. She stopped midway between the door and the Mercedes. "Oh. Hi, Tony."

"Darlene," Ramirez said. But his voice was softer than it ever sounded when he talked to Gabe.

Gabe shot him a look and grimaced. Ramirez's face had gone all dreamy, too. Few women ever ventured into the shop.

Darlene dragged her attention off Ramirez and speared Gabe with a glare. "When are you going to look at these résumés? We need to set up interviews."

Gabe glanced at the car. "I'm going to be tied up this week. And then I'm going away for a couple weeks. I trust you. Set up the interviews with the most qualified candidates. I'll approve your hiring decisions."

It wasn't like Gabe had never delegated work to her. He trusted her. Still, Darlene's mouth dropped open.

"A couple weeks?" Her voice rose into its upper register. "You're going on a vacation?"

Gabe's face heated. He picked up his socket wrench and twisted it, making a clicking sound. "Something like that."

"You haven't gone on vacation since..."

She didn't have to finish. Since his parents had died. Since he'd taken over at Beach Island. There was always too much work to do, ensuring the safety of his employees and guests. Besides, where would he go if he couldn't fly in a plane or ride in a car without white knuckles?

"I figured it was about time," he said. He couldn't tell her the real reason. If the DNA results were correct and he wasn't who they all thought he was, how would his relationship with Ramirez and Darlene change? He didn't want their questions. Their pity. Until he knew for sure, he had to be strong, stable. Just like always. He gripped the wrench in both hands.

Darlene opened her mouth but then pressed her lips together. She tilted her head. "Where are you going?"

"Somewhere sunny. I'll have my phone," he rushed to add. "You can call me for anything you need."

"All right." She tucked the papers under her arm. "I'll take care of this."

"Thanks. You're the best."

"You know it. See you later, Gabe. Bye, Tony." She nodded and left.

After the door closed behind her, a stream of air gusted out of Tony like a deflating balloon.

"You all right, man?" Gabe asked.

A few beats of silence ticked by. Ramirez shook himself. "Yeah." He straightened.

"Keep an eye on her while I'm gone, will you?" Gabe asked. "She pushes herself too hard."

"Got it, boss."

Boss? Maybe not for much longer. Was knowing the truth worth risking everything he had?

He was about to find out.

Chapter Seven

"You're staring," Cata said.

Sunny dragged her gaze away from the family at the next booth in the Waffle House. Two dads, two little girls. One dad was cutting up the younger girl's waffle. With its mountain of whipped cream and strawberries, it was too much food for her to eat, but they'd let her order it anyway. The way the men kept their attention on their daughters, helping them color on their placemats before their food came, their easy conversation and smiles, made her chest ache.

Cata pressed her lips together, and Sunny focused on her own cooling waffle.

"I still don't like it," Cata grumbled, setting down her fork.

She threw her arm around Cata's shoulder and hugged her tight. For the first time in a long time, nothing was looming over her: not her lack of acting prospects, not the hunk of unmoving Mercedes in the parking lot. She was about to drive her newly functional car to Los Angeles, where her agent—she hoped—had contacts who hadn't blacklisted her. It didn't hurt that she'd be sharing the ride with a man who'd made her salivate with a flash of stretched-tight undershirt. "Sometimes you just know. Same way I knew we'd be friends when we met last fall. Gabe's okay."

Cata flashed her a *bullshit* expression. "Text me every day. And we need a code so you can signal me if he's coercing you."

"A code? *Coercing* me?" Sunny grinned.

"Yeah. If he's looking over your shoulder to make sure you're saying you're okay, but you're really not. Tell me..." She drummed her fingers against her chin and looked up to the acoustic ceiling tiles like they'd inspire her.

"I'll tell you I've decided to give up acting."

"Perfect." Cata smiled at Sunny, but anxiety lingered in her eyes.

"I promise, he's a Boy Scout. He fixed my car. The starter, the brakes, all the belts and hoses. His friend, Ramirez, when he dropped off the car, said they'd gone to six junkyards to get everything, made sure the parts were perfect. Plus he added all these safety features, like a backup camera and forward collision warning. It purrs like a kitten now."

"A kitten, huh?"

Sunny shoved away her empty plate and wiped at her sticky fingers with a napkin. "Yeah. It's in better shape than when my grandma handed it down to me in high school."

Cata leaned forward to peer into her face. "Is it only your car's engine that's purring?"

Sunny crumpled up the napkin and tossed it into the puddle of syrup on the plate. In her best Scarlett O'Hara voice, she drawled, "Why, I have no idea what you mean."

"Maybe he wasn't just a cheap way to fix your car. Are you, like, into him?"

Sunny couldn't meet her friend's eyes when she said, "Of course not."

He had some sort of The Rock thing going on with his height and the muscles moving under his T-shirt and those big hands with their long fingers, her kryptonite. His face was pleasant, too. Friendly, before she'd handed him his DNA results. Open, except when she'd asked him about the driving. Even that stubborn bottom lip was a little sexy. Biteable. Sunny bit her own lip to contain the drool. Then she voiced the thing that confused her the most. "I don't get why a guy like that doesn't drive. He lives in a nice townhouse, wears the most gorgeous dress coat you've ever seen." Though maybe it was his inverted-triangle frame that made the coat look so good. "Dude could definitely afford a car. A nice one. He could probably rent one for less than what he spent on parts for my car."

Cata sipped her coffee. "Maybe it's some kind of power trip to be driven places. A Christian Grey thing. Maybe he's, like, a secret billionaire."

Sunny shrugged. He'd seemed pretty down to earth. Did secret billionaires get grease on their hands? His had been rough, callused, like he worked with tools and not at a desk like he'd said. The memory of his palm sliding across hers sent a shiver down her neck.

The best part? She'd be leaving his ass in Vegas. So even if he got those big hands on her lady parts, there was no risk of anything more. It was her favorite kind of relationship, the kind she couldn't screw up. One with a built-in end date. A seven-night engagement like some of the plays they'd run in high school. Not like her parents' decades-long sham of a marriage.

She checked her phone. "Time to go."

Cata slid out of the booth, and Sunny followed. Cata tugged her into a tight hug. "I'll miss you. Text me, okay? Even after you get to LA. When do you think you'll get there?"

Tightness gripped her belly. "The show starts filming in two weeks, but we can make the drive in four days, tops. I'll have plenty of time to get there, settle in, audition. Learn my lines if it all goes well."

At the register, Cata paid, which only made Sunny's eyes prickle more. Together, they walked out to their cars and stood between Cata's Honda and Sunny's Mercedes.

Cata sniffled. "Be careful out there. Wait, I'm supposed to say, break a leg."

"That's right. You be careful, too. Especially in the snow."

"You won't have to worry about that where you're going."

"No." Sunny wouldn't miss the icy winter roads. "You'll have to come up with an excuse to come visit me. A psychology conference or something. I'll show you the sights. We'll even take a tour of the stars' homes."

"I want to see J. Lo's house."

"'Kay."

They hugged, and when they pulled apart, Sunny's lungs felt tight, like she couldn't draw a full breath. But like her old drama teacher used to say, you close a curtain on one show to make room for another. She might be leaving Cata, but she'd be reunited with her parents and auditioning in a week.

Somehow, that happy thought didn't balance out her sadness.

After Cata's taillights disappeared from view and Sunny's breathing evened out, she checked her phone, which had been buzzing in her pocket.

Mom: When will you be home?

Sunny sighed and texted back.

Sunny: In a week, maybe less. Why?

Mom: We need to prep you for the show.

Prep me for the show? Did she mean run lines for the audition? If so, it'd be the first time her mother had ever offered to do that. Happiness fizzed in her belly.

Sunny: Don't worry, I'll be home in plenty of time.

Might as well start now. She opened the door that didn't creak anymore and slid into the driver's seat. She tossed her phone into her purse and set it in the back seat.

As grateful as she was for the free repairs Gabe had made, Cata was right. His request to be driven to Las Vegas was weird. Would he ride in the back seat like Cata had said, like a billionaire? If he were a billionaire, he'd have his own limo to ride in. And a driver.

Was this going to be uncomfortable? She wrinkled her nose as she turned the key in the ignition and the engine woke with a purr.

Not if she could help it. She channeled the leading ladies from every romantic comedy she'd ever watched. She'd get herself and Gabe over the weirdness. She'd play her role, like always.

Chapter Eight

S unny drove up in the car Gabe now knew intimately. He and the Mercedes had gone on a quest together. At the low point, when he'd found the faulty crankshaft sensor, he'd despaired that they'd both make it out alive. But they had, Cinderella—the name he'd given her after Ramirez's comment and for her silvery-blue paint job that reminded him of the dress the made-over commoner wore in the movie—now road-safe. Gabe was only slightly nicked with a bandaged knuckle, the bump on his head hidden under his hair, and a missing left pinky fingernail.

Sunny opened the driver's side door that no longer squeaked, rounded the hood, and then opened the rear door with a flourish. "Your carriage, sir." She smirked and bowed.

Scowling, Gabe tossed his bag onto the seat. "I'm not riding in the back." God, why'd she have to make things even more uncomfortable than they were? He opened the passenger-side front door, slid the seat all the way back, and folded himself inside. He shoved his shaking hands between his knees.

Her smile was gone when she got into the driver's seat. "Okay, you have everything you need? Your brother's address in Vegas?"

She might look like a fairy princess, but she was pressing every one of his buttons. Gabe didn't bother responding. Instead, he pulled out the printed directions and handed them to her. "Here's how I want you to go."

"Wait, what?" She wrinkled her nose at the paper. "No, this says it'll take eight hours to get to St. Louis. We'll just hop on I-70. We'll be there in six hours, including pee breaks. You can practically see it from here." She tossed the paper onto the console between them.

"No," Gabe said. "We agreed. I pay, you drive. And since I'm paying, no interstates." Just the thought of driving sixty-five or seventy made his breath shallow. She might weigh a hundred twenty pounds, but now he feared most of it was in her lead foot.

Sunny rolled her eyes. Somehow she did it so her entire body showed her frustration. "Fine." She grumbled something Gabe couldn't quite hear, something that sounded suspiciously like "Miss Daisy," as she started the car.

Gabe directed her along the route to the state highway. He tried to keep his eyes on the paper, but he had to keep checking the road for their turns. It wasn't so bad at first since traffic kept their speed low. But when they hit the state highway, the length of it stretched ahead of them, and the speed limit leaped to fifty-five. He couldn't see the speedometer without leaning toward Sunny, but he suspected they were going at least sixty.

He wiped his sweaty palms on his jeans and checked the taut-ness of his seat belt. "Slow down," he snapped. "I'm not paying for your ticket."

Her eyebrows slammed down, and her pink lips tightened. But she eased up on the accelerator. "It's going to take us an extra day to get there at this speed. Maybe two. I have a deadline, you know."

She'd said she had a job opportunity. But she hadn't said she was in a hurry. "When's the interview?"

She checked the rear-view mirror. "Audition. In two weeks."

Of course. She was an actress. "We've got plenty of time. No need to speed." He leaned over to try to glimpse the speedometer and caught a whiff of something sweet and floral.

She inhaled sharply. "Stop that."

"Sorry, I..." Had he meant to get into her personal space? He shook his head. Being in the car was doing funny things to his brain. He leaned back against the door, but it still didn't leave a lot of space between them. He shoved his hands between his knees. Not because he was tempted to touch her—God, why would he touch a stranger?—but to try to compact himself into the small cabin.

He'd be less anxious if he didn't watch the road. His gaze landed on Sunny where she sat, her shoulders stiff and her hands tightly gripping the wheel. He studied her profile. Her nose sloped straight until the tip, which turned up the slightest bit. It hadn't been broken like Gabe's, which still had a hard ridge right where a piece of metal from the track had slammed into his face during the accident. "You, ah, you going to stay in Los Angeles for a while?"

"Yeah. Now that my promising career in customer service is over"—one corner of her mouth quirked up—"I'm going to focus on acting. I'm hoping I'll get this part." She swallowed.

So she wouldn't be going back to Ohio. In her Beach Island personnel file, a note from her manager had recommended that they try to hire her for the summer season. So that wouldn't be happening. Too bad. For the entertainment director they still had to hire. He rubbed a hand over his stomach.

Picking up the paper with their route, he checked the next turn. He always did what others needed him to do. Not this time. He'd fixed her car, and he was paying for everything. This trip was about him and what he needed. And to avoid having a panic attack, he needed to keep their speed at fifty-five.

Sunny had plenty of time before her audition. He remembered she'd said her parents lived in Los Angeles. He envisioned a loving set of parents, just as gorgeous as Sunny. She was headed toward a joyful family reunion with banter and laughter. Not like the one-way conversation Gabe had with his parents at the cemetery the day before. When he'd asked them why they hadn't told him he was adopted, they'd remained silent.

Could Gabe be headed toward a joyful family reunion, too? Would his siblings accept him just as he was? Would they give him answers? If the DNA results were accurate, would they be able to tell him why his birth parents had given him up? And only him?

He looked down at his callused hands and rubbed the bandage on his knuckle. Maybe he hadn't fit in with them, either. They'd taken one look at him, with his shock of dark hair, his thick eyebrows, and his hands that must've already looked better suited to holding a wrench than a computer mouse, and decided he didn't belong.

No, he and Sunny had nothing in common.

He directed the heat vent away from himself and rolled up his shirt sleeves.

In his jeans pocket, his phone buzzed. He pulled it out. Darlene.

"Sorry, I have to take this. It's work."

The frown line between Sunny's eyes deepened.

Darlene started talking as soon as he answered. "I'm sorry to bother you on vacation—"

"It's not a vacation," Gabe growled without thinking.

"But you said—"

"Never mind. What can I help you with?"

"It's Brandon. He emailed me to ask for the latest financials and the historicals going back five years. Is it okay to give it to him?"

Why had he waited for Gabe to leave town to ask Darlene for them? Gabe would've provided them to Brandon himself. He liked that his cousin was showing an interest in Beach Island again. If Brandon wanted to be involved in the park, and if these people in Vegas really were his family, it might make a transition easier when Gabe needed to give up his role. Because that role wouldn't belong to him anymore. If it ever had.

"Gabe?" Darlene's voice startled him.

"Sure, go ahead. Give him the reports. He's going to the Expo next week. He probably wants to familiarize himself with the numbers before he goes. Remember, he's an MBA." Not like Gabe, who hadn't even finished his bachelor's.

"Okah."

Gabe clutched the phone. "Darlene, are you all right?"

A frustrated noise came through the phone. "Jus' a li'l slurry today. Don' worry."

Don't worry? What if her symptoms flared up while he was gone? What if she fell? "I'm going to have Ramirez look in on you."

"He's busy. I don't need a babysitter." The consonants crackled back into her voice, and Gabe eased up his death-grip on the phone.

"Then I need someone to make sure you're not slacking off while I'm gone."

Next to him, Sunny shifted in her seat.

Darlene knew he was joking. "If only I had the time," she said, airily. "I'm doing my job and yours now, you know."

"I owe you a vacation when I get back." Though her vacations might not be his to approve anymore.

"Yes, you do," she said, her voice tart.

"Anything else?"

"No, that's it."

"Thanks, Darlene."

"Take care, Gabe. And try to relax."

As he disconnected the call, he looked up at the road and caught a flash of tan and white. "Watch out!"

He braced one arm on the dash and one on the door as Sunny hit the brakes hard. *Don't go off the track. The road. Don't go off the road.*

He squeezed his eyes shut.

"Let's take a ride, see if we feel anything unusual." That was what Gabe had said, minutes before Beach Island opened that day nine years ago, after Ramirez and his crew hadn't been able to figure out what was making the trouble indicator flash. Sometimes it did that. Fright or Flight was young and capricious. She'd been closed the day before, and while Gabe worked the Guest Relations desk, everyone had chewed him out, disappointed that the most popular coaster in the park had been shut down.

Before the park opened that day, Mom and Dad had let him make the decision. Well, that's what they'd said. Their hopeful expressions and glances at the park entrance where guests already queued up at the gates told him they wanted to open the ride. So he'd gone along and said they would. After a test run, of course.

"First car," Dad had called.

That was okay. Gabe had always preferred the last car. The sense of weightlessness at the top of the first hill, the way it whipped over and down, made his heart leap every time.

Ramirez lifted off his ball cap and scratched his head. "We need to do more checks. It might be the train, not the light, that's malfunctioning."

"We'll tell you if we hear anything. Promise," Mom said, patting Ramirez's broad chest before she stepped into the car.

Dad slung an arm around Mom's shoulders in the front car and twisted back to look at Gabe. He winked and gave him a thumbs-up. Gabe tightened the belt over his hips and grinned back. Sure, Fright or Flight was temperamental, but she was the best ride in the park. His parents' favorite.

Sid's black curls bounced as she leaned over him to check the restraints. They'd dated the previous summer, and she tugged the belt a second time. "Enjoy the ride." She gave the thumbs-up to Calvin in the booth, who pressed the button that set the train in motion. Gabe's head jerked back as the car pulled forward. Then his body pressed against the seat as the train clacked up the first tall hill. Way up front, Mom's blond ponytail hung down beside the head-rest, framed by the pale early-morning sky.

At last, Mom and Dad raised their arms and disappeared over the top of the hill. For just a second, Gabe was jealous of the swoops in their stomachs, the empty track stretching ahead of them, the terror of facing the practically sheer drop. The rush of panicked pleasure. But four seconds later, his own car crested the hill, his butt lifted off the seat, and he plunged down, down, down, to join them careening over the hill.

Mom was a screamer, and she didn't disappoint. Her giddy "Eeee" wafted back, along with the rush of the wind on his face.

Gravity jolted back at the bottom of the hill, and the coaster flattened out. He braced himself for the S-curve. As his right shoulder slammed into the side of the car, he heard it. A clunk and a grinding roar that juddered into his bones. His chest slammed into the restraint, and his head snapped forward as the car screeched to a shuddering halt. Something smashed into his face, and the pain that sliced across his nose and cheeks made him squeeze his eyes shut.

When his vision cleared, the front car was gone. Mom didn't even have time to squeal before the thundering crash sounded below. A cloud of dust wafted up, stinging his eyes.

"Gabe! Are you okay?" Sunny's voice came to him from far away.

"What?" he blinked his eyes open. The Mercedes idled, unmoving, in the middle of the rural highway. The sun's angle was too low, the sky winter-pale and not July's bright blue.

"Everything all right?"

"Fine." He shuddered out a shaky breath. He couldn't feel his hands. "There was a deer."

She leaned her head back against the headrest and stared up at the car's ceiling. "I saw it. It was minding its own business at the side of the road." She scanned the road before easing back onto the accelerator.

"They can be unpredictable." He rubbed the center of his chest like he could slow his racing heartbeat.

"If you'd let me take the damned interstate, there wouldn't be so many damn deer. Stupid cornfields." One at a time, she wiped her palms on her jeans.

The fields stretched out to either side of the rural road, the dry brown stalks sticking up where the tops had been sheared off during the fall harvest. A pair of deer stood in the center of the field to the right, scavenging for fallen kernels and any bits of green that remained on the frozen ground.

"Listen, you've got to let me drive and chill the hell out," she said, her gaze on the road. "Your anxiety is making me twitchy."

"I don't have anxiety." It was a lie, and they both knew it. PTSD, too, if they were listing his issues. He closed his eyes and took a long breath in, held it, and let it out slowly like he'd done with his therapist. The breathing exercises she'd taught him were useful. Talking about his emotions? Not so much. He'd given it up a few years ago.

By the time they stopped for lunch in a small-town diner, Gabe's nerves were frayed, and if Sunny's tense shoulders were an indication, so were hers.

While he paid the check, she went next door to the drugstore. She met him at the car and pulled a bottle of iced coffee and a small canister of pain medication from a sack.

He couldn't stop himself from saying it. "You shouldn't take that while you're driving."

Glaring at him, she swallowed two pills with a swig of coffee. She rolled her shoulders.

Reaching into the bag, she pulled out a bottle of no-caffeine soda and handed it to Gabe. Then she held out a carton of sleeping pills.

"What's this?" he asked.

"You need to take one to relax. You're making me tense, and now I have a headache and sore shoulders. It's for both of us."

"I don't want to take it," he snapped. Who was she to make him take a sleeping pill?

"Look." She dipped her chin. "I could've ground it up and put it in your drink. You'd have never known the difference. But I'm asking you to take it so you can relax and we can make it to St. Louis in one piece."

She was right. He'd never have known. But she wasn't exactly offering him a choice. "Fine." He checked the recommended dosage and took it, choking back the pills with the soda. "Happy now?"

"Ecstatic. Now, do some breathing exercises or something." She flipped on the radio and hunted until she found a station playing classical music.

As she pulled out of the parking space in front of the diner, Gabe leaned his head back. She hadn't touched her phone or even fiddled with the radio while they drove. Her small hands were steady on the wheel. She seemed like a safe enough driver, if a little heavy on the accelerator. If he closed his eyes, he might not even notice how they hurtled down the lonely country roads. He focused on his breathing, slowly in and out, until his eyelids drooped.

Voices woke him.

He lifted his too-heavy head from where it rested against the window. Ouch. He rubbed the twinge in his neck.

Reaching for the glove box, Sunny met his gaze. "Oh, great, you're awake." But she sounded less than thrilled.

She handed the registration to the highway patrolman peering inside the car.

"You all right, son?" he asked.

What was happening? Where were they? "Mmm," Gabe grunted.

The trooper unclipped a flashlight from his belt and shone it into Gabe's face. Too bright. Gabe squinted and held up a hand.

All the good-old-boy softness left the officer's tone. "Have you taken any drugs, sir?"

Gabe's tongue was thick in his mouth. "Yeah."

"Gabe!" Sunny's voice was sharp. "Sorry, officer. My friend gets anxious in the car. He took a sleeping pill to relax, and he's still a little fuzzy. Want to see the package?"

Gabe leaned back in the seat and tried to keep his eyes from closing again. It wouldn't help Sunny's case if he looked like he'd taken more than an over-the-counter sleep aid. He bit his tongue to wake it up in case he needed to use it.

Sunny ended up showing the patrolman the pill carton and saying a lot more words that flowed past Gabe's sleep-fogged brain. Her hands fluttered around the car like butterflies, and he suspected those long eyelashes were getting a workout, too.

Finally, the trooper said, "All right, now. Slow down, and maybe give your boyfriend a lighter dose next time."

"Yes, sir," she said. Her back was to Gabe, but Sunny's dazzling smile was reflected in the other man's face. She waited for him to return to his patrol car, then she put on her indicator, checked the mirrors, and slowly pulled back onto the road. Her hands shook a little where she gripped the wheel.

"Did you just talk yourself out of a speeding ticket?" Gabe asked. Back when he used to drive, he didn't know that was even an option. He'd just sat, sullen, hands visible, while the police officer wrote the ticket.

"Yeah." She glanced down at the speedometer and eased off the accelerator. She flicked on the headlights.

"Really? You have New York plates. Those aren't too popular around here."

"All you have to do is be friendly and reasonable. And sparkle a little. It's easy. Though"—she glanced at him—"maybe reasonable and friendly aren't your thing."

Gabe grunted. He was plenty reasonable. Friendly, too, with his friends. Which Sunny was not. Sparkle, though, was beyond him.

The sun sank low ahead of them, melting into a red puddle at the horizon. The road had filled with a few cars. Brown fields still stretched out on either side as far as Gabe could see, but the houses had started to cluster together.

"What time is it?" he asked.

"Around five. We gained an hour with the time change. We're coming up on St. Louis."

She'd been driving all day. They'd taken a lunch break, and he might have missed a fuel stop while he'd slept. "You doing okay?"

"Yeah." The corner of her mouth quirked up. "Without your nagging, it was an easy drive. Until I got careless and hit that speed trap."

Sunny slowed at a stop sign, and instead of crossing the larger road, she turned onto it.

"Wait, I don't think you were supposed to turn there." Gabe fished on the floor for his printed directions.

"We're taking a detour."

"A detour?" That woke him from his sleepy haze.

"Don't worry, there'll be traffic. We won't move too fast."

She was right. Cars crowded around them, though far more cars were coming toward them, out of the city. Sunny drummed the wheel impatiently as she navigated through the tangle of interstates and across the bridge over the Mississippi River.

"There it is!" She pointed across him out the right side of the windshield.

The Arch looped, dark and gray against the thin clouds lit orange by the sunset. The buildings of downtown St. Louis huddled behind it, and in the foreground, the river flowed, sluggish, reflecting not one sparkle now that the sun had sunk below the horizon.

"I've only seen pictures of it," she said. "Do you think it'll still be open?"

Gabe looked it up on his phone. "The arch is open until six, but the tram—" He shuddered. No way was he going up inside that thing. "The last tram has already left." *Thank God.* "The grounds are open later. You can stand beside it if you want. I'll take your picture."

She shimmied in her seat. "Let's do it." Then she launched into "St. Louis Blues," and Gabe didn't mind the speed, the traffic, or the quick way Sunny changed lanes anymore. Her clear voice filled the car, belying the mournful lyrics. He wanted the song to go on forever.

In the end, Gabe was glad they stopped. The bright lights around the Arch illuminated the joy on Sunny's face as she ran her hand along the sleek metal exterior. Then, farther away, she made him take a picture so that it looked like she was hanging from the Arch like a child on the monkey bars.

Later, as they tugged their bags into a nearby Marriott, he said, "I thought you were in a hurry. We could've shaved an hour off the drive tomorrow if we'd stopped on the other side of St. Louis."

"Seeing the Arch was totally worth it. You have to stop and enjoy the world around you, Gabe."

That was what his parents used to say to him. Until they'd taken that last risk and stopped Gabe's enjoyment altogether.

The truth stiffened his resolve. No matter how attractive she was, how enchanting her voice was, no matter how much her joyful personality lit up the dark corners inside him, Sunny was a thrill-seeker who enjoyed the world in a way Gabe never could. She was a princess, off on an adventure, and he was the ogre, along for the trek. But this wasn't a fairytale. He and Sunny were only travelers on a journey together, much too different for a happily ever after.

Chapter Nine

Another day, another printout of fifty-mile-an-hour state highways.

Sunny gripped the steering wheel and checked the speedometer. She eased off the gas. No point in getting pulled over again. Talking her way out of tickets would take more time than if she just obeyed the speed limit.

Stupid speed traps.

She flicked a glance at Gabe. His color was better, but he still gripped the door handle and kept his gaze anywhere but on the straight stretch of road ahead. Car Gabe was very different from the version she'd met at his townhouse and in the parking lot of Cata's apartment. There, he'd been confident, sure. Sexy.

What was his deal? Had he been in a car accident? Or did he get motion sick? She hoped he didn't ralph in her car. It was old and the upholstery was a bit ratty, but it smelled decent. All it'd take was one puking incident, and it'd never be the same. He needed a distraction.

"So, Gabe," she said, "what should we talk about? We already covered the weather and the price of gas during breakfast. Got any interesting skeletons in your closet?"

She winced as soon as she said it. His parents were dead, so he had a matching pair of skeletons. *Great distraction, genius.*

"Don't answer that," she said. "Let's listen to some music." She touched the radio button and scanned to the first station. "Fool, I'm a Queen," the one hit from Gwen's brief foray into pop music, blared through the speakers. Wincing, she punched the power button for silence. *Not today, Mom.*

"I forgot about that new hands-free system you installed." She directed her phone's virtual assistant to play her Broadway playlist. "I hope you like showtunes."

His body was so big inside her Mercedes that she felt him shrug. Crap, mentioning his dead parents had gotten him stuck in his feels. Because no one shrugged at showtunes: they either loved them or despised them. But when "Let It Go" came on, he sat up straight.

"I know this one," he said.

"You must have some tween nieces." Sunny smiled. It was one of her favorites. Too bad it'd been played to death.

"Nah, I'm an only child."

Shit, shit, shit. She knew that. She should've played "Oops!...I Did It Again."

"We play this one during the winter wonderland show," he said, "on Saturdays."

"You mean at Beach Island?"

"Yeah, we do a whole number with a snow queen and dancing snowmen. We even make it fake snow on stage. Makes the guests feel cooler in the middle of summer."

Beach Island's costume department had a snow queen gown, yet she'd had to wear a nineteenth-century outfit that was more patches than dress. "I bet the kids love it," she said. "I wish I'd seen it."

"It's only on during the summer, when the high-school and college-age kids are working. We wouldn't have done it while you worked there."

"Too bad." It would've been fun to sing on a stage for a thousand people or more. She hadn't done that for a while, not since before she'd moved to New York.

As their conversation fizzled and died, Sunny checked the speedometer again and scanned the roadside for deer. She didn't realize she'd started to sing along until Gabe shifted beside her and brushed her arm. Shivers erupted under her sleeve.

She moved her elbow from the console and clutched the wheel with both hands. "What?"

"You can sing." His cheeks darkened. "I mean, I know you can, since you were a caroler at Beach Island. But you can *really* sing."

Warmth flooded her belly. "It's what I do. When I'm not doing customer service, that is." She flashed him a twisted smile. "I act, sing, dance, even play a little piano when coerced."

"I bet that took hard work and discipline."

She glanced at him again. Not the first thing most people said when they found out what she did for a living. Unexpected. "It did."

"I love the shows we put on at the park. I wish I'd seen your group perform. But I, ah, didn't really get out of my office during Holly Days."

"Oh." He was probably thinking about his dead parents again. She'd spent the holidays with Cata, and although her mother had unenthusiastically invited her on her annual ski trip, she'd never even considered it. Not without a job. Not without wheels or airfare to get herself there. Still, as cold and remote as her parents were, at least she knew they were out there, and she could call them whenever she wanted. The holidays had to be rough for someone who couldn't, no matter how much he wanted it.

He surprised her by asking, "Why'd you decide to become a performer?"

She smiled, remembering the karaoke bar she and some of her castmates had frequented after filming wrapped on Fridays. "I always liked the applause, the feeling I'd done something that made people happy. My grandparents used to say I sparkled onstage. That's why everyone called me Sunny. Except my parents, of course." How had that slipped out? She didn't want to talk about her parents. "It must be similar for you at Beach Island. You offer people a break from their daily lives, a chance to let loose and enjoy themselves."

But that didn't make Gabe relax the way she'd expected. Instead, he tensed.

"What's the matter?" She scanned the road. Not a deer in sight. Had she said the wrong thing?

"Nothing." He took out his phone and tapped it.

Shit. They'd almost had a moment there. She'd almost punched through the stone fortifications Gabe had built around himself. But that glimmer of softness he'd shown when she sang made her hope that if she tried a little harder, she could ease his pain for a while.

Not now. Tension built on his side of the car as he continued to type on his phone. "Is everything all right?"

"It's just work. I really shouldn't have taken time off."

His phone hadn't left his hand except while he'd slept in the car yesterday. Was that why his girlfriend had broken up with him? He'd spent too much time working and not enough time wooing? "Aren't you between seasons right now? What is there even to do at the park?"

Gabe scowled at his phone. "There's always something to do. Maintenance. A new ride we're thinking about buying. And I sent my cousin to a conference. He hasn't been too involved in the business to this point, and he has a lot of questions." He tapped out another sentence or two. "Plus, my assistant. She has some health issues. I worry about her."

"That is a lot." He sounded like a producer on a show. "What is it you do, again?"

"Back office," he muttered.

Okay, then. He didn't want to be asked about work. But she could still make him feel a little better.

After asking her phone to play "All That Jazz," she belted out the lyrics so that the melody filled up her Mercedes. She growled on the sauciest lines. If she could lighten some of grumpy Gabe's burden, she would.

Little by little, his stiff shoulders eased, and he leaned back into the leather seat. He slid his phone into his pocket.

The next song was "Come to Me" from *Les Misérables,* and she let the aching beauty of the song infuse her voice. When she'd performed it at a college production of the musical, she'd let pathos color it. But now, she kept it light, focusing on the peace Fantine feels as she approaches death, knowing her child will be cared for. Still, she hoped Gabe had never seen it. Today she couldn't go five minutes without bringing up dead parents.

When she stole a glance at him, though, he'd closed his eyes, and the faintest hint of a smile curved his lips. She wished she could gaze on that relaxed face, burn it into her memory for the next time he got all gruff and growly. But she dragged her attention back to the road.

Sometime when she wasn't hurtling along the road at seventy—whoops, fifty-five—miles an hour, she'd coax that expression out of him again.

Chapter Ten

When they stopped that night in a small town in Kansas, Gabe's muscles were stiff from being folded inside Cinderella like a Jack-in-the-box. He could tell by the way she rolled her neck, by her quick grimace when she shifted in her seat, that Sunny was aching, too. He almost felt bad about adding hours to their trip. Not bad enough to risk another panic attack, though.

The motel shared a parking lot with a diner. The good thing about taking the state highways was finding gems like this pair of small local businesses. As the CEO of a family-run corporation, Gabe felt a kinship with these buildings that had stood against the national chains. He hoped Beach Island could do the same.

When Sunny stretched beside the car and rubbed her shoulder, Gabe said, "I'll check us in. Why don't you go get us a table at the diner?"

She smiled, the one that dazzled him and made him forget she was the one who'd sent him on this terrible quest. "I bet they have a killer apple pie."

"I wouldn't turn down something sweet." He cringed. How did Sunny keep turning him into an awkward teenager? "Pie, that is. I'll meet you there in a few."

In the bathroom of the clean but shabby motel room, Gabe

checked himself in the mirror as he washed his hands. His eyes weren't as pinched as they'd been last night. His hair was probably flat in the back from the nap Sunny's singing had lulled him into. That day, he'd had only a couple of flashes back to the accident. Nothing like the thing with the deer the day before.

After checking that his door and Sunny's were locked, he strode back across the parking lot. The weather had been clear so far, and stars sparkled overhead. He breathed in the dry, cold air.

The diner was humid with the warmth of cooking and the bodies of many locals crammed inside. Gabe spotted Sunny at a small booth by the windows. Shucking off his coat, he made his way to her.

Uncharacteristically, she hunched her shoulders, almost like she was hiding behind the laminated menu sheet. She startled when Gabe wedged himself between the vinyl seat and the melamine table.

"What's wrong?" he asked.

"Nothing," she said too quickly. Her gaze darted to the counter and then back to Gabe, but the smile she gave him was brittle.

Gabe turned to look at the counter. A couple of guys in canvas coats and baseball caps stared at him. They were big, though not as big as him, and weathered-looking even though they couldn't have been older than thirty-five. The blond one squinted at him before he turned back toward the counter. The dark-haired one scanned Gabe from his casual oxfords to his khakis and all the way up to Gabe's set jaw. Slowly, he rotated on his stool so his back was to them. Gabe scanned the dining room, but no one else paid him any attention.

"Those guys weren't bothering you, were they?" He jerked his thumb back toward the men at the counter. He shouldn't have sent her in alone. He'd use his bulk to show everyone she wasn't unprotected.

"No," she said quickly. Gabe stared at the part in her hair to try to interpret that *no*. Had she said it because they *were* bothering her, but she didn't want Gabe to do anything about it, or did it mean that they weren't bothering her, and she was interested in one of them? Or both? Gabe hadn't yet seen this un-sunny, terse side of her personality. What did it mean?

When the waitress trotted over to take their orders, Gabe shook it off. He was hungry, considering all he'd done that day was sit in the car, but he went with it, ordering the meatloaf and apple pie for dessert.

His phone buzzed while they spoke with the waitress, and after she'd retreated to the kitchen, he pulled it out. Another text from Brandon. For someone who'd ignored the family business for the past eight years, Brandon suddenly had a lot of detailed questions about it: the annual attendance, the age of various rides, their profitability over the past five years. Gabe smiled. The expo must have sparked his cousin's interest. Maybe he'd like to come in and work with Gabe. He'd happily unload some of his responsibilities on his cousin. Not operations or safety—never that—but Gabe would be overjoyed to give up public relations or human resources. Plus, it'd be fun to hang out with his cousin the way they used to do.

A chill dribbled down the back of his neck. If he belonged to this family in Vegas, would Brandon still want to hang out? Or had he only been friendly because of their blood connection?

He looked up from his phone when a body loomed over their table.

"Hey, darlin'," the blond man from the counter drawled. "You're not from around here, are you?"

Sunny gazed up at him, and this time her smile wasn't brittle. It was glittering steel. "Nope."

"Though you look familiar." He passed a callused hand over his pale stubble. "You been here long?"

Sunny ducked her head. "No, just passing through."

"Around here, we pay better attention to our women than that." He tilted his head toward Gabe. Gabe's fingers stilled on his phone.

"That so?" Now her eyes glittered, too.

Was she flirting with this guy? Gabe wanted to crawl under the table and leave them to it.

"Yeah, I can show you the town. Leave this guy to his phone."

Gabe shoved the device into his pocket.

"What's there to see around here?" she asked.

"Bet you've never seen stars like we've got out here."

"Bet I haven't," she said. "And what more do you need than the stars on a night like this?"

"Only a little music and the love of a good woman."

Damn, this guy was smooth. Gabe could've never come up with a line like that. He leaned back against the squeaky vinyl.

"'I am constant as the northern star,'" Sunny said, "'Of whose true-fixed and resting quality/ There is no fellow in the firmament.'"

The blond man said, "Wait, I know that one. It's from *Romeo and Juliet.*" Gabe squinted at him. He wouldn't have pegged him as a Shakespearean scholar. He must have finished college. Unlike Gabe.

"*Julius Caesar,* but still, pretty good," Sunny said. "It means thanks, but no thanks. Have a nice night," she said, more gently.

He shoved his hands in his jeans pockets, and with a final sneer at Gabe, left the diner.

An awkward silence blanketed their table.

"I, ah, don't mean to get in the way of your...social life," Gabe said.

"Social life?" Sunny snorted. "You mean I could've gone out with that guy, given him some good lovin', and you wouldn't have cared?"

Gabe's stomach burned. Keeping his face neutral, he held his hands out in front of him. "Whoa. I just mean, you don't have to spend every minute with me. You can meet other people. If you want."

"We're leaving in the morning. Why would I want to meet anyone tonight?"

Another stab in his gut. Why did he care if Sunny spent time with anyone else? "I—we don't know each other very well. I don't really know anything about you." And she knew nothing about him. Aside from the obvious: that his birth family hadn't wanted him, and his adoptive parents had hidden the truth. He stared at the melamine tabletop.

Sunny tapped the top of his hand, and he looked up to find her biting her plush, pink lower lip. "You're right. Let's play a game until our food gets here. A game of Truth. I'll start. I'm not the kind of girl who picks up guys in diners. I mean, I'm into sex, don't get me wrong. But I usually have to actually like someone before I sleep with them."

"Are you seeing someone now?" The question popped out of Gabe before he could stop it.

Her lips twitched like she was suppressing a smile. "The game is Truth, not Twenty Questions. Now it's your turn."

Okay. Tit for tat. "My girlfriend broke up with me right before Christmas."

She made a sound like the buzzer at a hockey game. "You already told me that. New truths only, please."

Crap, he'd told her that in their very first conversation. "Fine. We'd dated for almost a year. I...I proposed. She said no. Said we'd stayed together because of inertia. And I was only proposing because I thought she expected it. Because I always do what people expect of me."

Sunny's grin faded, and she stiffened. "Was it true?"

"No questions. Your rule."

"Fine." She straightened her knife and fork on her paper napkin. "I guess I'm the same. Right now, I'm driving cross-country because my parents asked me. They're the ones with the job opportunity. Though I—" She looked up with a tight smile. "That's my truth."

He didn't know her well, but Gabe could see the pain hiding under her smile. Families were tough. A truth about his parents slid to the tip of his tongue, but he held it back. Instead, he said, "I have a cousin. Brandon. We're almost the same age, so we hung out a lot together." He rotated his cutlery roll on the table.

She grimaced. "You're terrible at this, Gabe. That's a fact, but it's not a truth. How does Brandon make you *feel?*"

Always having a friend across the playground at recess. Brandon and Gabe picking up each package from under Aunt Pat's Christmas tree, shaking it to guess what was inside. Late nights at the diner near Beach Island with a couple of girls after the park closed. "He always accepted me. Even though he looked like an Armstrong and I didn't. Aunt Pat—his mom—used to call me the family's black sheep. Only when my mom couldn't hear."

"Oh." Sunny's forehead wrinkled. "I'm glad he was nice to you. That you had a friend. An almost-brother. I never had cousins. Or siblings. I come from a long line of only children. Growing up was kind of lonely. Until I started acting. The other actors and I spent a lot of time together, so it was sort of like a second family. Better than my first family because they accepted me as I was. No expectations, even though... Anyway, it was a safe place where I didn't have to be *on* all the time, like at home." She dipped her finger into the puddle of condensation around her glass and drew a circle on the table.

Ah. He knew all about playing a role. Though his parents had never made him feel that way. Not until after they'd died. "Why'd you have to—"

"Wait! That's, like, four truths. Now you owe me at least two."

But Gabe had spotted the waitress coming toward them, plates in hand. He gave Sunny a fake sorry look. "Time's up."

She scowled at him. "Cheater."

"Definitely not," he said. "You can have that one for free. I'm the dullest, most consistent, dependable person ever. In high school, I was voted Most Likely to Stay Married for Fifty Years."

She looked up from the bowl of salad the waitress had slid in front of her. "That's sweet, Gabe."

"Yeah, I get that a lot. Exciting, not so much. I'm one hundred percent boring. Ask any of my ex-girlfriends."

"Exciting's overrated." She stabbed her fork into her salad.

"Exciting is never being in a relationship for more than three months. Spectacular break-ups. Jewelry throwing."

"Wait, jewelry throwing?" Gabe had seen rings thrown at cheating husbands on TV, but never in real life.

"This guy I was dating, Cade. We were at the beach one day, and he gave me a necklace. A heart with two gemstones, one for my birthstone, one for his. Ugliest thing you've ever seen. For our *three-month anniversary*, he said." She set down her fork and frowned. "I lost my shit. He was a nice guy, but when I thought about dating him for another three months, about carrying his birthstone against my skin, I felt like he was trying to put me in a box, just like that pendant. I tried to give it back, and when he wouldn't take it, I threw it, box and all, into the ocean. Then I ran." She blinked a few times, fast. "He called me a psychotic bitch on Instagram."

"That's terrible." Though Gabe knew the pain of thinking everything was fine and then finding out it wasn't. Of being rejected. The pain in his stomach returned, the one he felt every time he thought about his birth parents. He stared at his uneaten meatloaf and yearned, inexplicably, for Aunt Pat's dried-out version he always drowned in ketchup.

"Him or me?" Sunny's voice was almost too low for him to hear. But he wouldn't pretend he hadn't heard.

"Him, of course. Only cowards troll people online. He should've talked to you."

She grimaced. "He couldn't. I made sure of it. I was long gone by the time he was ready to talk." Her expression faded into something sadder. "I'm not cut out for long-term, so I knew we'd never last. I thought he did, too."

Pain stabbed through his gut, and he set down his pie fork. "Me, I'm no good at endings."

Sunny squeezed her eyes shut and rubbed her palm against her forehead. "I guess Truth and dinner isn't the best combination. Want to take our pie to go? It'll be good for breakfast."

Over dinner, Truth had been a game. And yet, the next day,

they'd be hurtling at fifty-five miles an hour toward his very real Truth.

His appetite might not be the only casualty.

Chapter Eleven

Why *did I have to open my big mouth and let all that truth fall out?* Sunny gripped her Styrofoam box of pie and brisk-walked into the motel lobby, her boots clomping on the tile. Anything to get away from Gabe, who knew too much now. She'd never told anyone about the blowup with Cade. Ever. Not any of her friends in New York. Not Cata. Certainly not her parents. To anyone who asked, she'd just said they'd broken up. And that she'd deleted her Instagram account out of boredom. She'd certainly told no one else that the hideous necklace had made her feel like a cornered animal.

The way Gabe had lowered his eyes to his plate of meatloaf proved he agreed with Cade that she was a psychotic bitch. And she hadn't even told him about her tantrum on the set of *New York Bomb Squad.* Or ripping off her badge at DN-YAY. Well, at least he'd have no regrets when they parted ways in Vegas.

Especially since she'd managed to remind him of his dead parents yet again. She was the tongue that couldn't stop touching the sore tooth. She was usually better than this. But being stuck in Ohio had messed everything up until she hardly knew who she was anymore.

The front desk was straight ahead. Shit, she didn't even know where she was going. *Elevators.* She swerved left, toward the sign.

But her left foot accelerated faster than her right. Like it was on ball bearings, it swept out in front of her, upsetting her balance. Her spine wrenched, right at her lower back. She flung out her arms—*save the pie!*—to offset her out-of-control left leg, but it was too late. She was headed for the hard tile floor. She braced herself for the impact.

An enormous hand gripped her biceps, hard, and she jerked upright. When her boots met the floor, the left one slipped again, but this time she stayed vertical, held by the upper arm like a kitten scruffed by its mama. She wobbled and set her left foot down. There was a tiny splash.

Gabe slowly eased his grip but didn't release her. "I've got you," he growled.

Tingles swept up her spine. And then a pinch. She grimaced and stepped toward Gabe, out of the puddle of water.

"Okay?" he asked, ducking down to gaze into her eyes.

Her cheeks burned. She wasn't normally clumsy, but she hadn't been watching, too focused on her own dark thoughts. And pie. She nodded.

Gabe led her to the front desk. He only released her when he stood in front of it and pointed back at the puddle. "There's water over there. She almost fell."

"Oh," said the young receptionist. "Sorry 'bout that." His eyes drifted down to his screen.

Gabe waited. Three beats. Five. "You're going to clean it up, right? And put a sign there."

"Yeah. Just a minute." The guy's attention was still focused on his screen.

"No. Now. That's a slip hazard. I'll wait." Gabe's gaze raked over Sunny, and she barely held back another shiver. That stern growl made muscles clench inside her. He turned back toward the receptionist, who'd finally gone through the door behind the desk. He returned with a mop bucket and a yellow caution sign.

Gabe waited until the guy made a halfhearted pass of the mop over the puddle and then propped the sign over it. Then he nodded to Sunny. She shivered again. Was sternness a kink? If so, she had it. Bad.

She forced her feet toward the elevators. When the doors slid open, she stepped in, gripping her slightly mashed box of pie. Gabe pressed the button for the third floor.

"Thanks for that. I thought I was going to hit the deck." Her nervous giggle surprised her, and she winced. Grown women didn't giggle.

"You okay?" He watched her face.

She rubbed her arm with the hand holding the pie box. "That's some grip you've got. I might have a bruise."

"Sorry," he muttered and dropped his gaze to her boots.

The door slid open, and when Sunny took a step, pain in her back took her breath. Gabe must have heard her gasp. "What's wrong?"

"Just a twinge in my back. Must've happened when I slipped."

"Can you walk?"

Was he offering to carry her to her door? "Of course I can." She bit her lip to distract herself from the throb in her back and brushed past him into the hallway. Right or left?

"This way." He turned left and walked halfway down the hallway. He slid a card into a slot in the door and pushed it open. "Yours." He handed her the card.

Sunny stepped inside and spotted her suitcase on the dresser. "Thanks."

"No problem. Need anything?"

"No, I'm fine." She still had the ibuprofen from their first day on the road.

"I'm next door if you change your mind."

Change her mind? What was he offering? But when she turned, he was already gone, the neighboring door clicking shut behind him.

That was best. She hadn't wanted a one-night stand with that blond dude, and she certainly didn't want a complicated week-long whatever with Gabe. Mr. Most-Likely-to-Stay-Married-for-Fifty-Years was a poor match for Ms. Three-Months-Max. Ms. Never-Repeat-Her-Parents'-Mistake.

She scuffed to the bed, lowered herself gingerly, and zipped out of her boots. It was only eight-thirty. Too early for sleep. Still, she changed into pajamas and cuddled into the laundry-softened sheets with her phone.

She was texting with Cata when a soft knock sounded on her door. Who'd be knocking in a strange city after nine at night? She held her breath.

"It's me, Gabe."

Oh.

She eased out of the bed and padded toward the door. She opened it to find Gabe, still wearing his coat, his cheeks flushed. Was it because he'd been outside in the cold or because Sunny was standing there, braless, in a tank top and pajama pants?

He shoved a plastic drugstore sack at her. "Here."

She took it from him and peeked inside. "A heating pad? And Tylenol PM?"

"For your back. Do you need anything for your arm?" He gazed at it. "Ice?"

Between text messages with Cata, she'd touched the fingerprints he'd left on her skin. Caressed, more like. They were red now and might turn purple tomorrow. "No, it doesn't hurt." She held up the sack. "Thanks for this."

"Anyti—"

She closed the door before he could finish. It was rude, and she was sorry. But she couldn't let him see the tears that had sprung up in her eyes.

She'd danced since she was five. And never, not in all those years, had anyone brought her as much as a bandage. Through broken blisters, lost toenails, sprains, and bruises, she'd carried her own first-aid kit. She'd bandaged, iced, and wrapped her own injuries—

and others'—without a second thought. Until today. Until Gabe had brought her a stupid heating pad.

And she was not about to let him know how his caretaking had wormed its way into her blackened heart.

Pale gray light stabbed through the gap between the motel's curtains directly into Sunny's face. She groaned and stretched against the soft sheets. The heating pad crinkled under her. It had turned off—of course Gabe had bought the kind with an auto-shutoff safety feature—but sweat had adhered it to her skin. She sat up and pulled it away. No more sharp pain, just a dull ache, barely there under the waistband of her sleep pants.

She'd had worse. Driving all day wouldn't be an issue. Not even with grumpy Gabe. When her lips quirked upward, she covered her mouth with her hand.

Stop it. He's not for you.

Although... They had to ride together. Enjoying his company wouldn't hurt anyone.

She rotated and swung her feet over the side of the bed. After a brief pause, she slid off the bed and headed into the shower.

Gabe had shared only a couple of truths at the diner last night, but she already understood him better than she had after sixteen hours on the road. His quick hands saving her from falling on her ass and then bringing her a freaking care package revealed the gooey center under his grumpy outer crust. The way he'd wanted to protect her from Blondie McFlirtyPants, the way he'd blushed when he'd admitted how "boring" he was, had given away even more. Gabe was one loyal dude, and those ex-girlfriends of his were idiots. If her parents' example hadn't proved love was a farce, she'd have made a move, sore back or no.

She turned off the water and patted her skin with the threadbare towel. Gabe was too smart for her moves. He'd be way too cautious to start something when she'd all but guaranteed she'd leave him broken-hearted.

She was a limited engagement, like Bernadette Peters' one-week show that she'd pulled every string she had to score a ticket to. Gabe was looking for *Phantom of the Opera,* the longest-running show on Broadway. God, how she hated *Phantom.* So creepy.

In the car, she played the original cast recording of *Into the Woods* and couldn't help singing along. Gabe didn't seem to mind. And when she sang, he didn't watch her speedometer. Still, a couple of hours later, she was squirming in the driver's seat. A fresh pain had erupted between her shoulder blades. Her lower back twinged again, too.

"What's wrong?" Gabe asked. She felt the weight of his dark-eyed stare.

"Nothing. Just a little stiff."

"Why don't we stop in the next town for coffee and a stretch?"

As much as she wanted to press on, her back needed a rest. "Okay. In the meantime, want to distract me with some mus—"

His phone rang, interrupting her.

"Sorry, it's work. I'll just be a minute," he said, already pressing the answer button. "Hi, Darlene."

She tried to sing in her head to avoid eavesdropping on Gabe's conversation with his assistant, but his normally calm voice rose, alarmed.

"I'll get Ramirez to call an ambulance."

Ambulance? Sunny glanced at him. His thick eyebrows hunched over his eyes, and his other hand clenched into a fist on his knee. He listened for a minute.

"No. You need to go to the hospital." He listened again. "Fine. Your doctor. And I don't care that no one's in the office. I'll ask Pat to go in."

Sunny shivered at the authoritative tone in his voice. Why did that turn her on? She stared hard at the road, trying to mind her own business, until he shocked her with his next words.

"I'm the goddamn CEO. If I say to go home, you leave and lock up the office. I'll close the whole damn park and have security come drag you out if I have to."

Whoa. She'd known Gabe's last name was Armstrong, but it was a common name, and she hadn't connected the dots. During the four weeks she'd worked at Beach Island, she'd discovered the peaceful little garden on the west side of the grounds, the one dedicated *to Luke and Lucille Armstrong, from their loving family.* A coworker had told Sunny the Armstrongs had died in an accident on the roller coaster that used to be there. Their son, who was now the CEO, had torn it down and installed the garden in their memory. How old had he been when they'd died? Had he witnessed the accident? Her chest squeezed, and she forgot all about her sore back.

He was still arguing with Darlene when signs warned of the reduced speed limit. Sunny slowed as a small town opened up around them. Seeing a storefront that advertised hot coffee, she pulled into the parking lot.

Gabe ended the call, scowling.

"Everything okay?" she asked.

"I wish—never mind. I need to call Ramirez to make sure she's going to the doctor." He finally looked at her. "My assistant has multiple sclerosis. MS. Sometimes she experiences numbness, and I hate it that she's alone in the office where she could fall and no one would know."

"I hope she's okay." The guy had a lot to worry about.

"I've had my maintenance crew chief keeping an eye out. He'll make sure she sees her doctor." He tapped his phone.

"I'll get us some coffee. Be back in a few."

He nodded, and Sunny got out, shivering in the shocking cold. Even with the buildings around them, the wind blew in from the plains, hard and chill.

She popped a couple of ibuprofen tablets while she waited for the coffee. By the time she turned to leave, cups in hand, Gabe was there to open the door and take one of the drinks.

"Is she all right?" Sunny asked when they were enclosed again inside the warm car.

"Ramirez is taking her to her doctor," he said. "He'll call me later with an update. How's your back?"

She shook her head. He went straight from worrying about Darlene to worrying about her. "It's fine. The stretch did me good."

After one more sip of coffee, she pulled back onto the rural highway. Once they'd left the town behind and she was up to speed, she glanced at Gabe. Unlike yesterday, he stared out the window, but she didn't think he saw the barren fields they passed.

"I, uh, didn't know you were one of *those* Armstrongs." She didn't normally hesitate, but it wasn't every day you found out you'd been driving your former boss across the country.

"Which—? Oh." He deflated beside her.

"I'm sorry about your parents."

"Me, too."

"You had to've been pretty young when you took over." The trees in Founders' Park weren't fully mature, but they weren't saplings, either.

"I'd just turned twenty-one."

When Sunny turned twenty-one, she went on a three-day drinking spree with her college roommates. She still couldn't stand the smell of rum. "That's a lot. Were you even done with school?"

"No. I dropped out. There was a lot to do at the park."

"Like rip out that coaster." As soon as she'd said it, she full-body flinched. God, was she ever going to develop a filter around Gabe?

He shifted away, toward the door. "Yeah."

"I'm sorry. I shouldn't have said that. Sometimes my mouth gets away from me."

"It's okay. It's true." He rubbed his hands over his thighs, making a rough scratching sound against the cotton. "It was my fault."

Sunny glanced at him. "I heard it was an accident."

"Even accidents have causes." His shoulders shifted. "Ramirez wanted to take the train apart for an inspection. But I okayed the test run."

God, how she wished her coworker had told her that so she wouldn't have gone and stepped in Gabe's guilt and tracked it all over the car. "You didn't make them get on the ride, did you?"

"No." His voice echoed off the window glass.

Then she remembered how anxious highway driving made him. That he no longer drove. She winced. "Were you on the ride, too?"

"Yeah. But I was in the last car. Only the first two went off the track. Listen, can we not talk about this anymore?"

"I'm sorry. Really. Want me to turn on some music?"

"Yeah, that'd be great."

She switched on *Mamma Mia!* because it was the peppiest soundtrack she could think of. Then she placed her right hand over his left. He didn't flinch away like she half-expected him to do. Instead, he rested his thumb on the back of her fingers. They drove that way on the long, flat road until it was time to stop for lunch, Gabe wrapped in his sad memories and Sunny gripping the hand of the strongest man she'd ever met.

Chapter Twelve

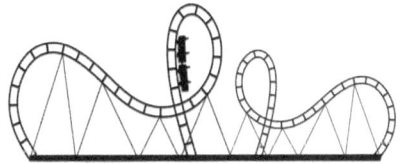

In high school, science had been Gabe's favorite subject, right up to the time they'd had to dissect frogs. His lab partner, Fiona Abernathy, and he had looked at the pickled frog, its skin wrinkly and its limbs stiff.

"I can't believe we have to do this," she'd muttered, squeezing her eyes shut. "I'm a vegetarian."

"By now, you should have made an incision and pinned back the skin," the teacher announced.

When Fiona didn't move to touch the scalpel, Gabe took a deep breath—a bad idea considering all the alcohol fumes around—picked up the knife, and, with a silent apology to the poor frog, slit its belly down the middle. His eyes burned as he made the horizontal cuts that allowed him to pull back its skin to expose its organs and tack it to the tray with pins.

Fiona crowded over his shoulder. "Huh. That's pretty neat. Move over."

She went on to become a surgeon.

Trapped inside Cinderella with Sunny, Gabe felt a new kinship with that frog. She'd slit him open and pinned back his top layers, and, like Fiona, she'd poked around inside.

It hadn't seemed to bother the frog. He was dead. Gabe, very much alive, didn't care for it.

"Oh, look! They have a Holiday Inn!" Sunny pointed to the lit-up billboard just outside the small Colorado town they were approaching. "I never thought I'd be excited about one of those. You think they have a bar? Or a restaurant?"

He grunted, which was enough for her. She navigated to the motel, which looked newer than the place they'd stayed the night before. Sure enough, it had a crowded bar where a couple of televisions showed a basketball game. Another TV showed a weather report.

They stepped up to the counter. "Checking in?" the clerk asked. He was older than last night's careless youth, but he kept one eye on the basketball game.

Gabe slid his license and credit card across the counter.

While the clerk typed on his keyboard, Sunny asked, low, "You okay, Gabe?"

"Yeah, just—just tired. How about you? How's the back?" He didn't touch her lower back, where it probably hurt. Instead, he laid a hand on her shoulder where it met her neck and kneaded the tight muscles there. Like holding her hand in the car, massaging the soft skin of her neck felt right.

She let out a groan better suited to a bedroom than the lobby of a family motel. "My back's not bad, but that's great."

He rubbed her shoulder until the clerk slid across a paper folio with two card keys inside. Gabe waited for a few seconds.

"Um." He'd been too busy touching Sunny to tell him what they needed. "We need two rooms, please. You have two rooms, right?" Gabe's heart slammed against his ribs. He needed quiet. And space. As much as he could get tonight. Sharing a room—he swallowed—with Sunny wouldn't allow him to stitch his skin back together.

The guy had already turned his attention to the Nuggets game, but he glanced at them. "Sorry, I assumed you...never mind." He returned to his computer. "Would next door be okay?"

Not really.

"Perfect," Sunny said. The clerk handed her another card key, and they headed toward the elevator.

Upstairs, Gabe leaned on the door of his room while Sunny inserted her card into her lock. Instead of going inside, she propped the door open with her bag and stepped over to him.

"Want to head down to the bar with me? I smelled food," she said.

"No, thanks." Flayed open, he craved touch, tenderness. He'd already gone too far by massaging Sunny's shoulder. Who knew what he'd do if they spent more time together? Something he'd regret, for sure. "I think I'll just lie down. It's been a long day."

"I could bring something up for you. We could watch the game together."

Then he remembered all the men in the bar. Would one of them come on to her like that guy at the diner last night? Harass her? "No, I...just let me set my stuff down, and I'll bring you whatever you want." He slid his card into the lock.

"Gabe." She laid her hand on his forearm, over his coat. "You're tired. I'll be fine. But thank you for offering. You're a good man, and I'm glad I know you."

She rose onto her tiptoes and kissed him. Not on the lips, and not on the cheek, but in that no-man's-land in between, just at the corner of his mouth. Her lips were soft, and the fragrance of her hair wafted over him. She hadn't used the shampoo from last night's motel, the stuff in the dispenser stuck to the shower wall. No, her hair smelled like the time Gabe had gone with his parents to visit the theme parks in Florida during spring break and they'd stopped at an orange grove, the trees heavy with white flowers and a fragrance he could've floated on. He hadn't wanted to get back into the car. And now he wanted to bury his face in Sunny's golden hair that smelled like Florida sunshine and happiness.

Too soon, she stepped back. She smiled, not the full-blown grin she sometimes flashed that warmed his chest, but a softer, more intimate smile that made her eyes soft as the twilight sky. His body didn't even know how to react to that one. Well, it did because it was definitely reacting, but clearly its signals had gotten crossed.

She laid her small palm on his chest, right over his heart, and said, "G'night, Gabe. Call me if you change your mind."

He nodded, not trusting himself not to say that he'd already changed his mind and try to follow her into her room. Instead, he turned the handle and walked into his own room.

Alone.

The first flakes fell while they ate rubbery scrambled eggs and a melon medley in the hotel's lounge the next morning.

Sunny, who should've known better after spending January in Ohio, jumped up and ran to the window. "It's snowing!" Gabe scowled at the flakes drifting down and drained his tiny paper cup of coffee. He picked up both of their cups, refilled them at the urn, and carried them back with more containers of vanilla creamer for Sunny.

When she bounced back to the table, he said, "You've lived in New York and Ohio. You've seen snow before."

"Oh, I have. But after growing up in southern California, it's still magical. Every time."

He picked up their empty plates and set them in the plastic bin. "You won't think it's so magical when you're driving through it."

"Oh." She slumped a little before she brightened. "But it'll be so pretty."

He snorted.

They retrieved their bags from their rooms and laid the card keys on the check-in desk. A different clerk, a gray-haired woman this time, peered at them. "You're checking out? Storm's coming in, you know."

"Yeah?" Gabe asked. "How bad?"

"Twelve to fifteen inches."

"Yeesh. Sunny, you sure you want to drive in this? We could stay here today."

"We have a heated pool with a hot tub," the clerk said. "Bingo in the bar later."

Sunny glanced out the window. "It's not even sticking yet. And it's February fourth."

February fourth? Oh. She'd told him she had to be back for her audition by the thirteenth. "You think they could've missed the forecast?" Gabe asked the clerk.

She shrugged. "Wouldn't be the first time. Still, be careful out there."

"We'll take it slow." Sunny winked at Gabe.

But Sunny's sassiness was gone an hour later as Cinderella's wipers struggled to keep up with the swirling snow, and ice crusted the windshield where the wipers didn't pass. No showtunes filled the car today, only tense silence. Gabe gripped the dash with one hand and the door handle with the other, dreading the curve ahead.

"Take it slow." His voice was more of a growl than he'd intended.

"Not what I need right now," she snapped.

"Okay, okay," he said. "You've got this."

"I bet the interstate's been plowed," she muttered.

It probably also had more cars and semis to avoid. On the two-lane highway, they were alone except for an occasional passing pickup truck with studded tires.

When Sunny braked to approach the curve, Gabe felt the car shimmy and slide as the tires slipped on the unplowed highway. In typical front-wheel-drive behavior, the wheels failed to obey Sunny's frantic yank of the wheel. The guardrail swam up at them through the blowing flakes. Gabe winced and braced himself, but at their creeping speed, Cinderella only tapped the guardrail and came to a rest against it.

Sunny's erratic breathing ripped through the interior of the car and fogged the driver's side window. Meanwhile, the wipers scraping against the windshield made the only sound outside. The snow blanketed the world in silent white.

"Think we can wait it out?" Her voice shook.

"Not here." Life would get much more complicated if another car lost traction at the curve and hit Cinderella.

"Okay. Just—just give me a minute." She took her trembling hands off the wheel and shoved them under her thighs.

Gabe glanced out the rear window. No headlights, but he probably wouldn't see them until it was too late. He hit the hazard lights and took a deep breath. "Let me try."

"Try what?"

"Swap with me," he said. "I've got more experience driving in snow than you do."

"But you—you don't drive."

With more confidence than he felt, Gabe said, "Stay in the car. Slide over the console." He opened his door and squeezed out between the car and the guardrail. Checking the road once more, he stumbled through the half-packed, half-powder snow to circle the back of the car and wedged himself into the driver's seat. He shut the door and pushed the seat all the way back.

It wasn't like he never drove. He'd driven Cinderella after the repairs he'd done to ensure the car was safe. Sure, he'd only circled Beach Island's empty parking lots, not a snow-covered highway, but after that understeering scare, Sunny wasn't in any shape to continue.

Gabe backed the car off the rail and put it in drive. Gripping the wheel so she wouldn't see the tremor in his hands, he eased onto the accelerator and continued down the road.

Snow obscured the pavement ahead, and Gabe kept Cinderella to a crawl. He heard every scrape of the wiper blades and crunch of the new all-weather tires in the snow. It was nothing like the coaster's clacking rush on that clear-sky morning. Plus, he wasn't alone. Sunny was beside him, her tense breath fogging the window on her side. He wouldn't let anything happen to her.

After twenty minutes, buildings appeared through the flying

snow. Sunny let out a shuddering breath. "Think they'll have a motel?"

Gabe pointed at the neon-lit sign. The *E* was dark, but it was clear, even through the heavy snow: *MOTEL*. He steered to the entrance on the left, bumping over the ruts in the snow. The low-slung, one-story building featured a long row of exterior doors in a single wing off the lobby entrance. A line of snow-covered cars sat in front. It wasn't nearly as nice as the Holiday Inn they'd left that morning. He'd bet they didn't have a heated pool. Bingo was a stretch.

He eased the car to a stop in front of the lobby door. "Wait here. I'll check if they have rooms."

"What if they don't?" Sunny asked. No grin, not even the hint of a smile cracked her pale face.

"I'll ask if there's a diner in town where we can sit and wait out the storm."

"Okay." She sounded just as unenthusiastic as Gabe felt about getting back onto the road.

The wind blew him into the lobby, where he stamped the snow from his shoes onto the mat.

"Pretty bad out there, huh?" said a white-haired man at the counter. He turned down the radio, which sounded like a sermon from the speaker's cadence. Which was odd, since it was Tuesday.

"Yeah. Got a couple of rooms?" Gabe approached the desk.

"Just one."

"One?" Gabe's voice rose, betraying his panic.

"Yep. We're not usually full this early in the day, but we're the only motel in town. Not many folks braving the roads." A ring flashed on his finger. Gold, with a cross cut out.

"Anyone else around here rent out rooms? An Airbnb?" Gabe asked.

The man shrugged. "Not that I know of. Not much need."

"Is there a restaurant in town?" They could wait it out with coffee and pie.

"Sure. There's a diner a little ways down the road. Not sure if it's open today with the storm, but there's a convenience store next door with gas and candy and whatnot." He lowered his bushy white eyebrows. "So, you want that room?"

"Double beds?" Gabe asked.

"Just one bed. It's a king, though. Should fit even a big guy like you. You alone?"

"Um." What was the best answer? *Yes,* clearly, but what if the man saw Sunny? Would he care? Gabe thought Colorado was pretty liberal. At least, compared to Ohio. But looming behind the man was Jesus. Painted life-size and floating above the rocky ground, eyes rolled up toward heaven, palms facing out, Jesus seemed to say, *Gabe, it's snowing. Why take the chance?*

Gabe opened his mouth to say, *Yes, completely alone,* when the door opened and Sunny breezed in on a gust of cold, snowy air. *God dammit.*

Chapter Thirteen

Sunny took in the portrait of the redeemer, the *Jesus Saves* sign on the desk, and the cross tattoo on the old guy's forearm—though it might've started out as an anchor. Gabe's horrified expression told her there was only one way to play this.

"Do they have a room, honey?" She skidded over to him on her wet boots and clung to his arm.

"One," he muttered, low. "And there's only one bed."

She slapped his biceps playfully and simpered up at him, squeezing his arm to telegraph her meaning. "Sweetie, now that we're married, we don't have to worry about that." She didn't have to try too hard to push the blush to her cheeks. Gabe's dark-eyed stare made her forget the chill outside.

To the old guy at the desk, she said, "He's not used to it yet. We just got married Saturday."

His gaze drifted to Sunny's hand on Gabe's arm. *Shit.* If she'd planned this better, she'd have flipped one of her rings to her left ring finger. Too late now. "In Vegas. We didn't even have time to get rings. He has such big fingers, you know." Her cheeks went surface-of-the-sun hot, all on their own, at the thought of what Gabe's big fingers could do to her in that one bed.

The guy was still squinting at them, so she dipped her chin and rounded her eyes innocently. "We wanted to avoid temptation." She'd learned a thing or two from a religious colleague at DN-YAY in Ohio.

His face cleared. "Rightly so. Mister, if you'll give me your license and credit card, I'll get you a key."

With a wide-eyed stare at Sunny, Gabe stepped away from her arm-hug and toward the man at the desk. Finally, she allowed the tension to melt out of her. Her muscles had seized up, even before the Mercedes had tapped that guardrail, and she'd concealed her trembling hands in her pockets while Gabe drove. Gabe, who hadn't driven in almost ten years. But he'd gotten them safely to the motel, and soon they'd be in a warm motel room. She didn't care if that one bed was twin-size. As long as the room had heat and they could wait out the storm in it, she'd be happy. If there was a crucifix in the room, she might even say a brief prayer of thanks near it.

When Gabe had the brass key in hand, they scurried out to the car, to escape either the man's suspicions or the wrath of God, she wasn't sure which. Sunny slid into the rapidly cooling car.

"What the hell was that?" Gabe asked, cranking the engine. "I was just about to tell him I was alone."

"If he'd seen me, it would've been trouble. This is better."

"Better?" he growled, easing the car across the snowy parking lot. "Now we're stuck in the one room with one bed, expected to do honeymoon-type things. I'll drop you off and head to the diner."

"No!" She clutched his arm, making him swerve a little too close to a parked car. "The roads aren't safe, not even for walking. We'll be fine."

"Fine?" He cranked the wheel, and the car slid into a spot, more or less, in front of the last door at the end of the building. "I don't know what's fine about this situation at all."

She shoved open the door, displacing snow that came past the lower edge. "It's totally fine," she shouted over the howling wind. "Much better than that death road."

After handing her the room key, he popped the trunk and lifted first her bag, then his. She slogged through the snow to the door and worked the key into the lock. The room smelled a little musty, like it didn't get much use. But she welcomed the respite from the chill wind and blowing snow.

Gabe's shoulders hunched. Was he religious, too? She had to lighten the situation, let him know she expected only refuge, not sex.

"Wait." She laid a hand on his arm. "Aren't you going to carry your bride across the threshold, Mr. Armstrong?" She tried to flutter her eyelashes at him, but snowflakes kept clumping into them.

He scowled at her and pushed inside. So much for lightening his mood.

She followed, grimacing at the clods of snow that fell off their shoes.

"Stay here. I'll get a towel." Sunny zipped off her tall boots and stepped out of them, leaving them at the door. She scurried in her socks to the tiny bathroom and grabbed a thin towel, which she laid down in front of the door. He untied his shoes and left them there for the snow to melt off.

The one piece of furniture in the room drew her eyes like a magnet. The bed was immense, and all Sunny could think was, how did they get it in there? It was shoved against the wall on one side, and a narrow path on the other side separated it from the closet and bathroom. There wasn't even a chair in the room, just the giant bed. On her trip to get the towels, Sunny had ascertained that there was no bathtub for her to curl up inside, only a shower she wasn't sure would fit Gabe's large frame.

"So," she squeaked, "it's cozy."

"I'll go." His shoulders huddled next to his ears when he shoved his hands into his coat pockets. "I can walk to that diner."

"Don't be ridiculous." When she propped her hands on her hips, her elbow slammed into the wall. She rubbed the stab of pain. "There's plenty of room here. I—I've got a deck of cards in my suitcase. And a bag of chips. It'll be fun."

One heavy eyebrow lifted. "Fun?"

"Okay, passable. But don't leave me here." What if he got lost in the snow? Or hit by a runaway snowplow? Or found something better to do than keep a washed-up actress company on her cross-country drive?

"Fine," he growled, sending shivers over her body. What the hell was that? She rubbed her hands over her arms, smoothing away the goosebumps.

When he set their bags in the corner, she scuttled over and dug through hers until she found the deck of *New York Bomb Squad* playing cards and the sack of potato chips. It was a small one, but if it kept Gabe out of the storm, he could eat them all.

Gabe sat gingerly on the edge of the bed as if he were preparing to take flight. Sunny rounded the end and scooted all the way into the corner, giving him as much space as she could.

"What should we play?" she asked. "Gin rummy? Go fish? Poker?"

He froze at the last option. Maybe the first thought that'd passed through his brain had been strip poker, too.

"Go fish ought to be safe," he said.

Safe. She leaned against the wall, glad they'd found shelter from the storm. But in the matchbox-size room, how could they be safe from the sexual tension that prickled across her skin, that kept him perched on the edge of the mattress? Maybe Gabe could figure out a way. If there was one thing Gabe was passionate about, it was safety.

Chapter Fourteen

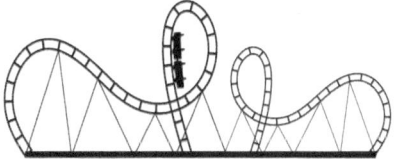

G abe woke in the dark, warm and safe, until a soft sigh next to him set his heart pounding.

When he lifted his head from the pillow, long hairs stuck to his lips. *Shit.* He was sharing a pillow with Sunny. And his hand was—

He snatched it off her smooth stomach where her T-shirt had ridden up. Unless he'd pushed it up. And that was when he realized his entire body was pressed up against hers. He was *spooning* her.

Gently, he scooted away. If he hadn't been so focused on how a particular part of his body felt against her backside, he might have realized he was already at the extreme edge of the bed. He teetered for a second and then slid onto the floor with a *whump*. His head cracked against the bathroom door, unreasonably close as it was to the side of the bed.

"Ouch! Dammit!"

"Wha—?" Sunny said. "Gabe?" Her low, sleep-rough voice made his dick spring fully to attention.

"What were you doing on my side of the bed?" he hissed.

She peered over the edge, her face a pale smudge in the dark. "I was cold. You were warm. Come back to bed."

"I—I can't. Not until you scoot over." No way was he going to let on that he had an erection.

"Fine," she said. The sheets rustled as she moved away. "Your virtue is safe now."

"Good," he muttered. Rubbing the back of his head where it'd hit the door, he clambered back up onto the bed. Clinging to the edge, he turned his back to her.

He'd almost drifted back to sleep when the mattress trembled. "Wha's th'matter?" he mumbled.

"Still cold. Can I come closer?"

Gabe sighed. "Mm-hm."

She said nothing, just scooted toward him, her knees sliding behind his and her hand—it was cold like ice—slipping over his side. Sighing, he lifted his arm, capturing her chilled hand in his, and pinned it against his chest. "Better?"

"Much." Her sigh tickled the back of his neck, and with their breathing synchronized, he drifted back to sleep.

Sometime later, a buzz broke the stillness of the room. When Gabe cracked open his eyes, sunlight shone in through a gap in the curtains. His phone buzzed again from where it lay, plugged in, on the floor.

When he reached down to grab it, Sunny's arm slipped off him. Before answering, he glanced over his shoulder at her. Still asleep. He checked the phone's display. Darlene.

Hopping off the bed, he took the phone into the bathroom and leaned up against the flimsy door. Goosebumps rose on his arms below his T-shirt sleeves. Outside the warm covers, it *was* a little chilly. "Hi, Darlene," he said, his voice as low as he could make it and still be heard. He rubbed his arms.

"Oh, did I wake you? I'm sorry." She didn't sound sorry.

"How are you feeling?"

"I'm fine. It was a relapse, but it doesn't seem permanent, at least so far."

"You sound good."

"Thank you," she said, enunciating the *k* so it popped in his ear. "How's the vacation?"

"Warm. Sunny. You know, vacation-y." God, he hated lying to Darlene. He rubbed a hand over his mouth.

"Hmm. It's twenty-three degrees here today, and we're supposed to get an inch or two of snow."

"Go home early," Gabe said. "I don't want you to slip or get caught out on the roads."

"I might. We'll see." She paused. "I called because Brandon is asking more questions about the business. This time, about the ownership agreement. I gave him the corporate attorney's number."

"Gabe?" Sunny's voice drifted from the bedroom.

"That's fine, Darlene. Good idea."

"But, Gabe, why is he asking about that? What could he need that information for?"

A knock at the bathroom door startled him, and then the handle turned. Gabe held the door closed with his back. Covering the phone's microphone, he said, "Just a minute."

Into the phone, he said, "I—I don't know. I'll text him later, okay?"

"Is someone there with you?" Darlene asked.

The panicked lie slipped out of him without thought. "No, just housekeeping."

"Oh." Her tone was suspicious. "Okay, but—"

"Sorry, Darlene, I've got to go."

"You'll let me know what Brandon says?"

"Of course. I'll text you later."

"Okay. Bye."

He disconnected the call and turned to open the door. Sunny blinked up at him, her eyes heavy-lidded and her hair tangled. "Sorry, I—I worried you'd left. What were you doing in the bathroom in the dark?" Her cheeks went bright red. "Never mind. Don't answer that. But if you're done, do you mind if I—?"

"Sure." He flipped the light on for her and stepped out. She went inside and closed the door.

After he'd pulled on jeans and a long-sleeved shirt, he crossed to the window and pulled the curtain aside. Outside was a winter wonderland. Snow covered all the cars in the lot, rounding their edges and making them a row of identical paper-doll cars. Deep ruts cut into the snow on the road beyond—or what he could only assume was the road. A lone pickup truck with chain-covered tires crawled by. Fat snowflakes continued to fall, not as thickly as yesterday. He shivered.

"Still snowing?" Sunny asked behind him.

He turned. "Yeah. Sorry, it looks like we're stuck here for a while longer."

She rubbed her hands over her exposed shoulders. His eyes burned to check out her nipple situation in her thin tank top, but he glued his gaze to her face.

"Better than being out there, driving in it," she said.

"You cold?"

"And hungry." On cue, her stomach growled.

He checked the old-fashioned round thermostat on the wall. It was set to sixty-eight, but the room temperature read sixty-two. He turned the dial to seventy-five.

"Put on a sweater," he said. "I'll go check if the front desk can do anything about the heat. And I'll find us some breakfast." A perfect excuse to escape Sunny's too-thin sleepwear and her orange-flower scent. A walk in the cold would clear his head. And settle his other head.

She'd already started to rummage in her bag, but she stopped and looked up. "Be careful out there."

"I will. Promise."

Slipping on his shoes and coat, Gabe shoved the door open, displacing the snow piled against it, and walked out into the snowscape.

Chapter Fifteen

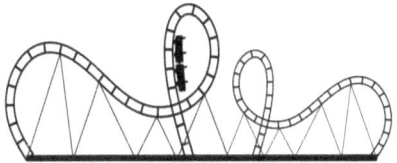

S unny huddled under the covers and stared out the window at the swirling white. Gabe had been gone an hour. Had something happened to him? She got up and checked the thermostat. It had risen to sixty-seven. Her hands weren't quite as chilled now, but she wasn't ready to shuck the comforter yet.

A knock came at the door just before the handle turned and the door opened to reveal Gabe, covered in snow. His shoes and the lower half of his jeans were crusted with white, and flakes clung to his coat, his hat, and the dark hair that stuck out under his hat. His normally olive complexion was ruddy, and the tip of his nose was bright red. Cold air blew in around him before he shut the door.

She flung off the comforter. "Gabe!" Why was she so unreasonably happy to see him? It must've been the smell of coffee that wafted around him.

"Take these." He handed her two plastic grocery sacks. She set them on the bed. "And this." He held out a cardboard drink carrier with four coffee cups wedged into it. Since there were no tables in the room, she carried it to the bathroom counter.

Gabe shrugged out of his coat and laid it on the towel along with his shoes. He tugged off his hat and ran a hand through his hair. In his flannel shirt, with his red cheeks and dark stubble, he looked like a mountain man. A sexy mountain man.

"I have good news and bad news. And more bad news," he said.

Had they been found out? Was the front-desk guy kicking their unmarried asses out of his motel? Were they going to have to brave the roads again? "Tell me the bad news first."

"The roads suck. They're plowing them every few hours, but the snow is going to keep coming until tonight. So it looks like we're stuck here another day."

Not so terrible. She'd figured as much. "And the good news?"

"Wait, I'm not done with the bad news." He checked the thermostat, nodded. "Pete, the manager, says because this room's at the end of the building, the HVAC doesn't work as well."

"What does that mean?"

"It means it'll be chilly in here."

"Oh." She snatched the comforter off the bed and wrapped it tightly around herself.

"He's agreed to knock twenty-five bucks off the rate and bring us more blankets."

Sunny slumped. "Is that the good news? Because it sounds pretty crappy."

"Where's your spirit of adventure?" He grinned. She'd never seen him crack more than a weak smile, and it transformed his face. With his teeth gleaming out of his shadow of a beard, he looked like Paul Bunyan. But sexier. Was sexy Paul Bunyan a thing? She was too dazzled by the smile to make any sense, even to herself.

He pointed to the bags on the bed. "The good news is the convenience store next door is open, and I brought provisions."

With the hand that wasn't clutching the comforter around her, she pawed through one. A package of cake donuts, three speckled bananas, string cheese, a jar of peanut butter, and a box of saltines.

"I had to fight a lady for the saltines. Fortunately, Pete from the motel talked to the store manager, Paul. He told him we were here on our honeymoon, so she had to settle for a box of oyster crackers."

The other sack held a pull-tab can of fruit cocktail, two packages of cup noodles, two sets of plastic cutlery, and a box of condoms. She held them up, eyebrows raised.

"On the house. A wedding present, Paul said." He ducked his head, but the blush on his cheekbones showed. "He may have done it to piss off Pete. They have some sort of bizarre rivalry going."

Sunny snorted. She and Gabe were stuck in the hotel room for the day with a box of condoms. And one bed.

"There's coffee and hot water for the soup. We should probably eat the soup while it's warm."

Noodles at nine A.M.? Her stomach didn't care; it rumbled. "Great. I'll just whip up breakfast for my husband." She winked at him. Grabbing the soup cups, she headed to the bathroom, where she poured the hot water over the noodles. She handed him a cup and checked the coffees. One was black and the other... She sniffed it and sighed at the blissful French vanilla scent.

Handing him the black coffee, she sipped the lightened one. "The convenience store had flavored creamer?"

"The coffee bar's not bad for a gas station." He sipped his own coffee and then sank to the floor, leaning back against the side of the bed.

Sunny copied his position, leaving a comfortable space between them. She poked a plastic fork into the noodles. "When I get back to LA, I'm going to my favorite ramen place with my bestie."

"Their ramen's better than this, I guess?" Gabe speared some noodles and slurped them.

"By a lot. But this isn't so bad. Warm food, shelter from the snow, and French vanilla coffee. Good company."

The corner of his mouth kicked up. "Tell me about your friend."

She shifted away from the hard edge of the box spring. "Her name's Leena, and we've been best friends since our middle school production of *Wicked*. She was Elphaba, and I was Glinda. It was my first big role, and on opening night I was so nervous I puked. She helped me through it."

"Yeah? What'd she do?"

"Held my hair. Then, after, she told me to imagine the audience was naked."

"That works?"

"Maybe. My problem was, my parents were in the front row. I saw them and froze. I was trying so hard not to imagine them naked that I couldn't remember I was supposed to speak, much less my first line. I was just standing there, silent, in that stupid bubble. Leena wasn't even there on stage, but she was standing offstage, and she chucked her nazar at me."

"Nazar?"

"An evil eye charm. She always carries it during performances. For luck. I guess it was all she had on her. She had a pretty good arm —used to play baseball, too—and it hit me square on the forehead."

"Ouch."

"Yeah, but it was like a reset for me. I remembered my lines and rocked that performance." She rubbed her forehead. She could almost feel where the warm glass had slapped her and reminded her that Leena cared about her.

"Your parents must've been proud of you."

She tugged the comforter more tightly around herself. "Yeah. They brought me flowers. But they forgot to give them to me. They were too busy signing autographs in the lobby afterward."

Gabe scrunched his forehead. "Autographs?"

Shit, she hadn't meant to tell him that. She'd liked that he thought she was just a regular person. Too late now. "They're sort of famous."

Gabe raised his eyebrows.

She sighed. "They're Gene and Gwen Lafortune. You must've seen their movies. My mom's been in, like, a million rom-coms. *Kiss Me Forever* was her big hit in the early 2000s. And my dad's—"

Gabe's jaw dropped. "Your dad is Mean Gene Lafortune? I've seen every one of his spy movies."

"Yeah." She stirred her noodles. *Don't ask—*

"What was that like? Growing up with such famous parents?"

She set the ramen on the carpet. "Lonely. They were always on location. Though I had plenty of nannies. And one housekeeper I was close to, Nadia."

"But you were their only kid. Weren't there times when you were all together?"

She thought about that day she'd worn the ruffled dress. Her dad had seemed happy to see her then. "I think their marriage started to fall apart when I was little. So they tried to stay out of each other's way. They focused on their careers. And kind of forgot about home."

"Sunny, I'm—"

"It's okay." She shook herself. "I had every luxury growing up. And all the singing, dancing, and acting lessons I could stomach. They paid attention to me when I performed. So I did that a lot. I was even on a TV show, though it only ran for one season. *The Brainiac Bunch?*"

He shook his head.

"It was a sitcom about a family of geniuses. And I was the dumb one. Kind of like *The Addams Family* mixed up with *The Brady Bunch.* But nerdy. Anyway, it was fun having a family for a while, even if it was only pretend."

"I'm sorry."

She shrugged. "It's why I got into acting. So something good came out of it."

He put a hand on her arm. "Something amazing. You have the best singing voice I've ever heard. And your acting skills were top-notch with Pete and that highway patrolman. You can't be older than twenty-five—"

"I'm twenty-seven." Practically geriatric for an actress looking for a fresh start in Hollywood. Still, his words warmed her better than the lukewarm soup.

"You've got your whole life ahead of you. I know you'll do great things. Regardless of who your parents are."

She stirred her noodles. "Family's hard." They had so many expectations. Ones she never seemed to meet. "But yours is going to be awesome. Like *The Brainiac Bunch.*"

Gabe set down his noodle cup and stared at the wall.

"Your family in Vegas will be so excited to meet you." Like the time she'd met up with her former castmates for a ten-years-later retrospective interview.

He sighed through his nose. "If they're even—maybe. We'll see."

"DNA results don't lie, Gabe," she said as gently as she could.

He turned to face her, his pain showing in the lines around his eyes. "But parents do?"

Oh. *Oh.* "I'm sure they had a good reason. Maybe your Vegas family will know."

He grimaced. "Maybe."

Why, *why* hadn't she listened to Cata and left poor Gabe alone? She was the last person who should advise anyone about family. He'd sounded so lonely, and she'd wanted to make it better. But she'd failed. She'd dragged him out here into the middle of the country and gotten him stuck in a freezing-cold room with nothing but cup noodles, saltines, and a dozen useless extra-large condoms.

Still, *he'd* tried to make *her* feel better. He was so nice. And caring. And brave. And sexy, with that Paul Bunyan stubble over that strong jaw. Not to mention the workingman muscles he'd hidden under his dress pants and cashmere coat. *No.* She had to ignore that tug she felt in his presence, the one that made her want to touch, to taste, to comfort. And take what those liquid brown eyes offered: affection, protection, loyalty.

Loyalty. Gabe Armstrong was a forever kind of guy. And she was the opposite. What was the opposite of forever? Right now. And right now, what she could do was distract him. Make him smile.

"So, husband, now that we've had breakfast, how are we going to entertain ourselves?" As soon as the words were out of her mouth, she wanted to pull them back. The bright blue box of condoms taunted her from the plastic sack on the bed.

Gabe jumped up like he'd been electrocuted.

"I meant...cards. Or a sing-along? Wholesome fun." Her face burned.

Gabe set his half-eaten cup of noodles on the bathroom counter. "I'm going outside to dig out the car."

"I—I'll join you." The last thing she wanted was to go back out in the cold, but someone needed to keep Gabe out of his dark thoughts.

He quirked an eyebrow and shrugged back into his coat.

Sunny shoved her feet into her boots. "One of us needs to charm Pete out of a snow shovel and a broom. And I doubt you're his type."

An hour later, breathless and warm under her pink puffy coat, Sunny skipped back into the room with Gabe behind her. The cold air and exercise seemed to have done him good. He wasn't smiling, but he wasn't scowling anymore, either. His jaw and shoulders seemed less stiff than before.

Sunny glanced at the sack on the bed where the box of condoms still lay. Why hadn't she thought to hide them in a drawer? Oh, right, there weren't any drawers in the room. She rustled through the bag and pulled out the box of donuts, shoving the condoms under the saltines. "Snack?"

"I want to wash up first." He held up his hands, red from the cold, and then ducked into the bathroom.

Sunny unzipped her coat and tossed it near the door next to her boots. When the cool air hit her skin, she dived under the comforter again and wrapped it around her shivering limbs. The squashy mattress shivered along with her.

The bathroom door opened, and Gabe chuckled. Sunny shifted so she could peer at him from underneath her comforter-hood. He leaned against the doorway, muscles bulging under his T-shirt, the hint of a smile on his face. God, he looked like a fucking centerfold in some manly-man magazine.

"Aren't you cold?" she asked.

"Not in here. I hate the cold outside, but indoors I run pretty hot."

That made her shiver, and not because of the chill in the room. But he didn't know that. He uncrossed his arms and ambled the two steps to the bed. He sat on it, making the mattress dip. Sunny leaned back against his gravitational pull. No matter how much she liked him, she had to respect his space. He had enough going on without her throwing herself at him.

He held out his arm. "Come over here."

"Really?" she squeaked. She could almost see the heat radiating off him.

He twitched his fingers. "Really."

She didn't hesitate. Dragging herself and the blankets over to his side of the bed, she nestled under his arm and arranged the blankets over them both. She tucked her icy feet between his shins. His chin rested on the top of her head.

"Better?" His voice was strained.

"Yeah. Am I squishing you?"

"No, I'm good." He tightened his arm around her.

She tucked her nose under the blankets. They smelled like fabric softener. But under the floral scent was Gabe. He smelled like the motel's soap—regular Dial—and...more. Leather, like the inside of her Mercedes, and something mechanical, motor oil, maybe. But on him it didn't smell bad, just...manly. She burrowed closer. *My man.*

Whoa. What was that? Regardless of the lie she'd told Pete, Gabe wasn't hers. They were sharing a ride. They were...

"Gabe?" She poked her head out of the blankets.

"Yeah?" He hadn't picked up his phone. He was just sitting there, cuddling her.

"Are we...are we friends?" She calculated the number of hours they'd spent together. They'd driven together Saturday, Sunday, Monday, and a partial day yesterday. Roughly twenty-seven hours together on the road, plus breakfasts and dinners. And they'd slept in the same bed the night before. She wasn't just his driver anymore. They'd shared some of their stories and secrets. She'd told him about her frosty parents, and she never talked about her parents. That was enough to call friendship, if nothing more.

He was silent long enough for her to wish she hadn't asked. But at last, he said, "Yeah, I think we are. Is that what you think?"

She buried her nose in his flannel-covered shoulder. "Yeah."

He rubbed his hand down her back from her shoulder to her tailbone and then again. He repeated the motion like he was patting a dog. Maybe he'd forgotten what he was doing. She lifted her nose from his shirt to the skin of his neck above his collar so she could inhale his scent. *Mmm.* She rubbed her nose against the prickle of his neck whiskers.

"Gabe?" Now she was performing a different calculation. They'd spent the morning and all yesterday afternoon here in the motel room. Close to twenty-four hours together, including sleeping in the same bed. How many dates did that equate to?

"Mmm-hmm?" he asked, his voice low and rumbly.

"Friends can kiss each other, right?"

"What?"

She lifted her face from his neck and focused on his lips, light pink and soft-looking beside his stubble. "Because I'd like to kiss you."

He tilted his face toward her, which was invitation enough. She'd already kissed him that night at the Holiday Inn. She hadn't quite hit his lips then, chickening out at the last second. But now, she touched her lips to his in her best approximation of a friendly kiss. In Los Angeles, friends gave air kisses hello and goodbye. In New York, it'd been common to give a cheek peck in greeting. This wasn't that.

She'd kissed her fair share of love interests in plays, plus Curt Suede on the TV show. She'd kissed plenty of people she wasn't romantically involved with. Sometimes it was awkward, sometimes it was nice. Every time she'd done it on stage, it was transactional. Work.

This wasn't anything like acting. After a moment of stiff surprise, Gabe responded, moving his lips over hers. His skin was dry from the cold air outside, and their lips tugged against each other until she licked his lower lip. After that, their lips slid together in perfect friction. His arm tightened around her, and she let go of the blanket to touch his jaw, angling his face where she wanted it to deepen the kiss. She traced her tongue over his lip again, and this time, he opened to her. He tasted like coffee and salt from the soup, and she loved it.

He pulled back gently, his broad chest heaving. "You kiss all of your friends with tongue?"

"Only the ones I really like." She grabbed his collar with both hands and tugged him back down to her.

Chapter Sixteen

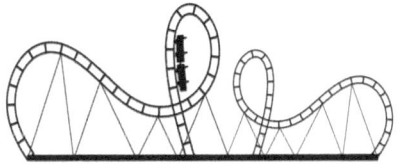

That stupid tug she kept feeling yanked at her heart when Gabe pulled away first, and she shivered despite the circle of his arms around her shoulders and his cheek resting on her head. When she breathed in more of his scent, it fuzzed her brain. Well, that and the things he'd done with his tongue. She squirmed, warmth pooling between her legs. If she'd gotten that turned on by a kiss, what would happen when his hands were on her? Because she and her Mercedes already knew he was great with his hands.

"Where'd you learn to kiss like that?" she asked, her words slurry.

"What?" He sounded a little drugged, too.

"A guy like you, all work and business, shouldn't have had time to learn to kiss like Zac Efron."

"Who?"

"Never mind. We're talking about you."

"Oh." He started rubbing her back again, which made her full-body shudder. "Beach Island. I worked there every summer from the time I was thirteen. There were lots of other high school and college kids who worked there. It was like a soap opera with all the relationships that formed. I'd date a girl for a few weeks, and then she'd move on to the next guy."

"I bet being an Armstrong made you a hot property." Had he been this big and burly as a teenager? Teenage Sunny would've swooned.

"Nah. I worked every job, from concessions to ride operation to janitorial, and I was treated the same as any other employee. Pretty soon, they all saw me as one of the gang."

She ran her lips up his neck to his jaw. "Ever date a guest?"

"No. My parents might've been free spirits, but there was a strict no-fraternization policy with park guests. Though there was a girl or two who slipped me her number, and I called them later."

"Huh. I wouldn't have thought you were such a playboy."

"Playboy?" He shook his head. "I was very committed to each and every girl. Exclusively. But we were kids, so our relationships ran their course pretty quickly."

Perfect. After today, they had another three days on the road, barring any other delays. They'd be just like those high-school relationships, full of fiery passion—and what he'd do with those hands —compacted into a short time together. And then Sunny would go on her way before either of them developed any dangerous feelings that might lead them down a path of folly like her parents.

"Their loss," she said between kisses on his jaw. She kissed her way back to his lips and turned the kiss dirty, sucking his lip between hers before plunging her tongue into his mouth. She buried her hands in his thick hair, holding him to her. He gripped the back of her sweater but didn't lift it. God, why didn't the lift it? She needed his touch everywhere. She squirmed on the mattress, chasing the friction of her own jeans.

This time, when he pulled back, he gasped for air. "Sunny, I... Should we be doing this?"

"What else are we going to do? We're snowed in here with all these condoms." She burrowed between his neck and his shoulder and nipped him gently.

Just as gently, he grasped her shoulders and pushed her back. There was a line between his thick eyebrows. "That's not who I am now, Sunny. Even when I was just a kid flirting with girls at the snow cone stand, I was looking for forever, like my parents had. Like my grandparents. But this—this isn't forever, is it?"

The F-word gave her a pang right between the ribs. "There's no such thing as forever, Gabe. I should know. Relationships are like roles. You play them for a while, and then you move on. Otherwise, you're famous for having a terrible marriage."

He still had his hands on his shoulders like she was the one who needed comfort. "Are your parents divorced now?"

She laughed, sharp and bitter. "No. They've been married for twenty-eight years. But living separate lives for more than twenty of them. They figured they could get more mileage out of being married than divorced. It's like a partnership. It's not uncommon in LA."

"My parents worked together and loved each other until the day they died. They had a business and a family." His grip on her shoulders had gone tight.

She shrugged, and his hold loosened. "That's not how it works in Hollywood. No one wants to cast a woman as a love interest when the tabloids are speculating about her baby bump. And in LA, all you have to do is eat an extra taco before they take a grainy photo, circle your stomach, and draw a big arrow with the word *baby* next to it."

He smoothed her hair away from her face. "That sounds terrible."

She traced a garish blue rose on the bedspread. "It's what I signed up for."

"Still, I'm sorry."

"Don't be. Besides, I'm terrible at relationships. Don't forget what I did to Cade."

"That wasn't—"

But she remembered what he'd shared that night at the diner. "Did you love Riley? When you proposed?" Why had she asked that? And why did it feel like she was pouring acid on her own heart? Coffee and noodles for breakfast had been a bad idea.

He was silent for a moment. "I liked her. It hurt when she left. But she was right. I wasn't ready to marry her."

Her heartburn eased. Why were they even talking about marriage? Sunny and Gabe weren't even really fake-married. They were just sharing a room during a storm. She unclenched her jaw enough to say, "Marriage isn't for me. I'd much rather enjoy life without all that nonsense getting in the way."

"You mean love? Fidelity?" The line in his forehead deepened.

"Monogamy is fine. An end date is better." Like a limited-engagement theater run. Everyone went in knowing exactly when it would be over. No one was hoping it'd be the next *Phantom of the Opera,* so no one could fail.

He lifted his hand from her hair and set it on the bed. "An end date."

She missed his touch. "That's why this is perfect. We'll have fun until we get to Vegas. No time to develop feelings. No promises to break." *No way to fail.* She ran her hands down his chest, following the contours of the hard muscle underneath.

He captured her roaming hands and pinned them to his chest. He stared at the window, but Sunny didn't think he saw the snow swirling in the twilight. "I think it might be too late. For the feelings."

"Oh, Gabe." Her lady parts were still on board, wet and swollen and needy, but her brain switched to platonic mode, like it had whenever she'd kissed Curt Suede on the show. *Feelings. Ugh.*

She scooted away from him, dragging the blankets with her. She needed them now that the cool air of the motel room came between them. Gabe was right; he was like her personal space heater. No, not hers.

"Do we have any of those donuts left?" she asked. She slid off the bed and dug into the grocery sack. Pawing past the box of condoms—*won't be needing those, now*—she pulled out the carton of donuts. "Want one?"

"Sunny, I...I'm sorry. I didn't mean to make you feel uncomfortable."

"Uncomfortable? Nope." But the high pitch of her voice betrayed her.

"And you don't...you don't feel anything for me?" He looked down at his big hands where they rested on the bedspread. The tips of his ears were pink.

Shit, now they were stuck together for the next who-knew-how-many days, and he'd developed *feelings*. She shoved a donut into her mouth and spoke around it. "Sorry. That's not how I roll."

"Oh." He looked at his watch again. She could've won an Emmy if she could've infused her voice with that much sadness.

She swallowed the donut. "It's not you. You're a great guy. You'll make someone very happy." She had to shove that word out between her teeth. She refused to think about why anger rose hot inside her when she thought about Gabe making some other woman happy. Instead, she ground down her emotions like a cigarette under her heel. "You'll have lots of big, handsome babies. But that's not for me."

She wished she could've walked out, given him some space to realize he'd confused arousal with emotions, but the snowflakes still flew thick outside. Instead, she tossed the box of donuts on the bed in front of him and grabbed the TV remote, which was attached to the wall with Velcro.

"What do you like to watch?" she asked.

"Doesn't matter."

Sunny flipped through the channels, trying to get a feel for the offerings in this out-of-the-way spot. But her attention snagged on a familiar-looking set. It was too early for *New York Bomb Squad* to be on, but it was a promo for the show. Which episode were they playing this week?

"Wait, is that you?" Gabe asked.

Sunny's face had flashed by. Now she knew the episode. It was the one where Curt Suede slept with Sunny's character for the first time after they'd solved a particularly grueling case.

"Yeah."

"You were on that show? Even I've heard of *New York Bomb Squad*."

"Yeah. Just for a few episodes after this one." Her stomach twisted when she remembered how her joy had turned to fury at that last table read.

"What happened?"

"I, ah. I don't want to spoil it for you." She grimaced. "We'll just say my character doesn't survive this season."

"Sorry."

"Me, too. I was a little...surprised. I didn't react well."

"Oh?"

Why was she even telling him this? She hadn't told anyone except for Cata, who'd turned on her psychologist mode and pulled it out of her. Maybe Gabe had taken psychology, too. "Yeah. My character had just gotten engaged to one of the leads on the show. I thought I was going to be a series regular. But my friend, they were going to kill off her character in the next episode."

She gave the TV a bitter smile, remembering the chill that'd raced through her at the table read. The twist in her gut from Odile's red eyes. "I threw a bit of a tantrum. Walked out on the director. You know, diva shit."

He didn't touch her this time. He was probably appalled. Hell, *she* was appalled at herself.

"You were defending your friend."

Was she? Or was she defending the bit of herself she saw in her friend? She shrugged.

"What happened then?"

She blinked. "They fired me on the spot. Had the terrorists blow me up with a car bomb instead. They didn't even need me to film it. They used some cut scenes." She felt the familiar dig between her ribs.

"I'm sorry."

She sucked in a deep breath. Let it out slowly. "Nothing's forever in television. Well, except *Meet the Press*. At least in the end, Odile got to keep her job."

He stared at the screen. "You looked—different."

"The show was supposed to have that gritty feeling. They used a lot of blue filters."

"I mean...unhappy. Not like you are when you're singing in the car."

She tried to remember acting on the show. Everything had been so serious. She guessed she had, too. "It was work. Not fun. Singing is fun."

"It is when you do it."

That warmed her up almost as much as sitting next to Gabe had.

"Come here," he said. "Now I'm cold."

He scooted back to lean against the headboard, and she settled next to him. He put his arm around her, and she arranged the blankets over them both. She flipped until she found an episode of her favorite baking show. "Is this okay?"

"Perfect," he said into her hair.

Chapter Seventeen

Another broken-sleep night. He'd lain stiff as a board beside Sunny, his arm a barrier to her encroachment, when all he wanted to do was hold her close, breathing in her scent, the way he had while they'd watched TV. Through the dark hours, he'd tried to stuff his burgeoning, unwanted feelings for her into a compartment inside him, next to the one where he'd kept his sorrow over his parents' deaths. They hadn't stayed. Neither would she.

Squinting in the bright sunshine, Gabe loaded their suitcases into Cinderella's trunk and plodded through the snow to the road. He scanned the asphalt like he was inspecting one of the Beach Island rides before the park opened. Plows had scraped away most of the snow, but a compacted layer remained. It was pocked and melting in places where the town had scattered ice melt pellets, but plenty of places were crusted with ice. What would the road be like outside town, where there was less traffic, fewer passes by the plows?

He trudged back to the Mercedes and winced at the scrape on the front bumper from the barrier they'd hit. He circled the car to the driver's side door and opened it. Sunny looked up and tilted her head.

"Slide over," he said. "I'll drive."

She didn't move. "What did you say?"

He took a big breath of cold air. Let it out in a cloud. "I'm driving. I have more experience driving in snow on partially cleared roads than you do."

"But you—"

"Slide over. Please." He shook his head in irritation. Why had he thought a drive through the plains and Rockies in February was a good idea? That was exactly it: he hadn't thought. Sunny had burst into his life, all strawberry-blond hair and self-confidence, and she'd spun stories of long-lost siblings for a lonely man. He'd been powerless to resist.

And he was even more powerless now that he knew her. Her fire. Her kindness. And those goddamned drugging kisses that turned his brain to soft-serve. Sunny was more dangerous than the snow-crusted road ahead.

When she levered herself over the console into the passenger seat, he tried not to look at her butt. Failed.

He lowered himself into the driver's seat and pushed it back. He checked the mirrors and flipped on the headlights. Silently, Sunny switched their coffees in the sturdy cup holder he'd installed to replace the broken factory-original one. He released the brake, checked the backup camera, slowly backed out of the parking space, and churned over the slush to the main road. The tires spun a little as he accelerated onto it, but they caught the road and held. He was glad he'd replaced the worn tires.

Driving, he wouldn't have to think about what Sunny had offered him and the pain that hid just below that offer. Focusing on the road meant he wouldn't spend the day regretting turning down no-strings sex with his dream woman.

He took careful sips of his coffee to keep the slightly burnt odor in his nostrils instead of the orange blossom scent of her shampoo that filled the car. Last night while supposedly watching that cooking show, he'd inhaled it shamelessly. When he'd finally fallen asleep despite the erection he couldn't do anything about, considering the paper-thin bathroom door, he'd dreamed about sitting in an orange orchard with Sunny, sunlight filtering through the canopy above. Well, not only sitting. Some of his dreams involved other activities.

Activities he wasn't about to do in his waking life with a woman who'd leave him without a backward glance once they hit Vegas. Even if they slept together, she might not even stop the car to punt him out of it on his relations' driveway. She'd said as much. An end date.

She didn't believe in the happily-ever-after he'd seen his parents living.

Gabe didn't do end dates. Usually, he was cautious about starting relationships because he knew once he was in one, he'd never want to stop. Like with Riley, even after they'd started to feel more like friends-with-occasional-benefits than soul mates. The only thing different about Sunny was how quickly it'd happened. Even now, sitting silently in the car with her, he wanted to reach out, take her hand, beg her to stay.

But she wouldn't.

Sunny was like a vintage pickup truck, all American-made steel, replacement parts, and duct tape; nothing was going to take her down. Gabe was one of those paper-thin fiberglass compact cars that'd crack if you gave it a stern look. If they slept together and she left, she'd crush his soft, aluminum heart.

She'd never make her heart vulnerable to begin with. She was reinforced steel, strong at the seams.

They were opposites, but Gabe couldn't figure if they were the kind of keep-them-separated opposites like fuel and flame or better-together opposites like red paint on a burly Jeep.

"Donut?" Sunny asked.

"No, thanks, not while I'm driving." He gripped the wheel. Still in the eastern flats of Colorado, the road was pretty straight, but they were headed through the mountains later that day. The peaks loomed ahead, white-capped blue in the distance.

"Don't be ridiculous." She shoved a piece of donut between his lips, and he fought not to close around her finger and suck off the sugar.

"Better than the boxed ones," she said.

"Mmm." Sweetness burst over his tongue, the delicate pastry melting in his mouth.

"Coffee's better, too. I'm glad old Pete sent us to that bakery."

Poor Pete. He was probably still praying for their souls. As good an actress as Sunny was, Gabe doubted they'd fooled him.

"How long do you think it'll take us to get there?" She licked sugar off her thumb.

Gabe ripped his eyes back to the road. "Another seventeen hours or so, according to the online map. Might take us another two days or a little more, depending on the weather and the mountain passes." A cold ball of dread settled in his stomach when he imagined the switchbacks coated in ice.

"It looks clear ahead," she said. "I can see the tops of the mountains. No clouds like the day before the storm."

He grunted. "You can turn on some music, if you like."

The music turned out to be a mistake. It was showtunes again, and when she sang along to "Defying Gravity," her voice was so clear and beautiful that it snapped his heart like too much sun on a plastic dashboard.

After lunch, they started to climb through the mountain passes. The disadvantage of avoiding the interstates was that while the small highway they'd taken had been plowed down to black asphalt, it had an unsettling number of curves without guardrails. Gabe slowed Cinderella to a crawl and kept his eyes on the road, hoping another car wouldn't come swinging wide in the opposite direction.

When Sunny sucked in a breath, Gabe stomped on the brake. "What?" Had she seen an avalanche? A mountain goat bounding onto the highway?

"Oh, sorry, nothing. It's just that it's so beautiful." She waved a hand toward the gorge below, its sides lined in tall evergreens and the bottom coated in snow like frosting. "I never get tired of seeing the mountains."

"It's pretty," he admitted. He'd never driven through the mountains, certainly never in winter. It was a lot for an Ohio flatlander to appreciate. He accelerated. Driving through the mountains in the dark was not something he wanted to do.

When they made it to Four Corners at sunset, Sunny insisted they get out. As she spun, arms out like a figure skater, on the medallion that marked the intersection of four states, looking utterly carefree, Gabe's heart split open a little more.

She held out her phone. "Take a video to capture the moment? I'm not sure I'll ever be here again."

"Sure." He hit the red button. Watched her spin, her grinning face turned up to the sky. Finally, she stopped, breathless. He almost asked her if he could send the video to himself, but that would've been creepy. And pathetic.

"Come here." She beckoned to him and tugged him to her side.

His arm went around her waist, and he didn't care that the strands of her hair slapped his face or that the wind blew away her scent. The soft warmth of her body was all he craved. More than he deserved.

Holding out her phone, she snapped a selfie of the two of them, the nearby rock formations lit up red in the background. "I'll send it to you, okay?" She dropped her phone in her coat pocket and laid a hand on his chest. "We'd have missed this if we'd taken the interstate. Thanks for bringing me here."

Gabe's gaze drifted to her lips, reddened in the cold. He didn't want to kiss her. He didn't want to feel the slide of her soft lips over his, mingle his breath, his soul, with hers, feel the warmth of her body pressed up to his like in the motel room yesterday. Still, he couldn't pull his attention off her mouth.

"God, you're annoying." Gripping the collar of his coat, she pulled him down to her and kissed him.

Her lips were cold, and so was her nose. Gabe wrapped his arms around her, sharing his heat with her, sharing this moment in the barren high plains. He burned it into his memory, recording the scent of her hair as it whipped around them, the chill breeze, the crunch of snow under their feet, and the last rays of sunset that made her hair glow like rose gold.

When he had it all down, he pulled away. "Let's get going. We'll stop for the night in the next town."

"Okay." As they walked back to the parking lot, she gripped his hand. Her power flowed into him through that connection. She'd shared her strength with him since they'd left Ohio, first pushing him to leave home and then propping him up as he'd allayed his fear of riding in the car and then of driving it. She was magical.

With Sunny by his side, he could've overcome just about anything. Too bad she'd leave him before he had to face his biggest dread: meeting the family that had thrown him away.

Chapter Eighteen

S ix days.

Sunny gave herself a stern look in the mirror in her motel room. Her very own motel room. Separate from Gabe's. No, she wasn't disappointed. Or lonely.

She ran the brush through her hair. She had six days before she had to be on set with her parents. She'd taken back the driver's seat from white-knuckling Gabe, but they'd crawled through the mountains and had to stop short of Las Vegas. It'd be an easy drive into the city the next day. She might even start toward LA that afternoon if Gabe seemed to be doing okay with his family.

She checked her lipstick. Why was she even putting on lipstick? It wasn't like they were going on a date. They were only going to dinner at the bar across the street. Their last dinner together. So what if she'd put on a dress? It was one of the few clean items left in her suitcase. She didn't bother to probe why she'd packed the form-hugging black dress at all.

A knock sounded at the door, the knock she already recognized as uniquely Gabe's. Four slow raps of his big knuckles, like he was holding his body back, restraining himself from being ungentle with the door.

After one last look in the mirror, she snatched her coat off the bed and opened the door. Gabe filled it, leaning against the frame. Instead of the parka he'd been wearing most of the trip, he wore that cashmere coat he'd had on the day she'd met him at his townhome. With a pair of dress slacks and softly shined shoes. He'd dressed up, too.

"Hey," she said.

He backed off a step, blinking those eyes she'd thought at first were hard like granite but now looked like a too-thin crust over the caramel-soft feelings that swirled just behind. He cleared his throat. "Ready?"

She shrugged into her coat and shut the red door behind her. The little town they'd stopped in housed an artists' colony, and everything was bright colors and sharp contrasts. The old roadside motel, a well-preserved throwback to the 1960s, was painted in turquoise and garnet. It reminded Sunny of her grandmother back in California who loved to wear garish flowered caftans and blue eyeshadow. Like the motel, she still looked good in it.

Even Sunny was at a loss for words as they crossed the street to the Donkey Kick Saloon under its blinking neon sign. They'd spent seven days on the road together, and they'd become friends. Friends who'd kissed, but that was Gabe's limit, and she had to respect it. Regardless, they'd part ways the next day. What more was there to say?

"Huh," was what he said when they stepped through the door into what Sunny had expected to be a honky tonk–style saloon. Instead, it was fitted with shiny red padded benches along the outer walls and reclaimed-wood tables in the center. On the wall opposite the bar was a stage with a screen behind it. Everything, from the bar to the stage to the bench-lined walls, was draped in multicolored Christmas lights. At only five minutes to seven, most of the tables had already filled with flannel-wearing diners.

The host, a tall, thin dude with a man bun peeking from underneath his knit cap, greeted them. "Do you want a table close to the stage?"

"What's the entertainment?" Sunny didn't see any instruments up there.

"Friday is community singing night," he said. "Members of the audience are welcome to perform."

"You mean karaoke?" she asked.

He grimaced. "We don't call it that, since it gives off the wrong sort of image. We prefer to think of it as a communal sharing of song."

"Away from the stage, please," Gabe said, scowling.

"It's okay," said the host, leading us toward the corner of the room. "You can hear the singing everywhere."

"Fantastic," Gabe growled.

She grabbed his arm. "It'll be fun. You can criticize everyone. Quietly," she added when the host shot her a sharp look. Gabe had seemed to enjoy her singing in the car. What was wrong now?

The host showed them to two seats in the isolated corner of the bench. Handing them menus, he said, "It's a very supportive environment. We encourage you to join in the singing. There are no catcalls or heckling of any kind."

When he'd gone, Sunny chuckled. "Poser karaoke. I hope the drinks are strong."

Gabe grunted. He didn't seem in the mood to talk, so Sunny gazed around at the other patrons. They were all more casually dressed than Sunny and Gabe, and many of them appeared to be fortifying themselves with booze for the karaoke—oops, *communal sharing of song.*

She let Gabe sulk in silence until their drinks came, then she raised her glass. Time to snap him out of it. "To our last night on the road." She'd be glad to be free of her Mercedes's stuffy interior when she made it to LA.

"Our last night together," Gabe echoed, tapping his pint glass against her martini glass.

She had to admit that she'd miss her driving partner. She slumped. "Now you've made it sad."

He rotated his glass on the table. "Sad? You'll be glad to be rid of me after tomorrow. You can speed off on the interstate. Go home to your family."

That was what she wanted. And yet. Her heart gave a weird twist-thump when she imagined Gabe in her rear-view mirror. She laid a hand on his arm. "No. Except for the driving-in-the-snow part, I had fun. I almost wish I'd met you sooner. When we both lived in Ohio."

"Almost?" He still didn't look up.

"If I had, I'd be even sadder to leave you."

He looked up then, searching her eyes. Finally, apparently satisfied she wasn't making fun of him, he said, "I'll miss you, too." Immediately, he snatched up the menu and hid behind it.

The emcee, a gray-haired Black woman wearing red cowboy boots, a short denim dress, and an electric purple beret, stepped up to the microphone. "Welcome to community singing night," she said. "We encourage everyone to come up and perform. Remember to kindly encourage our entertainers with applause. Any hecklers will be escorted from the establishment. First up, as always, is Miss Viola."

Miss Viola, an older Black woman, had gospel-soloist pipes. Sunny sat, rapt, listening to her belt out "Ain't No Mountain High Enough." If every one of the community singers was that good, they were in for a treat.

Sadly, no one measured up to Miss Viola. The rest of the community singers ranged in talent from James Corden's Carpool Karaoke to Mike Ditka's rendition of "Take Me Out to the Ball Game." Gabe kept his grumbling low enough that only Sunny could hear it, so no one offered to escort them out.

The food was simple but tasty, and the waiter kept the drinks coming. Someone sang an ear-piercing version of "Fool, I'm a Queen" that didn't quite break Sunny's martini glass but made her grit her teeth. She should've expected it; it was a standard on karaoke machines from New York to Tokyo. When the last, warbling high C faded away and relieved applause began, she stood.

"Come on. It's our turn." She held out a hand to Gabe.

"What?" His eyes went wide, and he gripped the table like it was Rose's door in *Titanic*.

"We have to return the favor. Everyone else has entertained us. Now we entertain them."

He shook his head. "I don't sing."

"Everyone sings," Sunny said. "Some just do it better than others. Now come on." She wiggled the fingers of her outstretched hand. At last, he grasped it.

As she dragged him to the stage, she asked, "Do you have any favorites you like to do?" It was always best to let the newbie choose.

"I don't sing," he repeated.

Sunny kept from rolling her eyes. Barely. "Okay, I hear you, but you're singing tonight. Do you know 'Shallow' from *A Star Is Born?* Ever see the movie?"

"Yeah," he muttered.

They'd reached the stage, and before mounting the step, she looked at him, raising one doubtful eyebrow.

"Riley liked it. I watched it with her once." He heaved out a resigned sigh. "Okay, a few times."

"Okay." God, she wished he hadn't said *her* name. Now she had to picture him cuddling in front of the TV with someone who wasn't her. Shaking it off, she went to the machine and queued it up, thankful they didn't have to do "Don't Go Breaking My Heart." He probably didn't have Elton John's range. Besides, the female part on "Shallow" was stronger.

"Remember, you start," she said, shoving a microphone at him. "Lyrics there"—she pointed at the screen at the front of the stage— "and hold the microphone close. Ready?"

His wide eyes told her he wasn't, but the audience shifted restlessly. She hit the button to start the music.

Maybe Gabe didn't sing on the regular, but his voice wasn't bad. It was low with a rasp to it, kind of like the country singer Chris Young's. It pleased her ear and made her smile, the way his growly speaking voice did.

But Sunny realized her mistake while he was still singing his first solo part. When he sang, "I'm falling," and turned those deep brown eyes on her, glinting in the stage lights, she saw that she'd tripped right into the trap of musical duos everywhere. Johnny and June. Sonny and Cher. Beyoncé and Jay-Z. Even, long ago, Gene and Gwen in that teen musical where they'd met. The soulful lyrics, sung with his heart in his eyes, twisted around Sunny's heart like ribbons and daisy chains and all that romantic bullshit. She almost forgot to come in at her cue.

She wanted to watch the audience as she sang, or else close her eyes and let the music soothe her, but she couldn't drag her gaze away from Gabe. A delighted smile played on his lips while he listened to her, and a full-out grin stretched his cheeks when she hit the high notes.

She had to poke him to join her in the last part of the song, and he stumbled over the final syllables. Still, the audience rose to their feet when they finished. Blushing, Sunny grasped Gabe's hand and pulled him down into a bow beside her before they scrambled off the stage.

The next singer stopped Sunny with a hand on her arm. "Aren't you Sunny Lafortune?" she asked.

Sunny never hated being recognized, but now wasn't the time, with her body quivering with need. For Gabe. She glanced at him, and he nodded, a proud smile stretching his face and crinkling his eyes.

"Yes, I am." She stuck out her hand to shake the other woman's.

"I knew it! Your voice is just as beautiful as your mom's. And I love *New York Bomb Squad*. And between you and me"—she leaned in close to Sunny to whisper, tequila on her breath—"your boyfriend's hotter than that Curt Suede."

"I know, right?" Sunny leaned away, grinning. *My. Boyfriend.* Just for the next twenty-four hours or so. "Break a leg."

The woman hopped up the step and launched into Patsy Cline's "Crazy."

Still clutching Gabe's hand, Sunny met his gaze. His brown eyes sparkled like smoky quartz, and crystalline tingles traveled from his hand up her arm. She shivered.

He tugged her close and spoke in her ear so she could hear him over the singer. "Want to get out of here?"

As much as she'd enjoy soaking up praise from the other patrons, she couldn't stay in the bar with the electricity coursing through her. They paid their bill and, Gabe's hand in hers, jogged across the street to the motel.

She fitted the heavy key into the red door while he waited. "Come in?" she asked.

He nodded and followed her in.

Somehow, she'd strewn most of the contents of her suitcase across the room. She might've gone through an outfit or two trying to find the perfect one for their not-date. Sunny scooped clothes off the bed, and Gabe sat in the cleared-off space, humming "Shallow."

While she shoved her belongings back into her bag, Gabe said, "I'll miss hearing you sing. Do you think you might do something with music when you get to LA?" Clutching an open-weave sweater in her hand, she didn't miss the yearning in his eyes.

He needed her.

Suddenly, LA didn't seem as appealing as it had earlier that evening. Staying a couple more days wouldn't hurt.

"You know, I don't need to be in LA until next Thursday. Maybe I could meet your family. Just to make sure they're not, like, serial killers."

Once she left for LA, she'd never see Gabe again. And she wasn't yet ready for the Gabe-free part of her life to begin.

Chapter Nineteen

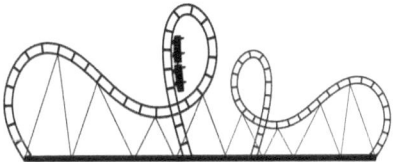

"You'd do that? For me?" Gabe asked. It was all he could do not to launch himself off the bed and across the room, fall to his knees, and cling to her while begging her never to leave him.

That song had undone him. Stolen his resolve. Flung him off the mountainside and left him hanging only by his own hope. She'd locked those electric blue eyes on him like she cared about him, like she meant the words she was singing about diving into love. He'd almost believed she was falling for him as hard as he'd already fallen for her. The last locks on his heart had failed, and the atrophied, desiccated thing was open to her, waiting for her to pick it up or step on it. Either way, it was hers.

And now she was offering to stay with him. Could a few more days be the start of forever?

"Yeah," she said. "I would." Gabe had lived without love, without hope long enough that he could pretend she'd answered yes to his unvoiced question.

She closed the suitcase over the pile of unfolded clothes and crossed to the bed, not stopping until she stood between his knees. Gabe shuddered when she dug her hands into his hair and scraped his scalp with her fingernails. She tilted up his face and lowered hers until they breathed the same air, until her face blurred in his vision. He fisted his hands in the comforter to keep from touching her.

"I can't—I can't do this and never see you again." The words rumbled out of his chest. He had no illusions she'd stay with him until he figured his life out. She had her own life in California. But long-distance relationships weren't so bad. Maybe he could get on a plane. There had to be some drugs that'd help him survive a flight from Columbus to LA.

She pressed her lips together, and he knew she'd walk away. Just like all the other women in his life. Better to know it now than after he'd given her his heart.

When her lips met his, all those swirling thoughts stilled. He didn't think about cars or planes or Los Angeles or even his as-yet-unconfirmed family in Vegas. The soft press of her lips against his set off fireworks inside him, lighting him up like that karaoke bar.

He let go of the comforter and touched her then. Her soft hair. The back of her dress, the one that clung to her curves, same as his eyes had all night. Gracefully, she dropped into his lap without breaking their connection. With one arm behind her back, he pressed her to him. His other hand cradled her cheek.

She opened and ran her tongue across his lip until he opened, too. He explored the wet warmth of her mouth, tasting the sugar and lemon from her martini that mixed with the orange scent of her hair, growing an entire citrus orchard around them in his imagination. One he never wanted to leave.

She tugged her lips away and kissed along his jaw to his ear. "Gabe, I need you," she whispered.

And with those words, she slayed him. His heart was already open to her, but that phrase was the password to his soul. Now when she went to LA, it'd follow her there, leaving him an empty husk.

She shifted to kneel over him, her slinky skirt lifting to the tops of her thighs. He gripped the round swell of her butt to steady her.

Who was going to steady him? When she arched her back, her breasts filled his vision, half-contained in the V-neck of her dress. He kissed the upper curve of one, then the other, making her moan out his name.

With trembling fingers, he reached behind her to locate the tab of her zipper. Slowly, he dragged it down as far as it'd go. He helped her shrug out of the top of the dress until it pooled at her waist, and then he took a moment to admire how the red lace of her bra cupped her breasts. Reverently, he ran his fingers along the lower cup, feeling her warmth through the raised texture of the lace.

He kissed over the curve of her breast until he found her nipple. Gazing up at her face, he met her heated stare, daring him to go farther, to take what he wanted, to give her what she needed. When he licked the nub through the lace, she gasped and arched, shoving it into his mouth. He licked and sucked until the fabric was wet like a second skin, clinging to her.

Trailing his hands down her back to her sweet curves, he tugged her close until her core nestled against his erection, straining toward her through his pants, just a tease so she could feel how much he wanted—needed—her, too.

Then he nipped her breast, and she arched again, sighing out his name. He moved both hands under her skirt to find her bare skin underneath. A thong. Was it red like her bra? His dick pulsed against his pants.

Tracing a finger up to her hip, he located the strap of her thong and followed it down in front. He ran his other index finger across the dampening satin that covered her core.

"Is this okay?" he asked.

"Mmm, yes."

"Can I keep...going?"

"All night if you can. I want to feel your fingers on me."

He wanted it, too. Slipping them under her thong where she was wet and warm, he circled her core once and then swept up her folds to her peak, where he found her clit swollen and waiting. He'd just barely touched it when she arched and stiffened.

"Oh, my God, Gabe, I've been waiting so long."

He ran a deliberate figure-eight pattern over her. "We just got started."

"We've been on this road trip for seven days, and at least the last four have been goddamn foreplay." She lowered herself to grind on his hand. "I about went off in the car the other day when I fed you that donut."

He flicked her clit, and she sucked in a breath. "Want me to suck your nipple or your finger while I do this?" he asked.

She shuddered. "Yes."

She still had her hands buried in his hair, so he kept going on her breast, tonguing and nipping it through her lacy bra. At the same time, he thumbed her clit, learning what made her breath hitch, what made her stiffen, and, finally, what made her cry out his name. By then, his dick throbbed, but he held her up against his chest, easing her back from her orgasm.

After a minute, her eyelashes fluttered against his neck, and she sat up with a lazy grin. "Thank God for Paul's wedding gift." She leaned over to open her handbag, which she'd tossed onto the bedside table, and pulled out a condom. She set it on the bed next to Gabe and went to work on his belt.

He put his hand over hers. "I—I'm not sure I can last long."

"Do that thing with your hand again, and I won't care." She unfastened his belt buckle and unzipped his pants. He stood, and she shimmied them down his legs, taking his boxers with them. It put her at eye level with his flushed penis, which pointed straight at the object of its desire. She only smiled and launched herself back onto the bed.

Gabe finished what she'd started, taking off his shoes before kicking out of his pants. He stripped off his socks and tossed them in the general direction of his pants. Right then, he didn't care about trip hazards. Burying himself in the sexiest woman he'd ever met was worth a face-plant later. Finally, he turned to face her, lying with her dress half-off on the bed. He unbuttoned his shirt slowly and watched her sultry smile turn sulky.

"You fuck like you drive. Too slow."

"Deliberate," he said. "And you didn't complain earlier." He unbuttoned the cuffs and slid off his shirt, finally naked before her. He kneeled on the bed and crawled toward her. "Sit up."

She shoved up on her elbows, and he reached behind her to unfasten her bra. He peeled it off her and then paused to admire her. Her nipples had pebbled and reddened from the attention he'd given them earlier. He'd come back to them later. He tugged her dress over her head, and then, at last, rolled off her black thong. Her naked skin glowed golden in the lamplight, and, at least for tonight, the most beautiful woman he'd ever known was his.

He stroked her from her shoulder, over one breast, across her ribs, over her hip, and down her leg all the way to her instep. God, every part of her was so small next to his big hand. "Any requests?"

"The thing with your hand again. And I want to watch this time."

His dick gave another hopeful throb. He'd gladly take orders from this woman for the rest of his life. He pushed her legs so her knees bent and her feet were flat on the mattress. Ignoring his own painfully hard erection, he kneeled between her feet and touched her glistening pussy. Then he traced up to her clit and circled it. She propped herself up on her elbows and watched as he rubbed the nub again with his thumb. Her legs trembled.

But he wasn't about to take her over the edge yet. With his other hand, he explored her opening before slipping a finger inside. He checked her face. Her eyes were glassy, but she didn't take them off his hands. He switched from making circles to fluttering his thumb over her, and she arched up off the bed, her muscles squeezing the finger he still held inside her. He kept up the motion until she squirmed, and then he switched to pressing the heel of his hand against her. She surged against him once, twice, and then went boneless, her knees flopping off to either side.

"God, Gabe, if I'd known you were that good at this, I'd have jumped your bones that first day."

He leaned over her and kissed her, gently. "After all your

Driving Miss Daisy comments, I don't think I'd have done such a good job."

"In this context, that sounds like a porn flick."

"Huh?"

She reached for the condom. "I think it's time for you to drive Miss Daisy." She nodded down at Gabe's dick, swollen and straining toward her. "Let's see that bad boy."

He slid his finger out of her and straightened, as if presenting himself for inspection. He must've passed because, making an appreciative sound in the back of her throat, she sat up, tore open the condom wrapper, and placed it on him, slowly, tortuously rolling it over his length.

"Lie back," she commanded.

He did, taking her place on the pillows and shoving the sheet and comforter out of the way. She straddled his hips and ran a finger down his length, over the latex. His dick jumped in response. Gabe groaned, desperate to be inside her. But he wanted her to take the next step. After that, he'd take back the driver's seat.

She lifted and rubbed herself over his dick. He tried to imagine what it'd feel like without the rubber between them, and his dick jumped again. Any more teasing, and he'd shoot his load before he was even inside her. To distract himself, he started to name and visualize the parts of her Mercedes's engine. Timing chain. Ignition coil. Crank. Shaft. His heart slammed against his chest.

When she finally lifted onto the head of his dick and started working herself down, he added the carburetor to his mental exercise. But the tight squeeze had all the blood rushing downstairs, and he couldn't visualize whether Cinderella took the straight or tapered air filter. Sunny stopped when her hips met his.

"Are you okay?" she asked. "Your face is all squeezed up."

He opened his eyes to find her biting her lip. "Just—just trying to hold off for a few minutes. You feel so good."

She rolled her hips once, experimentally. "So do you."

He gripped her bottom, his fingers splaying over her cheeks. "Wait. Just for a minute." He wanted to savor the feeling. Even though she'd agreed to stay with him long enough to meet his family in Las Vegas, how long he could keep her? Women like Sunny didn't date men like Gabe long. Tonight had to last as long as it could.

At last, he moved his hand around to rub her clit with his thumb. At the same time, he bucked his hips into her. And that's all it took. He'd danced on the edge too long. When she shrieked and clenched around him, he went off, his brain fuzzing.

The next thing he knew, Sunny was draped over his chest, strands of her long golden hair in his face. He scraped it off to the side and tugged the covers up over them. He had to get up in a minute to take care of the condom, but for now, he wanted to luxuriate in her closeness. The silkiness of her skin. The mingling of their scents. He rubbed his hand over her smooth back, and she sighed.

"Was that all right?" he asked. "I warned you that—"

"Gabe." She levered herself up and put a finger over his mouth. "Stop fishing for compliments. You're a sex god, and you know it. You've ruined me for all other men. Now be quiet and cuddle me, you big teddy bear." She lay her cheek back on his chest.

Even her mention of other men couldn't stop the grin that spread over Gabe's face or the warmth that rose inside him.

For now, she was his, and he'd do whatever he could to make her want to stay.

Chapter Twenty

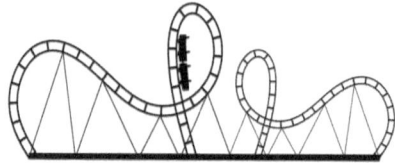

S unny woke from a sexy dream about Gabe to find his stubble rasping against the inside of her thigh. The red glow of dawn that came in at the edge of the window blind gilded the unruly tips of his hair.

"What are you doing?" She stretched, lazy and catlike. Her abdominal muscles squeezed in anticipation.

"I figured you wouldn't mind my morning breath down here." His words puffed over her pussy, making her gasp.

"Is this okay?" He shifted closer to where she wanted—needed —him.

"Yes, please." The *please* came out as a whine.

"So polite." His chuckle made her squirm.

"Do it fucking now, Gabe."

"That's more like it." When he closed his lips over her clit, she lost the power of speech. He sucked her higher and higher until she fell apart, trembling and groaning his name. Not only had he ruined her for all other men, but he'd ruined her for her favorite vibrator. When she got to LA, she'd have to find a new one that was more Gabe-like.

He wiped his face on the sheet and prowled up to the pillow. His erection bumped against her hip as he lay beside her in the queen-size bed that wasn't quite big enough for the both of them, considering Gabe took up so much space.

Sunny took his cock in her hand, smearing the precum at the tip down his length. "One more for the road?"

"Not if you're sore," he said.

She was, a little. It'd been too long since she'd had a partner, and Gabe was big. Not that she was complaining, but after the marathon session they'd had the second time, she was feeling a little stretched, and all the orgasms had given her abs a workout.

But her pussy wanted what she wanted, and she wanted Gabe again. Her center was already pulsing, needy, at the thought of being filled.

"I think there's a condom somewhere..." She patted the bed.

He tugged it out from under the pillow. "Got it."

He rolled it on and then lay back on the bed, lifting her by the hips to straddle him.

She resisted, curling a hand around his shoulder. "Come here."

"I'm too heavy for you," he said.

"Not if you prop yourself up on your elbows. I want to feel you on top of me."

Carefully, doubt crinkling his eyes, he settled between her legs, holding himself up in a plank her former trainer would've died to see. She was dying a little at the way his biceps and pecs bulged.

"Relax." She smoothed her hands over his shoulders and tucked her legs around his, tugging him closer.

He lowered himself to one elbow while he guided himself inside with his other hand. When he entered her, they both sighed, two halves completing the whole.

Slowly, he raised and lowered his hips. "Okay?"

She'd learned last night that this was his M.O.—check in first, and then take over. She didn't know why that'd surprised her. He was that way out of bed, too. But most guys she'd been with wanted Sunny to take charge. Some, attracted to her forceful personality, assumed it carried over to the bedroom. Others wanted to dominate that force and snuff it out. She never slept with those guys again.

Gabe was different. He checked that she was on board, and even took requests, but after that, there was no question about who was taking care of whose needs.

"Is that smile a yes?" he asked. "I want you to say it."

He was sunk to the hips inside her, lighting up nerves she didn't know she had. "Yes, Gabe. Please fuck me now."

He reached between their bodies and tweaked her clit so she gasped. "Less sass, more crying out my name."

He didn't have to tell her twice.

After, they separated to shower. She'd have suggested that they shower together, but she was starting to worry that she'd need ice for the two-hour drive. Not to mention that the little things she was learning about Gabe when they were naked were blurring her purpose.

Like this trip. Once she got back to LA, she'd reboot her acting career. Sure, she'd had a setback in New York. Despite what her parents thought of her, she'd have done it again. She was proud of herself for standing up for Odile. And if the role for her mother's project didn't work out, she'd shake it off and go to another audition and another until she landed a job.

But the longer she stayed on the road with Gabe, the less she wanted to get to LA. Gabe was real. When he told her he loved her singing, it wasn't so she'd tell him she loved his or to get her to do something for him. It was because he truly enjoyed it. And, unlike some of her former friends in New York who stopped speaking to her when she got herself blacklisted, he cared about her. From making her car safe to keeping her from falling on her ass to the heating pad, he showed her he cared in small ways. And not-so-small ways.

The look he'd given her when she'd offered to check out his family...it was full of hope, and longing, and something more. Something she wouldn't name because it'd tempt her to change her dreams. And she'd vowed never to do that. Not for love, which wouldn't last.

So, yes, she'd fulfill her promise. She'd even do long-distance if he still wanted that. Her mouth watered at the thought of phone sex with him. She could watch his enormous hand fist his gorgeous cock for hours. But it didn't mean she had to give him her heart. If she even had one to give at this point.

When she was dressed and packed, she rolled her suitcase next door and knocked.

Gabe came to the door wearing khakis with a razor-sharp pleat and a white T-shirt that clung to his muscled torso. He kissed her, the taste of mint toothpaste on his breath. "Sorry, I just need a minute, and then I'll be ready to go." He returned to the ironing board set up beside the bed and passed an iron over the front of a blue dress shirt.

The way his muscles bunched while he gripped the handle made her core give a hopeful clench. She blinked, hard.

"Oh, my God. You're *ironing?*" She tried a laugh, but it came out as a yip. "You're just going to get wrinkled in the car."

"Mm-hm." His tongue stuck out between his lips as he guided the iron between the buttons.

He lifted the shirt from the board and held it up, inspecting it. Satisfied, he slipped into the sleeves. His hand trembled as he fumbled for the button at the cuff.

The sharp pleats. The trembling fingers. They were meeting his siblings today, and he was fighting a massive case of performance anxiety. That, she could work with.

She grabbed his hand to still it. "Let me help."

When he nodded, she buttoned the still-warm cuffs for him, then she moved to the front buttons and fastened them all the way down. She smoothed her hand across the placket, over his flat abdomen. "It'll be fine, you know. They'll be just as sweet and kind as you are, and they'll love you."

"Yeah?" His brown eyes searched hers.

"Yeah." She wrapped her arms around him and squeezed. "Oh, oops." She released him. "I don't want to wrinkle you."

His smile was gentle before he kissed her. "I don't mind."

Sunny blinked hard and told her lady parts to stand down. Breathless, she said, "No more stalling. Time to go, tiger."

His face paled a little before he turned away to unplug the iron.

When they got to the car, he protested he wasn't hungry; still, she made him sit down in the nearby diner to eat breakfast. He'd be friendlier with a full stomach. As long as he didn't do his big, scary, gruff act, she knew they'd love him. Just like—

She took a sip of the scalding-hot coffee. No. Not like anything. She and Gabe were friends who'd fucked. Who were oddly sexually compatible, considering it'd been their first time together. And who'd be separating in a couple of days, as soon as she knew his family wouldn't hurt Gabe's soft, squishy heart.

And before Sunny could do it herself.

Chapter Twenty-One

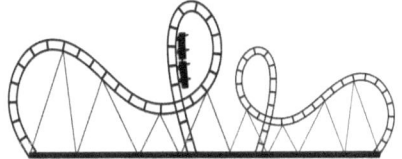

At the first sign to Las Vegas, a cold trickle of sweat ran down Gabe's neck.

Great. Sunny was right. He was going to meet his siblings —*potential* siblings—with a wrinkled, sweaty back. He dabbed the perspiration at his temple.

"You okay there, big guy?" Sunny asked, slanting a glance at him. She reached across the console for his hand and squeezed it, sweat and all.

"Fine." His voice cracked on the word. He could've been a teenager again, riding with Dad to pick up his date for the freshman dance.

"Breathe," Sunny said. "It'll be great. They'll love you."

"Will they?"

"Of course they will. Just be yourself. But less grouchy. The way you've been..." She cleared her throat and turned up the stereo. She was playing showtunes again, and "My Shot" from Hamilton popped, staccato, through the speakers.

She meant how he'd been with her, lowering the shield he held up all the time, ever since his parents—adoptive parents?—had died and left him to hold everything together. The only way he'd been able to keep Beach Island running was to box up his grief, same as he'd boxed up his parents' clothes and their Funko Pop collection, and hide it deep inside himself, holding up that shield to conceal the debilitating emotions that didn't help anyone. His arms were so tired now.

He turned down the volume. "What should I say?"

She glanced at him before turning her gaze back to the straight, flat road. "You're good at direct. Maybe try, 'Hi, I'm Gabe, your brother.'"

"I mean"—he swallowed—"after."

She was silent for a moment, and Gabe passed a hand over his face. Maybe he didn't have to keep his shield up with Sunny, but did he have to expose his squishy softness to her?

She turned the stereo off. "You mean, how do you talk to your brothers and sister?"

"Yeah, I...what about my...my birth parents?"

"Oh." The word dropped like an iPhone off Twister of Terror.

"Never—"

"No," she said. "I just hadn't thought about it, is all. They weren't on the DN-YAY report, so I sort of assumed they were... gone, you know? But maybe they just didn't take the test."

Gone. That'd make two pairs of dead parents. A good hand in poker, not so great in life.

"We'll start off easy. I'll be your sister."

"What?"

"A little role-play. For practice."

Role-play? This was her specialty, not his.

"I'll start. Hello, Gabe, I'm your big sister, Mary."

"Hi, Mary," Gabe muttered. But all the questions he wanted to ask stuck in his throat. They'd expose too much of his pain. *Do you remember me? Why did our parents give me up? What was wrong with me?*

A minute passed in silence. "Okay, maybe role-play isn't your thing," Sunny said. "Mary was five when you were born. She won't remember much. Michael might remember more. When you meet them, start off slow. Try to keep your focus on your lives now. On what you've been doing. They'll probably be curious. And then you can find something you have in common. Maybe they hate interstates, too."

"Maybe." It came out as a mumble.

"I didn't grow up with siblings, either. But I made friends who are like family. Like Cata. She and I both like walking in the city when it snows. And New York–style pizza. And boba tea."

"What's boba tea?"

"Oh my God, Gabe." She moaned. "It's sweetened tea, with these little pearls in it, and you drink it with a fat straw to suck up the bubbles."

"Bubbles, like air?"

"No, no, they're made of tapioca. They're chewy."

"You have to chew your tea?"

She snorted. "Never mind. I'll take you sometime."

"Yeah?"

She blinked and shook her head. "I bet there's a place in Vegas. We could try it before I go."

"Oh. Right." Even after what they'd shared the night before, she was leaving. He'd needed that reminder. Once he'd met his siblings—potential siblings—she'd be on her way. He wasn't even sure what exactly he wanted, but he wanted more. More time. More Sunny.

Her voice was airy when she continued. "On *The Brainiac Bunch*, the character I played was always doing bratty things to get her siblings' attention. One time, she told a guy her sister had a crush on him. After she apologized and the sisters made up, they did something they loved doing together: they went to Coney Island and rode the Cyclone. It's a—"

"I know the Cyclone."

"Oh, sure. Anyway, they rode it together, and it reminded them of how much they loved each other."

"But I don't have any old memories of my—of the Forzas."

"That's what I mean." She squeezed his shoulder. "You have to make them. Together."

"I haven't liked coasters since...a while." He caught her wince and rushed to smooth over the moment. "Vegas has a Ferris wheel. Those aren't so bad. And—and shows. I definitely like shows." Either one would be heaven with Sunny at his side.

"A show, then, with your siblings. Or maybe one of them drives an old clunker of a Mercedes you can work on."

He stroked a hand over the dash. "Cinderella's not a clunker. She's a tough old girl. She'll protect you." He was glad now he'd spent so much time on the car. She'd keep Sunny safe after she left him.

"Cinderella?" Sunny quirked an eyebrow.

The back of Gabe's neck heated, and he rubbed it. "We, ah, spent a lot of time together. The paint color reminds me of her dress. The blue one. My—my parents took me to meet Cinderella at Disney World when I was six or seven. That was the first time I fell in love." Even the swish of her wide skirt had been magical.

She smiled. "That's sweet, Gabe. Talk about stuff like that until you find something you have in common."

"What about...what about my birth parents?"

She paused so long he thought she might not answer. Finally, she said, "I'm not sure I'm the one to coach you on relationships with parents."

He'd much rather talk about her parents than his. "Why not?"

She stretched her back in the seat and stared out at the road for so long he thought she wouldn't answer. "I told you my parents were always on location. And that I took all those dancing and singing classes. That performing was a way to get their attention."

Gabe waited a minute for her to continue. Then he prompted her, "You're an amazing performer. I'm sure they were impressed and proud." His parents—the Armstrongs—had praised him every time he'd made a good tackle, hit a home run, or brought home an A on an assignment.

"They—" She grimaced. "They have high standards. Being box-office gold, you know. So once I got old enough that I wasn't adorable anymore, they took it seriously."

"You're still adorable."

She snorted. "Not six-year-old adorable. Anyway, nothing I did was good enough. *The Brainiac Bunch* being canceled after one season humiliated them. My dad made this face." She turned and did a passable impression of Gene Lafortune in the remake he'd done of *MacArthur,* the expression that made the young private piss his fatigues.

She turned back to the road. "He got me the audition in New York. He was proud I got the job, but it was only television. My parents think television is for B-list actors. Still, it was a relief to be far away and out of their sphere."

She was talking about her feelings. With him. His chest warmed. "But now you're going back."

She barked out a bitter laugh. "Yeah. Can you believe it? They actually asked me to come back."

"It's kind of you to do that for them." Gabe knew all about family obligations. Once upon a time, he'd wanted to follow in his parents' footsteps and run Beach Island. Until those footsteps ended.

Gabe stroked the scratched face of his watch. Which was worse: having supportive, loving parents who'd died too soon, or having negligent, critical ones? Gabe thought he'd pick the living-parents option, but maybe he was wrong.

"Oh my God, Gabe." A nervous laugh erupted out of her. "We're supposed to be talking about you and your family, not mine. Anyway, you should probably do the same with your Vegas family. Find common ground. You can talk about the hard stuff later."

"I don't know that I can." How could he say surface-level things when those questions bubbled right below the surface? *Why did you keep Raphael and not me?*

"I'll be there to hold your hand, I promise. I'm good at small talk. I'll help you."

His belly warmed like he'd swallowed some of her sunshine.

"Siblings are easy, though," she continued, her voice breezy, like she could blow away any obstacles with her confidence. "They'll love you. It's like—like a friend you've known all your life. I've had girlfriends like that. My friend Leena. We come together like we've been apart hours and not months. You've got a cousin, right? It'll be like that."

Gabe and Brandon hadn't been close since his parents died. Since Brandon had offered to take over Beach Island and Gabe had refused. They hadn't hung out, hadn't really talked other than *How's it going* at holidays. Maybe it was the awkwardness of what to say to someone who'd lost his parents. Or maybe it was the double-edged pain of Gabe refusing the offer he'd desperately wanted to accept. For whatever reason, there'd been a wall between them. Invisible, but there all the same, pushing them apart.

It'd be easier with Sunny. She'd take the conversational reins. Whenever he was near her, he felt better. Shored-up. Stronger. Like she was a steel support beam. Like it wasn't just him anymore.

It all rushed to the tip of his tongue, but the words tangled there, refusing to come. Just as he opened his mouth to force them, Sunny pointed.

"Look! It's the Strip!"

Electric signs and glass high-rises rose before them. Towers stabbed the cloudless blue sky. And in the foreground, rising high above the city, was the Ferris wheel. It rotated lazily in the mid-day sunshine. They had one at Beach Island. It wasn't a popular ride, mostly attracting older folks and teenagers who wanted to recreate the scene from *Love, Simon*. Its safety record was perfect, though, and if Gabe ever felt the need to get on a ride, it'd have been that one. So far, though, he hadn't.

"Mind if we take a cruise down on our way to your brother's?" she asked.

He ripped his gaze away from the soaring wheel. "No, go ahead." The closer they got to his family—*maybe* family—the more his guts squeezed. Could he convince her to put it off to tomorrow?

Once they turned onto Las Vegas Boulevard, traffic slowed to a crawl. Gabe's stomach unclenched a little when they passed the wheel, but his gaze snagged on another loop farther down. Red like the kiddie coaster at Beach Island, but taller. Not a poisonous tangle of purple and black like Fright or Flight. Still, the unexpectedness of it made him suck in his breath as he glanced away, pinning his gaze on a yellow taxi.

Sunny reached across the console to grip his hand and tug it onto her thigh. "Hey. You okay?"

"Yeah." He cleared the roughness from his voice. "Just wasn't expecting it. The—the coaster."

"We'll stay at the other end of the Strip. Or away from the Strip entirely. Somewhere we can't see it. Though..."

"Though?"

"You don't have a problem with other people riding coasters?" she asked. "Because I love them. I miss going to the parks near LA. It might be fun to do before I leave. If it won't bother you. I promise you don't have to watch."

He forced a smile. "No, I don't mind." Though he'd check the ride's safety record first.

He kept his eyes straight ahead until they left the Strip. And as they moved away from the neon and through the parts of the city that looked more like neighborhoods and less like an amusement park, his breaths came more easily. Maybe Sunny was right, and he'd fall right into this family the way she did with her friend. Maybe they'd plug the hole that Sunny would leave behind.

For the first time, he hoped DN-YAY hadn't gotten it wrong.

Gabe wiped his palms on his pants as Sunny pulled the car into a parking lot a couple miles from the Strip. Out there, the neon and the traffic were a memory, and it looked like Columbus in the summer—but with more cacti and palm trees.

"What's this?" he asked. He'd expected a house or an apartment building.

"This is the address I have for your brother Michael. Look." She stopped the car and pointed at the sign on the metal building at the center of the lot. "Forza Elite Motors. It's got his name on it."

The sign also had a white tiger, its mouth open wide in a roar. Gabe's heart gave a hopeful skip.

"See?" she said. "You already have something in common: he likes cars, you like cars. You'll have plenty to talk about."

The parking lot was half-full of exotic vehicles: limousines of every variety, from the standard town car to Hummers; convertibles; even a few classic Mustangs. The weight in Gabe's chest lightened. Clearly, Michael liked cars, too. Gabe had never met a gearhead who was a jerk.

Sunny parked in a space in front, and they got out. The sun beat down on her dusty Mercedes with the scrape on the front bumper from the blizzard, making it look sad next to the shiny-clean cars. He'd have to give it a wash and a tune-up before she continued to Los Angeles. Check the belts and the tires. She had more mountains to cross.

The heaviness settled back in his chest. But at least for now, Sunny was still with him. He grabbed her hand and plodded toward the open garage door. Prince's "Little Red Corvette" played from a speaker somewhere.

A stretch SUV with its doors open was the only car inside the garage bay. Familiar scents of motor oil and gasoline, plus those cardboard pine tree air fresheners, washed over Gabe. A broad backside wearing faded blue coveralls poked out of one of the doors.

Gabe cleared his throat, but the music was too loud for the person to hear it. He tried again. "Excuse me," he said in a voice that boomed off the concrete floor and windowless white walls.

The person backed out of the vehicle and straightened before turning to face them.

It was like looking in a mirror. After a sleepless night. Or a mirror that aged you ten years. The man shared Gabe's dark hair, but his skin was tanner with more crinkles around his brown eyes. He was clean-shaven like Gabe, and even the shape of his mouth was the same as it opened in an expression of shock.

"Wh-who the fuck are you?"

Gabe's heart pounded against his sternum. But he knew exactly who he was. "I'm your brother. Gabriel."

Those thick eyebrows slammed down in a scowl. His gaze traveled from Gabe's face down to the pressed front of his blue dress shirt, his shiny leather belt, his car-wrinkled khakis, to the shoes he'd polished last night. The man jammed the cloth he'd been using into his coveralls' pocket. As if there was any doubt, a patch on his chest was embroidered with his name. *Michael.*

"Didn't think you'd show your face here after all these years," he snarled.

Everything Gabe wanted to say died in his chest. All the oxygen had been sucked out of the garage. Sunny squeezed his hand.

"Do you...do you know me?" Gabe asked.

"Never saw you before, but I know who you are." Michael crossed his arms over his broad chest. He was a couple inches shorter than Gabe, but his bulk made up the difference.

"You do?" God, why hadn't he and Sunny role-played this scenario? *What do you say to your brother who hates you on sight?*

"Of course. I was eight when you were born."

Sunny nudged him, and Gabe tried to remember what they'd rehearsed. Michael had the manual, and Gabe couldn't assemble the parts.

"I'm Gabe Armstrong." Gabe stepped closer and held out his hand. "And this is Sunny Lafortune. My girlfriend." He didn't know why he gave her that label. They hadn't talked about it. But he needed something to hold on to. A throw rope in the sea where he was now adrift.

Michael looked at his hand but didn't shake it. "Looks like you did fine for yourself," he said, staring at Luke Armstrong's classic Omega on Gabe's wrist. "I don't know what you want from me."

"I—nothing." What did he want from Michael? From any of the Forzas? Suddenly, it seemed foolish to have come all this way. Why hadn't he called? Emailed? Heat crept up his neck. "I found out I might've been adopted and wanted to see for myself." He dropped his hand to his side and took a step back.

Sunny stayed where she was. "Gabe took a DNA test and found you. He wants to learn about his birth family."

"His birth family?" Michael sneered, the expression strange on a face so similar to Gabe's own. "He's not a part of our family. Obviously, he doesn't need us. And we don't need him."

The heat left Gabe's face, and ice trickled through his veins. Michael's face and his words had proved that Gabe had been one of them once. But they still didn't want him. Where did he belong now?

"Sorry to bother you," he croaked. Still holding onto Sunny's hand like she was a life preserver, he turned and strode back to her Mercedes. He wanted to drive, to be in control of something, but his hands shook, out of control. Instead, he opened the driver's-side door for her. After closing the door behind her, he rounded the hood on unsteady legs, keeping his gaze away from the garage. He slumped into the passenger seat.

Sunny started the car. "Are you okay?" she asked in a low voice like people had used around him in the funeral home.

He looked out the side window at the white tiger on the sign. Now the heat spilled over his cheeks. Michael had sliced him open, revealing the ugly thing underneath Gabe's skin. He wished Sunny hadn't seen it.

"I—I'm sorry that went the way it did."

"Not your fault." It was her fault, though. She'd bullied him into coming all the way out here. She'd painted a rosy picture of a family that was looking for him, wanted him. But the truth was that they didn't. He stared at Cinderella's dusty dashboard to avoid looking at the white tiger he'd taken as a sign that he had something in common with the Forzas.

Maybe if he'd known how screwed-up Sunny's family was, he wouldn't have started out on this trip. As it turned out, Gabe knew more about functional families than she did. And now it was time for her to continue on her way. "Just—just drop me off at a hotel."

She backed out of the parking space and headed past the rows of shiny cars back toward the street. "I'm not dropping you off anywhere. We'll figure out our next steps. Together."

The words ripped out of his mouth. "Our next steps? You're on your way to LA. You can drop me at the airport. I'm going home."

She stomped the brake, flinging him forward against his seatbelt. Throwing the car into park in the lot, she stared at him, hard. "You've come too far to give up now. My acting coach always said that if you fuck up your lines, you keep going and try harder next time. If I'd given up, I'd never have gotten the part on *New York Bomb Squad.*"

"But you did give up." Gabe was sweating again, and it wasn't the Vegas heat or even nervousness anymore. It was fury. "You worked that crap job at DN-YAY for months. Who are you to tell me to go crawling back to Michael Forza and ask him to reconsider?"

"I—" She stared at her hands in her lap. "You're right. I'm sorry. I know nothing about siblings or adoptions or families. I shouldn't tell you what to do."

His anger melted like ice cream on asphalt. He unbuckled his seatbelt and reached over the center console to fold Sunny in his arms. After a second, she wrapped her arms around his back. "I'm sorry I yelled at you," he said into her hair.

"God, he's such an ass," she mumbled against his neck.

"Must be a genetic trait."

"Gabe." She loosened her hold on him and pinned him with a fierce stare. "You're not—"

Just then, his phone rang. Hope flared inside him until he realized it couldn't be Michael calling to apologize and welcome him back. Michael didn't have his number. It was Darlene.

He held up a finger to Sunny and answered the call. "Hi, Darlene."

"Hi, Gabe. Are you checking your email? Brandon called an emergency board meeting. Noon tomorrow. Are you going to be home by then?"

Relief flooded through him. She was okay. But an emergency board meeting? Who'd let Brandon call one of those? And why? To make it home by noon tomorrow, he'd have to leave today.

"I—I don't know that I can make it ho—back by then." He'd almost said *home*. What was home anymore?

"Then I'll set up a conference call for you and text you the details. Just in case. Any idea what it's about?"

"No, Brandon hasn't called me. I guess I'll find out tomorrow."

"He's not a member of the board. Can he even call a board meeting?" she asked.

He heard the worry in her voice. "Maybe Aunt Pat asked him to get us together."

"Maybe so." She didn't sound like she believed it.

"I'll try to call him later and ask him about it."

"Okay. Are you all right? You sound...not like yourself."

Gabe snorted. Like himself? Who was he now, anyway? But that wasn't what Darlene needed to hear. "I'm fine. I'll call you if I find out anything."

He disconnected the call and slid his phone into his pocket.

"Everything okay at home?" Sunny asked.

"Fine. Just work stuff."

She smoothed a finger between his brows, and the muscles in his forehead relaxed. "You do so much for them. For everyone. Maybe it's time to think about what you want to do for once."

Now there was a concept. From the second he'd leaped out of the car that day, clambered down the coaster's scaffolding to the ground, broken through the circle of horrified onlookers, and checked his parents' broken bodies for a pulse, people had looked to him to lead. To take his parents' place. To care for everything and everyone at Beach Island. But now that he knew he'd been adopted —Michael's face was better proof than a birth certificate—it was time to examine his life. Who was Gabriel Forza, and what did he want?

Sunny waited, lips parted, blue eyes darting between his. He knew exactly what he wanted. Lowering his face to hers, he kissed her, gently at first, but when she opened to him and licked over his lower lip, he poured all his frustration, his anger, his longing for things to be different into it. Grinding over her lips and flicking into her soft mouth with his tongue, he showed her what he wanted. Who he wanted. With one hand, he cradled her cheek. He trailed his other index finger down her neck, over her collarbone, into the valley between her breasts. Delving into her bra cup, he rubbed his callused fingers over her nipple the way she liked.

She pulled back, breaking the kiss, her breath heaving. "Hotel."

He took his time dragging his fingers back over her hardened nipple and out of her bra. "Hotel," he agreed. He'd take a few hours to show her what she meant to him, and then he'd think about what his next steps would be. What else he wanted.

She reached for his hand and squeezed it. "I know just how to make you feel better. And then we'll figure it out. Together."

He leaned over and kissed her, filling his nostrils with her scent. "Together."

One thing was right in his world: that this woman was by his side. At least for now.

Chapter Twenty-Two

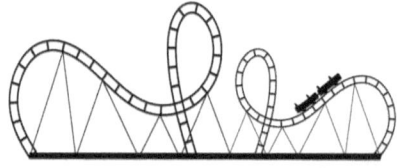

"Meet the Forza family, take two." Sunny turned off the Mercedes in front of a little stucco house in the near suburbs.

Gabe couldn't keep the words inside. "I don't know about this." Sure, Mary had seemed nice when Sunny passed him the phone. She'd apologized for her brother Michael's behavior at the shop and invited them to dinner.

Sunny turned to him, her eyes wide as if to keep from rolling them. "We drove two thousand miles to meet your family. They want to get to know you. And now we're here. We're going in." She reached over the console and tucked her hand into his, the way she'd been doing since they'd walked up to Michael yesterday, the way that sent a jolt of courage through his veins. He could do it if she was with him.

"Okay." Gabe reached between his knees for the bottle of cabernet and shoved open the door. The cool desert air hit his too-warm cheeks. He wiped his palms on his pants, then reached into the back seat for the bouquet of flowers Sunny had picked out. She met him at Cinderella's hood, and together they walked up to the house.

They didn't have to knock. Mary threw open the door like she'd been watching for them. She wore a white apron with the Italian flag on the top, and the scent of fresh basil wafted around her. "Gabriel!" she squealed, launching herself at him. She was tall for a woman, with a curvy build. Her thick, dark hair tickled his nose.

She stepped back and bent to hug Sunny. "I'm so glad you called. I can't believe Michael didn't even take Gabe's phone number." She scowled, but the expression cleared when she let go of Sunny. "But you're here now. You look just like Rafe." She hugged Gabe once more. "What are we doing standing out here on the porch? Come in, come in."

His lips trembled so that he could only mumble, "For you." He held out the wine and the flowers.

"Thanks," Mary said. "But you're family. You didn't need to bring anything." She took the gifts and led the way through an arched doorway into the bright kitchen.

Rafael—Rafe—stood in front of the stove. He'd been wiping his hands on his jeans, but he froze when he saw Gabe. If he'd thought looking at Michael was like looking into a mirror, looking at Rafe was even more so. They were almost the same height, and he had fewer lines around his mouth and eyes than Michael did. Like Michael's, his skin was tanned like he spent time outdoors.

Mary said, "Rafe, it's Gabriel. He's come home."

Tears welled up at that, and Gabe blinked hard. What would his brand-new family think of him if he cried?

Rafe strode over, paused for a second, then hugged Gabe. His hair held a spicy scent; that was what made a tear roll down Gabe's cheek and soak into Rafe's button-down shirt. Gabe squeezed back. Hugging Rafe was nothing like hugging his Ohio family; he'd always been afraid if he squeezed too hard, they'd break.

He shouldn't have worried, though. Rafe sniffled as he thumped Gabe on the back before releasing him, and when they parted, Mary's face was wet with tears.

"I can't believe it's you," she said. "We'd given up hope you'd ever come back."

He was glad now that Sunny had been so tenacious and made

him meet Mary and Rafe. He glanced around for her and spotted her hanging back at the doorframe. He reached back and tugged her to him. "Rafe, this is my girlfriend, Sunny." That was twice he'd called her his girlfriend. They hadn't talked about it, but the word gave him the anchor he so desperately needed in the face of all this uncertainty.

Rafe shook her hand. "I hope you're hungry. Mary doesn't know how to cook for less than a dozen people."

Gabe's stomach contracted. Sunny answered for them both. "Starving," she said. "It smells delicious."

"I thought Gabe would enjoy our great-grandmother's lasagna recipe," Mary said.

"Oh, is she...still living?" Sunny asked, a hopeful tilt to her mouth.

"No," Mary said and crossed herself. "We've got an aunt or two still with us, and cousins, but the rest of the older generations passed on. Dad died just last year. But we'll talk about all that over dinner." She pulled a platter of meats, cheeses, and olives out of the refrigerator. "Antipasti?"

The appetizers smelled delicious, but the weight in Gabe's stomach kept him from eating. He'd missed meeting his father by only a year? And he couldn't keep his gaze away from the front door, anticipating—dreading—the moment Michael would walk through, scowling, and make him feel like a stray dog. With mange. And fleas.

Gabe didn't miss that Mary watched the door, too. But after half an hour of small talk, wine, and cheese, she tapped the counter. "Let's eat. Rafe, help me get dinner on the table."

Sunny and Gabe offered to help, and Mary kept them so busy Gabe almost didn't notice when Rafe took the fifth place setting off the dining table. He poured everyone another glass of wine, and they sat down. The dishes and silverware looked modern. Apparently, the only heirlooms were the recipes themselves.

After Rafe mumbled a blessing, Gabe raised a forkful of meaty lasagna to his lips. The smell of tomato sauce, spices, and garlic almost made him forget the boulder in his stomach that stole his hunger. When he popped it in his mouth, the flavors burst on his tongue. Basil. Oregano. Salty cheese. Tangy tomatoes. It tasted like home, but not his home in Ohio.

"This is delicious. You said it's a family recipe?" Sunny patted her lips with a napkin.

"Our family's from Napoli originally. Naples. Our grandparents were born here, but their parents came from Italy. We've preserved their traditions. Gabe, did you grow up in an Italian family?"

"No." The Armstrongs had lived in the U.S. for generations; any traditions they'd brought from northern Europe had long disappeared. But he wasn't ready to talk about his Ohio family yet. His brain was still processing the certainty that this was his biological family. If there'd been any doubt about it after meeting Michael, it had disappeared when he'd met Rafe and Mary. Being with them was like seeing one of his old baby pictures. Familiar in a distant way, like the memory dangled just out of reach.

Mary's forehead wrinkled at his terse response, but she picked up a thread of their pre-dinner conversation about Sunny's acting work. She'd recognized Sunny from *New York Bomb Squad*.

"What's your next project, Sunny?" Mary passed Sunny the basket of homemade rolls.

Sunny pulled a chunk off the roll and buttered it. "My mother lined up an audition for me."

Mary's eyes widened. "That's right! Your mother is Gwen Lafortune. I loved her in *Kiss Me Tomorrow*. And you look just like her."

"Thanks," Sunny said. "But if that doesn't work out, I'll call my agent to ask him to line up some auditions. If he's still speaking to me." She said the last part under her breath.

Gabe shook himself out of his self-absorption at that. "Of course he'll find you a role. You're the most talented person I know. You should hear her sing," he said to Mary.

Mary's dark eyebrows arched. "I can imagine. Gwen had that hit song, 'Fool, I'm a Queen,' you know."

"Oh." Sunny's cheeks went red. "I'm not at their level. I took some lessons, but I'm still working on my craft."

"You're amazing," Gabe said. "Any production would be lucky to have you."

"Thanks." When she smiled at him, all his discomfort melted away. It was like they were back at Four Corners, twirling in the sunset. She turned to Mary. "Gabe's not so bad himself. We sang a duet at community singing night."

"Community singing night?" Mary's eyebrows disappeared into her curly bangs.

"Karaoke."

"You sing?" Mary asked.

He snorted. "No, but Sunny encouraged me." It was the best night of his life. He found her hand under the table and interlaced his fingers with hers.

"I can be very persuasive." She winked at him.

She turned back to Mary, but the sparkle in her ocean-blue eyes, the soft smile that played on her lips, the pink in her cheeks that was just for him and the memories they'd made together on the trip were burned into his vision. In that moment, he knew there was nothing he wouldn't do if she asked. He loved her.

Yet she was leaving. Soon. She had to be in LA in four days. Should he ask to go with her? Would she let him? Or would she insist on her end date? She'd already told him she wasn't interested in forever. But four days wasn't enough. Would she give him more if he asked?

"Gabe! Gabe, are you all right? Do you not like the lasagna?"

He blinked and found three sets of eyes on him. Picking up his fork, he cut a bite and shoved it into his mouth. Spicy sausage and sweet tomatoes burst over his tongue. He lifted the corners of his mouth and nodded his approval. Rafe's big shoulders lowered an inch or two.

Mary laid down her fork and dabbed at her lips with her napkin. She speared him with a kind but no-nonsense stare. "We want to know all about you. About what brought you out here. I don't even know where you live now."

He swallowed with difficulty and sipped some water. In a few sentences, he summed up Sunny's phone call from DN-YAY, her reckless visit to his house, and their cross-country drive. His siblings didn't question any of it: not Sunny's meddling, not the drive, not the lack of a phone call or email. He got the sense they'd have done the same thing.

Then, as economically as he could, he told her about the Armstrongs and Beach Island. She interrupted with questions about growing up, school, the family, and his life now. When he told her—as briefly as possible—about how his parents died, she burst out, "They never told you that you were adopted?"

"No, I—I don't know why. Maybe they were waiting?" He'd thought a lot about it ever since Sunny told him. He supposed he'd never know why they'd kept it from him. From the entire family. They'd never been too focused on the past, not like Gabe had, anyway. Probably, they'd just thought they'd have more time. And they would have, if not for Gabe's decision that day.

After that, Mary eased off with the questions. Rafe asked nothing at all, just kept his attention on his plate and looked up at Gabe occasionally, as if he was checking that his brother was still there.

When Mary brought in the dessert—Sfogliatelle, she called the shell-shaped pastries—she said, "You probably have a lot of questions."

"I do." Questions he didn't know how to ask.

"Let me tell you what I know." She split open the flaky pastry to expose the custardy filling but didn't take a bite. "Mom and Dad never had a lot of money. Dad worked as a mechanic at a garage, and Mom waitressed nights at a bar. Apparently, Rafe here was a surprise, and he wasn't six months old when Mom found out she was pregnant again with you. I was too little to understand, but I imagine growing the family so quickly and unexpectedly put a lot of strain on them."

Gabe pictured what she hadn't said. Parents who worked in shifts, tired all the time, maybe not quite enough food in anyone's belly. The Armstrongs had worked hard, and their hours at the park had been irregular, but when he wasn't in school, he'd accompanied them to work at Beach Island. He'd spent hours playing there, never far from their loving gazes. And there'd always been plenty of food, new clothes when he outgrew his, whatever he needed or wanted.

She looked over at Rafe, her brown eyes liquid. "Michael had just turned eight, and I was five. If we'd been a little older, maybe they wouldn't have been so overwhelmed, but...anyway, they decided adoption was the right thing to do. We're Catholic, you know. Mom had you baptized at the hospital, so I guess you are, too."

Gabe's chair was going to crack with the extra weight. All this history he'd never known, and now Mary had thrust a whole religion on him, too.

"Mom met your parents at the bar. They were staying in Vegas for a while, and all four of them got to be friendly. She was showing by then, and they came to an agreement. I don't remember, but Michael says your parents hung around, bought us presents, made sure Mom went to her prenatal appointments. They were there the night you were born, you know. And when Mom was released from the hospital, they took you away."

Rafe nudged her with his elbow. "Tell him."

Mary's lips tightened. "They gave our parents a lot of money. Enough for Dad to buy the garage where he worked, and his first limo. He drove it himself until Mom went back to work, and then he kept doing it on her nights off. He was determined to make a better life for us all."

Gabe was frozen, unable to speak or move. His parents—the ones he knew, his adoptive ones—had bought him. And his other parents had sold him. Like a car.

"It looks like he did a great job," Sunny said, filling the silence. "The business is impressive."

"Dad started it, but Michael's the one who really built it up," Mary said.

"You said he died." Gabe's voice came out scratchy, like he hadn't used it for hours. "What about..."

"Mom?" Mary's smile was sad. "She died, too. A couple years after you were born. She never was healthy, and she just didn't bounce back from those last two pregnancies. Rafe doesn't even remember her."

She'd died because of him. Because he'd been born. The pastry turned to dust, and he choked down what was in his mouth. He tensed, preparing to push back from the table and flee.

Sunny gripped his hand, and Mary reached across for his other hand, pinning him in place. "Dad and Michael took care of us until I was old enough to help. Then Michael started helping Dad at the shop. Michael was like a second dad, always taking care of us, making sure we ate right and did our homework. Rafe and I even went to college. So we all turned out fine." She smiled at Rafe, then at Gabe. "Especially you."

But he didn't want Mary's doe-eyes on him. He didn't want anyone looking at him. If he hadn't been born, they might still have their mother.

He tugged his hands away from Mary and Sunny and scraped back his chair. "I—I think we should go."

Sunny's eyes went wide, but she stood with him. "You've been so kind. Thank you for dinner," she said. "It's a lot to take in. I'm sure you understand."

"Gabe, I..." Mary's proud smile had faded, and a furrow divided her dark eyebrows.

"Thank you for telling me. I just need..." But he couldn't finish. He didn't know what he needed. He walked straight out the front door and stood on the front porch, gasping in the cool, dry air that didn't smell like a great-grandmother's recipe, like a heritage he didn't know about, like guilt.

After a couple of minutes, Sunny stepped out onto the porch.

She stood beside him for a minute, staring out into the suburban street. "Gabe, you—"

"Don't," he said, harshly. Cruelly. "I need another minute, okay?"

Her eyes glinted in the porch light. "I'll meet you in the car." She walked away, leaving him alone on the porch.

The screen door slammed, and Rafe stood beside him. He didn't look at Gabe, just stared down the street like Sunny had done. Finally, he spoke. "I felt guilty for a long time. Like it was my fault she...she died." He shoved his hands in the front pockets of his jeans. "But it's not my fault, and it's not yours, either. No matter what Michael thinks."

That made Gabe's stomach roil. He bit his tongue, trying to keep from losing Mary's delicious dinner in her bushes. "He thinks it's my fault?"

"It's complicated. He has a lot of guilt himself. According to him, if he'd helped more, paid more attention, maybe she wouldn't have gotten so sick. But you weren't here, so you were an easy target for the part of the blame he didn't take himself. I've tried to get him to go to therapy like I did, but..." Rafe rocked on his heels. "Without the money, we wouldn't have the shop. And he loves the shop. That might be the hardest part of it all for him. You should talk to him."

"It didn't go so well last time."

"Try again. Family's worth it." He clapped Gabe on the shoulder then disappeared into the house.

But was it? Was it worth the pain he'd already caused, already felt? Was it worth digging that knife even deeper into his gut?

At last, he forced his feet down the walk to Sunny's car. Before he got in, he took a deep breath. He couldn't blame her for any of this. She'd meant well. She hadn't intended to ruin his peacefully ignorant, happy life. Just like he hadn't meant to ruin the Forzas' by being born.

Before he'd even closed the door, she turned to him, her eyes soft and pleading. "Are you okay?"

He grunted. He couldn't lie and say yes. But she didn't want to hear the *no* that was closer to the truth.

Gabe woke up to the sun streaming in through the curtains they'd forgotten to close and the buzz of a text message on his phone. Sunny's small hand rested on his chest, pinning him against her, and soft puffs of her breath tickled the back of his neck. He closed his eyes, shutting out the sunlight.

The bed was warm, and Sunny was soft. How many more mornings did they have together? Not many. And the box of condoms that'd seemed laughably huge when Paul at the convenience store had handed them to him now seemed like a countdown clock, measuring their remaining time together in dwindling prophylactics. Only two remained. Somehow, it felt presumptuous to buy more.

His phone buzzed again, insistent, on the nightstand.

Carefully, he disentangled himself from Sunny's embrace and scooted away to check the phone's display. What could Darlene need so early on a Monday? His heart pounded. Was she okay?

He flicked open the message. *How'd the meeting go?*

How did Darlene know he'd met his family yesterday? He hadn't told her, or anyone back home, about it. He hadn't wanted to reveal his uncertainty, his vulnerability, until he'd seen proof. He needed answers to the questions they'd fire at him.

Wait. She was asking about the board meeting. The one Brandon had scheduled yesterday. The one he'd forgotten. How had he missed it? He'd have to call home and apologize.

He sat up and moved to the chair by the window. From this angle, Sunny was a tangle of white sheets, red-blond hair, and warm, pink skin. He flicked the curtain to block the sun from the bed.

He checked his email. Sure enough, Uncle Bobby, who served as the board secretary, had sent out the meeting minutes. He'd flagged them "sensitive," so that explained why Darlene had asked Gabe about the meeting. She couldn't open any sensitive emails.

He tapped to open it, and when he saw the heading, he shook his head. Brandon had received a buyout offer from one of the larger park chains.

Unlike eight years ago, it wasn't only talk about selling. It was a real purchase offer. Gabe couldn't simply explain to Brandon that it was a bad idea because it'd compromise the security of their employees and, potentially, the safety of the patrons. No, his cousin had done an end-run around Gabe by taking the offer to the board.

They wouldn't agree, would they? He was almost positive they'd refuse the offer. While Grandpa, Uncle Bobby, and Aunt Pat hadn't worked in the day-to-day operations for years, they'd rotated through the park like he had, and they had to remember their responsibility to the employees and the patrons. Didn't they?

On their most recent tour through the park, no one had said anything about selling. Though Grandpa had complained about his knee. They were all getting older. Eventually, they'd have to pass their responsibilities to the next generation. Which included Brandon. How long could Gabe hold him off? How much longer could he protect Darlene and Ramirez and the hundreds of others who depended on Beach Island?

As quietly as he could, Gabe changed his pajama pants for jeans and a blue Beach Island T-shirt. He put on his sneakers in the hallway and went downstairs to compose a response to Brandon and the rest of the board.

An hour or two later, Gabe was finishing up a call with Darlene when he spotted Sunny standing at the door to the café. He couldn't tell Darlene about the offer, but he assured her everything was fine. And it would be. Gabe would ensure it was. He told her some white lies about how much he was enjoying his vacation. Though, looking across the café at Sunny, it almost felt like the truth. But then he remembered that a third of the family he'd come out to meet hated his guts.

"Gotta go, Darlene," he said. "The masseuse is here." He smiled at Sunny as she approached him, her blue flowered sundress making her eyes glow.

"Masseuse?" Darlene's voice dripped with doubt.

"Bye, Darlene." He stood and pulled out the chair for Sunny. "Morning."

She reached up on her tiptoes to kiss his cheek. "G'morning. How long have you been up?"

"A couple hours, maybe. I had some work to do."

She yawned and flipped over her coffee cup. "This early on a Monday? When you're supposed to be on vacation?"

"When you're in charge, sometimes you work on vacation."

The waitress came to pour Sunny's coffee. Sunny dribbled in French vanilla creamer and sighed after she took the first sip. Her radiant smile made his heart twist in his chest. Another morning with Sunny ticked away.

"What was your urgent Monday-morning business?" she asked.

Since the offering organization was publicly traded, he couldn't give her specifics. He hadn't signed a nondisclosure, but he couldn't afford to have their corporate lawyers fight him. "I—I missed a meeting yesterday, and I had to deal with that."

"You. Mr. Worked-All-the-Way-Here, Mr. Works-on-Vacation, Mr. Responsible-for-Everything-and-Everyone. *You* missed a meeting."

"I was distracted." He shrugged.

Her lips pinched. "Maybe it's a sign. Have you ever thought—really thought—about what it is you want?"

I want you. But he couldn't say that. And it wasn't what she was asking. "I guess not. People had expectations, and I did what they expected."

"But this could be an opportunity for you."

"This?"

"Finding out who you really are. Not that you're any less an Armstrong than you were before." She held out her palms to him in a *whoa* gesture. "It's a good time to think about whether or not you want what the Armstrongs forced on you."

"They didn't force—"

"Sure, they did. And maybe that's okay. Or maybe it's not. Regardless, you should think about what you want to do with the rest of your life." She stared into her coffee.

What would his life look like without Beach Island? Without Uncle Bobby, Aunt Pat, and Grandpa? Without Darlene and Ramirez? He'd have only himself to worry about. If they sold the park, he could stay on this break from reality forever. He could stay with Sunny as long as she'd let him.

No. He'd spent his whole life at Beach Island. He'd poured everything into it for the past nine years. He knew the park and the community that surrounded it better than anyone else. Selling wasn't right. And he had to tell the rest of the board. Maybe they'd vote him down. Maybe they wouldn't listen once he told them he'd been adopted. Still, he had to try.

"The board has a vote scheduled next Saturday. I need to be back in Ohio for it."

Her smile dissolved. "Oh. I have to be in LA for the show on Thursday. I can't drive you back."

"I know." Gabe sorted the sugar packets in the dispenser by color. "I'll fly back."

"You think you can? Have you flown since the—the accident?"

"No, but"—he smirked to hide his doubts— "it can't be any worse than your driving, can it?"

"Ha, ha. I happen to be an excellent driver. Just not in the snow."

"You won't have to worry about that in LA." And just like that, he'd popped the delicate bubble of his own happiness.

She traced the rim of her cup with her finger. "No, I suppose not."

"So, when are you—" He cleared his throat to get the waver out of it. "When are you planning to head west?"

She gripped his hand. "Not until you've worked out your shit with Michael."

"We both might miss our deadlines if we wait for that."

She narrowed her eyes and then trailed her gaze from his T-shirt down to his sneakers. "Let's take our coffee to go. I have an idea."

Since that first day, Sunny hadn't driven him past the roller coaster at the New York New York. Today's route, though, gave them a side-on view of the Ferris wheel. In the daylight, it seemed smaller.

"Maybe we can ride the Ferris wheel together before you leave." Stopped at a traffic light, he tilted his chin at it, through her side window. "Now it seems a lot less terrifying than the Forzas."

She grimaced at his weak joke. "You're pretty intimidating yourself, you know." Her gaze trailed over him. "With your sharp pleats and that cashmere coat you wear. That chiseled jaw. Those"—she gulped—"steely eyes. The first time I met you, I almost ran the other direction."

Standing on his porch that day, her delicate jaw had been set, and her Cinderella-blue eyes had flashed. "You did not. You stood right up to me. Even though I wasn't so nice to you."

"No, you weren't." The light turned green, and Sunny eased the car forward.

"What about now?"

She glanced at him, a smile curling her lips. "I think you're pretty nice now. Especially when you do that thing with your fingers."

His fingers itched to touch her now. All he had to do was ruck up the short skirt of her dress. It was already at the middle of her thigh. He fisted his hands in his lap. Not while she was driving. It wouldn't be safe. "I hope your idea involves going somewhere private where I can do it to you again."

She chuckled. "Tempting, but my idea's better."

Her idea culminated in barely slowing down to boot him out of her car in front of Forza Elite Motors. "I'll pick you up in a couple of hours," she called just before she drove off.

Gabe stood alone in the parking lot. Monday morning at a limo rental shop. Sure enough, the *Open* sign in the window was unlit.

He'd be sitting here by himself until Sunny came back to pick him up.

But after Cinderella roared away, the guitar riff of "When Doves Cry" leaked out of the open garage bay. Gabe followed the synthesizer run through the entrance and leaned against the wall. His brother Michael squatted in front of the open driver's side door of a midnight blue '66 Mustang.

A bolt plinked onto the concrete floor, and Michael bent at the waist to lift the door from its hinge.

"Whoa, whoa!" Gabe peeled himself off the wall and jogged over to help. He gripped the outside of the door and supported as much of the weight as he could. "This is a two-person job. Why would you do it alone?"

Michael only grunted and tipped his chin toward a drop cloth on the floor where the other door already lay. Together, they carried it over and laid it gently on the cloth. Michael propped his hands on his hips and scowled at the pair of doors. Gabe picked up a rag from the workbench to wipe his hands. He'd gotten grease on the hem of his Beach Island T-shirt, and he rubbed half-heartedly at it. It'd never come out.

"If you're going to stay, put on some coveralls," Michael growled.

"Yeah?" He wasn't kicking Gabe out?

He nodded at a rack in the corner. Gabe crossed to it, found the biggest one, and stepped into it.

"These, too." Michael held out a pair of safety glasses.

Gabe zipped up the coveralls and held out his hand for the glasses. "What are you doing here on a Monday, anyway?"

"I had some cars to turn," his brother said. "When you're in charge, sometimes you work on your day off."

"Someone's taking this one out today?" Gabe asked, raising his eyebrows doubtfully. The Mustang didn't look like she'd be ready for customers anytime soon. Not with the doors off and the paint peeling at the bottom.

"Nah, she's a pet project. Clears my mind." He stared at the engine compartment.

"Need help?" Gabe asked.

"Not afraid of spoiling your manicure?"

"Screw you." He kept his voice cool and held his brother's stare. "I just saved your back by helping you with that door."

"Fine. Help me take off the dash."

The men worked together in near-silence, communicating mostly in grunts and one-word instructions to replace the corroded instrument bezel and install a reproduction lens over it.

Finally, when they had the Mustang put back together, Michael captured Gabe in a sideways stare. "Not bad for someone who works at a desk all day."

Gabe shrugged. It wasn't the time to argue with his big brother. Not while he craved Michael's approval. As kind as Mary and Rafe had been last night, he knew he needed it to be fully accepted into the Forza family.

"Let's go for a ride." Michael plucked a set of keys off the wall and nodded at the passenger seat. As little as he wanted to get into the car, Gabe obeyed his eldest brother. He breathed a little easier when he found the car had seat belts. He buckled his.

Michael started her up, and she idled at a low rumble. As he rolled her slowly out of the garage, he said, "Mary called me last night. Said you were upset about Mom." He exited the parking lot onto the street.

"I just—it was a lot to take in. You know?"

He snorted. "It was a lot to live through."

Gabe turned to him, but his brother kept his eyes on the road. "I—I wish…" He didn't know what he wished. That he hadn't been born? No, not that. Riding through Vegas in a vintage Mustang, still bearing its grease on his hands, made him happy to be alive. That he hadn't been adopted? That he'd been around to grow up with the Forzas, putting more financial strain on the family? That he'd found out sooner and gone back to help? That he'd never come to Vegas at all?

Michael shook his head. "You came back, stirred up all those feelings. I thought I'd dealt with them but...I guess not."

"I had a good therapist back in Ohio. I could ask her to recommend someone out here."

Michael's lip curled. "Therapy's for—" He glanced at Gabe. "Never mind. What would *you* need a shrink for?"

Now it was Gabe's turn to stare through the windshield. "I lost my parents, too. My adoptive ones."

"Car accident?" Michael nodded at the way Gabe gripped the dash.

"Something like that."

"That sucks."

"Yeah."

His brother guided the Mustang around a corner, and they were back at the garage. He parked her in a covered spot and, together, they tucked a tarp over the car.

"You're not bad with a torque wrench," Michael said. "I don't know what your plans are, but I could find a spot for you here. God knows I've found jobs for more useless people."

If that was Michael's way of welcoming him into the family, Gabe hoped Michael left the public relations to Mary.

"I've got some stuff to sort out back in Ohio. But I'd like to come back and visit again."

Michael grunted. "Sunny going back with you?" Her powder-blue Mercedes had just made the turn into the lot.

"Nah." Saying it felt like an ice pick in his heart. "She's an actress. She belongs in California."

And now that he'd sorted his relationship with his family, she could go on her way.

Chapter Twenty-Three

From the narrow passenger seat of Mary's candy apple–red Corvette, Sunny spotted an overflowing trash barrel and an abandoned traffic cone. The flickering streetlight cast a yellow glow over her black skirt. She already missed the well-lit theme-park cleanliness of the Strip.

"Why am I doing this, again?" Sunny should've been sitting in LA traffic by now, almost home. Gabe had reconciled with all three of his siblings. Mission accomplished.

But when she'd gazed into his big, brown eyes, she couldn't leave. So she'd put it off. Again.

Mary switched off the engine, and they stepped out onto the cracked asphalt of the parking lot. The top of the Ferris wheel glowed in the distance, lit in blue and purple against the blue-black sky. Most of the street was quiet except for the jangle of music that seeped from a long, low, windowless building. Its red door stood out in the street packed with gray industrial buildings. Here, there were no roaming mobs of bachelors and bachelorettes in search of a good time. Quieter, smaller groups and pairings disappeared through the red door.

"I'm bonding with my brother's girlfriend." Mary beeped the locks.

"I'm not—"

"Whatever you call it. I've missed years of this with Gabe. Besides, this place has the best music in town."

"Better than Mariah Carey?" Sunny's voice dripped with doubt.

"I think so. It's...honest. Not something you get a lot of in this town."

On the other side of the red door, the place was dark, lit mostly by the neon-lined bar that wrapped around three sides. Spotlights washed out the stage at the back, which held two shiny black baby grand pianos. A shortish, older man sat at one in an Elton John getup, complete with fedora and red-tinted glasses.

Mary nodded at the bouncer and led the way to a table near the stage. "I hope Sam's here tonight. It's fun when they play together."

"Dueling pianos?" There weren't any peanut shells on the floor, but Sunny had been to her share of bars like that.

"More like duets."

The man at the piano launched into "Your Song." His voice wasn't as smooth as vintage Elton John, and it had a rasp to it, fading at the emotional lines. Still, he sang the song as if he'd written it, his heart pouring out over the shiny surface of the piano.

When the song ended, the server came to get their drink order. She delivered the news that Sam was out sick, and they hadn't gotten a replacement because of the short notice. When she left, Mary frowned.

"This guy is good, though," Sunny said. "What's his name?"

"Rick. But he doesn't sound as great as he usually does."

"I hope he's not coming down with whatever Sam had." When Sunny glanced up at the stage, Rick guzzled water and hoarsely announced a ten-minute break. It didn't bode well for their night of honest music.

When the server returned with their drinks, she hesitated, staring at Sunny. "Are you that actress, Sadie from *New York Bomb Squad?*"

"Oh, um." Sunny shot a quick glance at Mary, who smiled at

her and shrugged. "Yeah, I am. Sunny Lafortune." She held out her hand, and the waitress shook it.

"My girlfriend's a big fan. She loves all those cop shows." She blinked. "I mean, yours is the best, of course."

"Of course," Sunny said, chuckling. "It's okay. It wasn't the greatest show, but I had fun."

"Actually, that one episode you did a couple weeks ago, the one where you got engaged, that was pretty awesome. We both cried."

Sunny'd had some good lines in that one. Had it aired so recently? If so, her big exit was coming up soon. Probably for February sweeps.

"Would you mind...?" The waitress's fingers twitched toward the stack of cocktail napkins on her tray.

"Not at all." Sunny couldn't keep the grin from her face. She asked for her girlfriend's name and scrawled it with her signature on the napkin. The waitress carefully tucked it into her apron, thanked her, and left the women alone.

"That happen a lot?" Mary asked.

"Not as often as you'd think. *New York Bomb Squad* was getting good ratings, but my part was small. I wasn't in every episode until Sadie became a love interest for Curt. And that didn't last long."

"What?" Mary asked. "They wrote you out?"

"I'm not supposed to talk about it because it's a big reveal later this season, but yeah."

"What'd they do, kill your character?" Mary sipped her gin and tonic.

Sunny shrugged.

Mary set down her glass with a plunk. "Oh, my God. They fridged you?"

Sunny wrinkled her nose. "What?"

"They do it all the time in the superhero comics my brothers used to read. They kill the hero's love interest to deepen his motivation to fight the villain or some bullshit. Last one I read with that in it, I threw it across the room. Michael was pissed because it crinkled the corner." She smiled at the memory. "I'd sneaked it out of his room."

"Oh." Sunny thought back on the season's arc. "Yeah, I guess so. I assume Curt's character was going to go after the bad guys who did it. And Odile—" It was hard to say her friend's name. Though it wasn't Odile's fault she'd gotten to stay while Sunny had to go.

"I hate that," Mary said. "And I hate that they did it to you. I'm sorry."

Sunny lifted a shoulder. "If it hadn't happened, I wouldn't have met Gabe." Cold washed through her body. What had she just said? She hadn't really meant that being with Gabe was better than acting on a hit show, had she? No. Way. She stared at her half-full lemon drop martini. She couldn't be drunk already. And that couldn't be how she really felt about Gabe.

Could it?

She drained her glass and squinted at Mary. "Did you bring me here to liquor me up so you could find out all my secrets?"

Mary sipped her sparkling water. "Your secrets or Gabe's. It's always worked for my other brothers' girlfriends."

The server set another lemon drop in front of Sunny. She rotated it on the table. It wasn't her place to spill Gabe's secrets. How long had Rick been on break? He had to come back soon and put an end to Mary's interrogation.

"So," Mary said, "how long are you staying?"

"Not long." It was Monday night. Three days until she had to be on set. "I'm supposed to be in LA by Thursday."

"Will you come back after? I was going to offer Gabe my spare bedroom if he wants to stay awhile. There's room for you, too."

"Gabe's staying?" They hadn't talked about it. When they'd gone back to the hotel after Gabe had bonded with Michael, he'd tugged her into the shower and done that thing again with his fingers. And then his tongue. It was a good thing Sunny was leaving soon; they'd run through almost all the fake-honeymoon condoms. She'd coaxed him into bed for a nap he needed badly, and he'd woken up just in time to mess up her lipstick before she'd gone downstairs to meet Mary. Their kisses had grown desperate as the days—hours, maybe—counted down.

"I was hoping he'd stay," Mary said. "Michael says he's a decent mechanic, and we could use his help in the garage. We've missed so many years with him. I want to get to know him better."

"He's got his business to run back in Ohio. I don't think he'd leave it." Would Gabe let his cousin Brandon take over? The calls and emails from Darlene never ended. Gabe was working even on his fake vacation.

Mary's glance was sharp. "Not even for you?"

Sunny thanked whatever force called Rick back on stage at that moment. She couldn't look Mary in the eye and tell her there was no place in her LA life for her brother.

Rick sat at the piano, swallowed hard, and rasped into the microphone. "Sorry, y'all. This next set is gonna be instrumental."

He launched into a rollicking piano version of "Benny and the Jets."

The familiar tune soothed Sunny's curdled stomach. After she'd performed it at an elementary-school talent show, Mom and Dad had stopped shooting dagger-eyes at each other long enough to hug her. They'd—accidentally—almost touched each other. "This is my favorite."

"Then get up there, girl, and help him out."

Mary must've known that she'd had just enough vodka to obey. Sunny rose and found the steps up to the stage. Out of the corner of her eye, she saw Mary stop the bouncer, who'd approached to drag the drunk girl off the stage.

Sunny nodded at Rick, who watched her warily while she lifted his microphone off its stand. She breathed in deep. Holding it to her lips, she belted out the lyrics with just as much enthusiasm and more skill than she'd done in elementary school.

Some members of the audience looked shocked, but most took it in stride. They probably thought she was a plant. Maybe some of them recognized her from the show, like the waitress had, and figured she was just another attention-craving C-list actress. Which she totally was, but she was also helping Rick.

After she sang a few bars, he got into it, molding his accompaniment to her voice, supporting her. At the end, he grinned. "Not bad, blondie."

"Not bad yourself." Sunny smiled back.

"Another?"

"Yeah."

He played and Sunny sang another set. She even sat at Sam's piano for a duet of "Don't Let the Sun Go Down on Me." After that, her voice was almost as raspy as Rick's, but her nerves buzzed from the performance. It'd been too long since she'd performed for a live audience, and her insides glowed.

As the last note faded, she hugged Rick, then descended the steps to rejoin Mary at the table.

Mary smiled, smug. "Not bad."

"Not bad?" Sunny yelped. "That was amazing! I—"

A man in a suit, no tie, loomed up next to their table. "Hey, Alex," Mary said. How much time did she spend in this place?

"Mary. You going to introduce us?"

"Sunny, this is Alessandro Villa, but we call him Alex. He owns the place. We grew up together, went to the same church. Alex, this is my brother's girlfriend, Sunny." Sunny didn't miss how Mary emphasized *girlfriend.*

Alex shook her hand then reached behind himself to pull up a third chair to the table. He straddled it backward.

"Nice job up there, Sunny. Thanks for the help. You a singer in one of the shows?"

"No. Just passing through."

Mary's mouth turned down at that.

"Too bad," Alex said. "I could use another performer. If you wanted to extend your stay, I'd make it worth your while."

For a second, she imagined coming back to Vegas during a break in filming. Gabe would be overjoyed. As she performed, he'd sit in the audience transfixed, the way he'd been in the car that time she sang "Defying Gravity." Then they'd go home together, not to Mary's guest room but to a little apartment or even a bungalow of their own. He'd do that thing with his fingers every night.

She shook it off. She couldn't tell her parents she'd become a nightclub singer. In Vegas. She had bigger dreams than that. Besides, she and Gabe would grow apart, just like her parents. She wasn't built for long-term.

"No, sorry, I really am just visiting. But thanks."

Alex stood and replaced the chair. "Mary knows where to find me if you change your mind. Thanks again for the entertainment tonight."

Sunny smiled and watched him walk back to the bar. Mary, she noticed, watched him, too.

"Grew up together, huh?" Sunny smirked.

"Yeah." The corner of Mary's mouth quirked up. "We know way too many of each other's secrets."

"That's a bad thing?" Sunny sipped her drink. It'd gone all watery, but it soothed her throat.

"Well." She winked. "Mostly."

The question about their history perched on Sunny's lips. Until she realized she'd gotten invested in Mary, too. First Gabe, and now his sister. She had to cut those ties, fast, or they'd grow too thick, too painful. Too hard to leave.

"But you," Mary said, "you should think about Alex's offer. You were really in your element up there. You glowed."

"I can glow as an actress, too." Though Sunny remembered what Gabe had said about her on *New York Bomb Squad.* Maybe she wasn't cut out for gritty TV. She should try out one of her mother's rom-coms. Though everyone would find her lacking, compared to Gwen.

"Of course you can." Mary patted her hand. "You're great at whatever you put your mind to."

When they walked out of the bar into the cool, dry Nevada night, Sunny looked up again to the Ferris wheel, still glowing above the buildings.

She pointed. "Have you ever ridden it?"

"No," Mary said, "I'm more of a thrill rider. I've been on the roller coaster at New York New York a couple times. That's fun."

"I bet you get a good view from the top."

"Of the roller coaster? No, it goes too fast. There's a loop, though, so there's that."

Right then, Sunny was on a roller coaster, hurtling toward LA, her parents, the audition, her next show. Gabe had thrown her for a loop, sure, a momentary thrill. But she was about to straighten out and ride the train to arrive back home with a lurch.

Too late, she realized she should've been riding the Ferris wheel the whole time. At the top, she could see her life laid out in front of her. Then she'd know what to do next.

Chapter Twenty-Four

S itting against the headboard in their hotel room, Gabe flipped the last page of the purchase agreement for Beach Island. Aunt Pat, Uncle Bobby, and the rest of the board wouldn't vote to sell, would they? The agreement contained no guarantees about retaining the employees. All of them, from Old Jeff in the ticket booth to that high school kid who'd arrived early every shift to be the first to ride Mystery Mountain, whooping so Gabe could hear him all the way in the executive offices if the window was open, would be out of a job.

Not to mention the patrons. They wouldn't be Gabe's responsibility anymore if they sold. He wouldn't have to worry about anyone falling off because of a poorly maintained harness or hitting their head on a low-hanging branch. That'd be the new owners' responsibility. But would it? He'd cared about them for so long. Could he stop after it wasn't his name on the deed?

That was why he'd emailed Brandon, copying the board, to lay out his long list of concerns about the purchase order. It might not be his place, considering he wasn't really an Armstrong anymore, but he'd done it all the same. He'd worked in the park since he was thirteen. Been the CEO for nine years. They might not let him vote once he revealed what he'd learned, but he had opinions, and he'd expressed them.

The door clicked, and Sunny stepped in, humming "Piano Man." Her cheeks glowed with more than rouge, and her eyes held a sparkle they hadn't when she left.

Until she looked at Gabe. The smile that'd been playing on her lips faltered for a moment. She stopped humming. Then her lips lifted, but the spark didn't return to her eyes. "Hey, I didn't think you'd be up."

"I was just reading." He tossed the papers onto the bedside table. "Did you and Mary have fun?"

"We did. She took me to a piano bar, and I sang a little."

"Karaoke?"

"Something like that."

Why did his chest twinge? It wasn't like karaoke was their thing. As he'd told her, he didn't sing. She did. And he should've loved that she and Mary had fun together. But he and Sunny had so little time left. Was she leaving tomorrow? Or the next day? Definitely by early Thursday. He coveted every minute she had left.

He kicked his feet over the edge of the bed and walked to her. She stood still while he cradled her delicate jaw in his hands. Leaning down, he kissed her lips. She didn't want him to say the words that burned in his chest, but he'd show her. With his touch, he'd tell her he was grateful for what she'd given him. That he'd grown to care about her. That he wished she'd never leave.

"Let me take care of you tonight," he murmured against her lips.

She blinked up at him, her eyes glassy, and nodded.

He eased her coat off her shoulders and lay it over the chair, revealing the black dress that hugged her body, the same one she'd worn the night they'd done karaoke. He shut his eyes, remembering the first time he'd taken it off her. They'd been wild that night to get to each other's skin, to taste, to touch, to relieve the pent-up longing that had built on the long drive. Not tonight. Tonight, he'd savor her. He'd create a memory he could pull out like an old photograph to comfort him on the lonely nights to come.

Gently, he turned her to face the bed. He looped up her long hair, twining it around his fist, and held it against her shoulder. In the lamplight, some strands glowed golden, and others blazed ruby red. He wished he had time to catalog them all. It'd take weeks. Maybe years.

When he kissed her nape, she shivered. Slowly dragging down the zipper of her dress, he placed kisses along each vertebra as it was revealed. When the zipper reached the end of its track just above her thong, he pushed it off her shoulders and supported her as she stepped out of the puddle of fabric. He made her wait, trembling with need, while he picked it up and laid it over the back of the chair with her coat.

She stood in her black bra and purple-striped thong a couple feet from the foot of the bed. This gorgeous woman had chosen to be his. At least for tonight. He wanted to fall to his knees and beg her to stay so he could worship her always, but she would've snatched back her dress and left him right then. So, instead, he'd treasure the moments they had left.

Standing between her and the bed, he pulled off his T-shirt and pajama pants, down to his boxer briefs. They didn't hide how turned on he was, and as he adjusted himself, her gaze arrowed to his barely contained erection. She licked her lips.

He circled around behind her, letting her feel the warmth of his body.

"Gabe—" Her voice was strangled.

"Shh. Shh. I've got you." He started back at her nape and laid a trail of kisses from there along the top of her right shoulder. Lifting her arm so it was perpendicular to her body, he kissed over it, down to the elbow, then to the back of her hand. He kissed each fingernail. Then he circled around and kissed the pad of each finger, her palm, her wrist—she squirmed at that. Then the inside of her arm, the crook of her elbow, with a tiny nip there, up the inside of her arm and across her collarbone, carefully avoiding her breasts. He'd come back to give them the attention they deserved.

He kissed along her other arm, front to back. Then, starting at her shoulder blades, he planted row after row of kisses all the way down to the waistband of her thong. He made the kisses on her buttocks in narrowing circular patterns. She twitched and moaned but let him continue.

Kissing each leg from the curve of her bottom down to each heel, he ended with his cheek pressed against the carpet. Then he circled around to her front and started at her toes.

Maybe she realized it, maybe she didn't, but he was laying claim to every inch of her body. Even if no one else, including Sunny, knew, Gabe would know that whenever she left, she was going out into the world with the print of his lips on every part of her. It'd be like the time someone had tagged the wooden fence at one side of Beach Island. They'd painted over the graffiti a half-dozen times, but if the sunlight hit it just right, you could still see the old words, a ghostly reminder.

The closed-mouth kisses Gabe placed on the triangle of her thong were promises he'd return. He breathed in the scent of the soaked fabric. Her arousal was a gift, and he'd anoint himself with it later.

He moved up her flat stomach, circling her navel with his tongue. That made her shiver, too. He kissed over her ribs, noting how they heaved with her breath. Finally, he reached behind her to unclasp her bra. It whispered to the floor.

His own arousal gnawed at his control, urging him to hurry, to bury himself inside her and mark her there, too. He observed the sensation, the pleasure that tugged at his gut with a hint of pain, and set it aside. Soon enough, he'd give in to it. Not yet.

His kisses around her breasts turned to nibbles and, at last, full-on licking and sucking. She wobbled, and, finally, he used his hands, banding them around her waist to hold her up. She rubbed her thighs together as he tongued her nipples. He imprinted the scent of her on his brain.

Her breathing coming in pants, she buried her hands in his hair and held him to her. He pulled her nipple into his mouth and flicked the tip with his tongue. When he looked up, her mouth was open on a silent scream. He released her nipple, and when he repeated the action on her other breast, her whole body quivered.

He guided her to the bed, where he arranged her now-pliant body face-down, with her hips at the edge. Rolling down her thong revealed her plump, glistening lips. He kneeled and, spreading her legs with his shoulders, feasted on them and her beckoning clit until she shuddered and froze, crying out this time. He licked her through her orgasm, gently, reassuringly, murmuring, "I've got you." He squeezed his own dick at the base through his shorts to calm it. *Later.*

"Gabe, I—"

"What is it, love?"

As soon as the words were out, he wanted to claw them back. His heart pounding, he covered the slip with a playful tap on her ass cheek. "Move up on the bed." Maybe she'd believe it was only sex talk.

He pulled back the covers and let her crawl inside. Still wearing his briefs, he spooned up behind her, cradling her like the precious gift she was.

"Gabe, I—I want you inside me. Just you." She didn't look at him, but she ground back against the ridge in his shorts. "I have an IUD. And I've been tested. All clear."

God, another gift. One he couldn't accept. "I haven't been tested since before my ex and I broke up, and we—we didn't use condoms. I don't think she...still, I can't. As much as I want to. Besides." He rolled to the bedside table and shook the box. "We have one last honeymoon condom."

"It's really all right. I trust you, Gabe."

He kissed her shoulder. "And I trust you. But we're using the condom."

He shucked off his underwear and rolled on the latex. They made love face to face, and Gabe held off as long as he could, making sure she had one last orgasm before he came and came, shuddering, above her.

Only later, when he was sure from her long, even breathing that she was asleep, did he whisper the words that'd been tearing at his chest all night.

"I love you, Sunny."

Chapter Twenty-Five

I *love you, Sunny.*
The words echoed in Sunny's ears hours later as she blinked open her eyes. The sun wasn't quite up, but it was past six, so she could legitimately stop pretending to sleep and get up.

She'd rolled to the edge of the bed after the whisper he hadn't meant for her to hear, so she didn't disturb him when she dropped her legs over the side of the bed and stood.

Gabe's face was smashed into the pillow, and his arm splayed out toward her side of the bed like he'd reached for her during the night.

He'd always be reaching for her.

She needed to go now before...before...

It was already too late. But she'd rather shave her head the day before an audition than admit she loved him, too.

Tiptoeing into the bathroom, she checked her phone. Texts from Mom and Dad waited for her reply. Increasingly urgent reminders that they needed her there in two days.

Long-distance wasn't an option. Not living in LA with her celebrity parents. The tabloids had cataloged her early dating life, and she'd built up a reputation as a love-em-and-leave-em heartbreaker until she'd learned to keep her dates on the down-low. LA was too much to ask of him.

Though between projects, she'd have time to visit him in Ohio. Could the magic of their road trip, the days and nights in sparkly Vegas, survive a phone-only relationship until then?

If anyone could do it, it was Gabe Armstrong, the most loyal person she'd ever met.

She turned on the shower. She didn't want to scrub off the million kisses Gabe had placed on her. She didn't think she could, anyway. They were part of her skin now, like freckles or moles or pores. Like an invisible tattoo marking her, reminding her.

Maybe he'd be different. Maybe he wouldn't reject her. Maybe they really could build a relationship like his parents', one that was real.

She'd ask him about long-distance. But first she'd pack her things in case he said no. If he rejected her offer, it would crush her.

Rejection sucked. She knew that from a lifetime as the unexceptional Lafortune.

After turning off the shower, she slipped on jeans and a T-shirt, brushed her teeth, put on makeup. Not wanting to make noise with the dryer, she combed through her hair and left it to air-dry. Then she gathered up all her things from the bathroom and opened the door.

Gabe was awake. He sat up in all his massive nakedness, his broad shoulders pressing against the headboard and the sheet puddled around the vee of his hips. Acres of tantalizing olive skin contrasted with the whiteness of the hotel bed.

He said nothing right away, but the way he scanned her from her damp hair to her armful of beauty products told her he saw straight through to the whirling fear in her brain.

"You're leaving." It wasn't a question.

"You know I have to be there by Thursday. And I need some time to prep for the audition. My parents keep calling to remind me." They didn't trust her to follow through. She had to show them she would.

"Don't do it like this. Don't run away."

"I'm not running anywhere. The point of this trip was for you to meet your family—which you've done—and for me to get back to LA. It's time for part two of this adventure." She dumped the stuff onto the bed and went to the closet for her suitcase, hoping he hadn't heard the tremor in her voice. *Ask me to call you.*

"Will you come back?"

She set the suitcase on the bed and zipped it open. He wasn't talking about coming back to Vegas or even about going back to Ohio. He was talking about coming back to him.

"Maybe. I—"

"Or let me visit you?"

She'd never expose her gentle giant to the entertainment media. In LA, they'd dig up his painful past and splash it across the internet and onto the covers of those checkout-line magazines. Was a long-distance relationship fair to either of them, considering she knew it couldn't last? She was a Lafortune, and Lafortunes could play romance on screen but couldn't manage it in real life.

"I need to do this audition with my mom." She tossed the items from the bathroom on top, not bothering to pack it well. So what if her shampoo bottle opened and spilled all over her clothes? She'd always associate the clothes with this trip, with Gabe. She'd have to burn them.

"I get that. I understand about family. But stay long enough to have breakfast with me. I'll get dressed. Give me ten minutes."

Of course he understood about family obligations. More than that, he understood her. His steady brown eyes bored into her. Pleading for a few more minutes. Her own traitorous heart skipped in answer. It was too late. She'd already stayed too long to leave unscathed. When those brown eyes turned cold like her father's, it would hurt that much more.

The answer came from the primitive part of her brain that didn't care about any of that. The one that craved more time with this beautiful, kind, strong man. "Okay." She zipped her suitcase and tried not to ogle his naked body as he passed her. "I Cain't Say No" from *Oklahoma!* jangled through her head.

When the shower came on, Sunny checked the room for anything else she might have left behind. If everything was packed, she could grab it and go after breakfast. She wouldn't be distracted by all the places they'd made love—no, *had sex*—in the room. She wouldn't get sucked down into Gabe's brown eyes, yearning for another sexy growl.

Her phone charger. As she reached for the plug next to the bed, Gabe's phone rang on the bedside table. The ring she'd heard several times a day since they'd left Columbus, always Darlene and work. The display read *Brandon*. After a few rings, it stopped. And three seconds later, it rang again. *Brandon*. Maybe it was a family emergency. Should she pick it up? It was crossing a line to touch someone else's phone. The ringing stopped. But when it started right up again, she answered it.

"Gabe's phone. Sunny speaking."

"Who?"

"A—a friend. He can't come to the phone right now."

"A friend." Suspicion sharpened his tone.

"That's right. Can I pass on a message to him?"

"I'm sorry, but I don't know you, and I know all of Gabe's friends. How do I know you haven't stolen his phone?"

It was kind of sweet, actually, that he was so protective of his cousin. So she played along. "You're Gabe's cousin. You went to some fancy business school and now you're helping with Beach Island while he's away." She wanted to say "meddling" instead of "helping," but even though she might never see Gabe again after today, pissing off his relatives wasn't kind.

"Fine. You're his friend." His tone softened. "How's he doing?"

Oh. Gabe must've talked to him before he and Michael had made up. Of course he'd told his cousin how anxious he'd been about reconnecting with his birth family. And now Brandon was worried about Gabe and how he was feeling. Sunny's heart swelled.

Gabe would be okay. He had family, both biological and adoptive, to care for him after she left.

"He's doing better now," she said. "He and his brother bonded. Later today they're going to see if the state has his real birth records."

"His real birth records?"

In those four words, she knew she'd screwed up. Her jaw dropped open. No words came.

But they didn't let just anyone into fancy business schools. Brandon was a smart guy. "You're saying Gabe was adopted?"

"I didn't say that. He's totally not." She squeezed her eyes shut. Shit, what had she done?

"Where are you two, anyway?"

"Gotta go. I'll tell him you called." She mashed the button to disconnect the call.

"Who was that?" Gabe's voice behind her made her jump.

She whirled and found him shirtless, drying his hair with a hand towel. "I—I'm really sorry. Brandon kept calling, so I picked it up. I thought it was an emergency. And I—I didn't know you hadn't told them. I'm sorry."

His face turned the color of ash.

Chapter Twenty-Six

"**W**hat?" He'd heard her fine, but he couldn't believe what had just happened. Brandon now knew he was adopted. Questions exploded in his brain like popcorn kernels in a popper. Would it change their relationship? Would he question Gabe's role with Beach Island? Would the board? Would they vote him out before he made it back to Ohio? Could they?

He'd wanted to reveal the truth in person, on his own terms. Use the opportunity to present his arguments against the sale. Now they might not let him in.

"I'm sorry," she said for the third time.

"I was going to tell them," he said. "Just not yet." It'd taken him until last night to figure out the answer to the question Sunny had asked him in the hotel café the morning before. He wanted to remain a part of Beach Island if they'd let him. It was what his parents—Luke and Lucy—wanted. For him to nurture what they'd built. But more than that, it was what he wanted. To protect their employees and guests from the big corporations that focused only on the bottom line. To continue the Armstrong tradition of treating them like family. He needed a minute to plan how to have that conversation with the board. Now that time was gone.

Because of Sunny.

As if she hadn't already hurt him enough with her armful of makeup. And the bottle of orange flower–scented shampoo, gone from the shelf in the shower.

"Is there anything I can do?"

She looked small, delicate, standing there next to the bed. But then her suitcase caught Gabe's peripheral vision. She was leaving him. Like all four of his parents: Forzas and Armstrongs. Like Riley and every one of his girlfriends. Only Sunny was taking his heart with her.

"You've done enough, haven't you?" he snarled. "And now I guess it's time for you to leave. God forbid you'd stay to fix what you broke. But that's what you do. Leave when things get difficult."

Her eyes went wide, and she blinked. "What?"

"Poor Cade." He hadn't realized her ex's name had stuck in his brain. "He didn't stand a chance, and I was a fool to think I did. No, you'd rather make the big, dramatic exit scene than quietly do the work. Because relationships are work, Sunny. And sometimes that's not fun. But I guess you're only here for the fun parts."

Her lower lip trembled. But his heart was bleeding out, and he had no comfort to spare for her.

"That's what you think of me?" She cleared the tremble out of her voice. "That I'm only interested in fun? I've been on my own since I was seven. Nannies and housekeepers aren't the same as parents. At least you had those. I thought you'd understand that I need to go back, try again with mine. Prove to them I'm worthy by following through on what I promised."

She flung a hand at herself, at the exquisite body he'd worshipped the night before. "Exercise. Injuries. Hours of memorization. Singing until I was hoarse. None of that was fun. But I did it anyway. And now I'm off to join my family's business and finally get some goddamn recognition for it."

Gabe understood the pull of a family business all too well. He had his own job to do. A job she'd made infinitely more difficult. By forcing him to confront his past. Question his identity. And then by worming her way into his heart with her gorgeous voice and her encouragement and her goddamn sparkle. In the end, she'd broken him. "Fine!" he roared. "Give up on us. On what we had. On what we could've been!"

"What we could've been? I saw my parents' relationship. I did everything I could to hold it together. And I learned it doesn't work. I don't want any part of that. Any part of this." She gestured at the invisible tension, the jagged words between them.

The connection they'd built over the past two weeks severed like the train his parents had ridden that terrible day.

She yanked her phone charger out of the wall. "Maybe I don't have my shit together like you do. Maybe I've made some mistakes. But at least I'm not stuck in the past. I'm focused on the future, and I'm the only one I can rely on for that. I have dreams, and I'm not letting you or anyone get in my way." She snatched up her suitcase and purse. With one last flip of her red-gold hair, she walked out, letting the door crash behind her.

The hotel room went silent like the Sunny-shaped void in his heart.

Was that what he'd done? Tried to stand in the way of her dreams? He hadn't said that, had he? She was right about one thing: he'd been living in the past. If he'd spared one thought for the blissful present he'd experienced over the last few days, he'd never have said those hurtful words to her. Now all that remained was his Sunny-free future.

You drive. I pay. Their agreement from weeks ago echoed in his head. Because she'd driven. And his shredded heart had paid the price.

Gabe was still staring at the door when his phone rang. Was it Sunny, calling to apologize yet again? Or offering to give him another chance? He leaped for it over the bed.

Brandon. Crap. He sighed and answered.

"Is it true, what that girl said?" Brandon asked without a hello.

"Her name is Sunny. And, yes, it's true. Turns out, I was adopted. I'm in Las Vegas meeting my birth siblings." What was the point of hiding anything now?

"Yeah?"

"Yeah. I'm like the ugly duckling. I finally found my people." He sagged onto the bed, which still smelled like sex and Sunny's orange-flower shampoo.

"You're no swan, coz."

"No." Gabe rubbed his hand over his mouth, his bristly jaw snagging the calluses.

"So you like them."

"The Forzas? Yeah. They own an exotic car rental company. I got to work on a '66 Mustang with my oldest brother. It felt right, you know? Like where I belong."

"Right?" Brandon's voice rose into its upper register. "You belong in Ohio. With us. Or don't the past thirty years mean anything to you?"

What the hell? It wasn't like they'd spent much time together since Gabe's parents died. Still, Brandon was the closest thing to a brother he'd ever known until he'd met the Forzas. "Of course I—"

"You like these...these strangers better than us? Than me? After all we've been through? Don't forget that time the cops caught us with those twins in the back of your dad's pickup, and I had to talk them out of calling our parents."

A weak joke was better than Brandon's uncharacteristic anger. "Not better. It's not *or,* it's *and.* At least, I'd like to think so. You'll always be my cousin."

"Hmm."

Had he really hurt Brandon's feelings? Gabe wished he could see his face. "Brandon, you okay?"

"Yeah, just thinking."

"So why'd you call me?"

Brandon paused for a moment, and when he spoke again, his voice was business school–slick. "I have some concerns about your email. About the purchase offer."

"Oh?"

"A sale is what's best for the family. The older generation is getting older, and they'd like to retire. Selling would give everyone a nice nest egg, some security for their golden years."

Was that what Aunt Pat wanted, to retire? Gabe couldn't picture it, but Brandon was her son, and he'd know better than Gabe would. When she found out the truth, would she think it was still his business to care about her?

"Plus..." Brandon paused for a long moment. "I think it's what's best for you. You've shouldered too much responsibility for too many years."

"Someone had to do it," Gabe snapped.

This time, the silence stretched on so long Gabe pulled the phone away to check that the call hadn't disconnected. "Look, I'm concerned about the employees. There's nothing in the agreement that says the new owner would keep them."

"I'm sure they'll be fine. Who else would they hire?"

Lots of people. Unqualified, untrained people. People they brought in from their other parks. Speaking of which... "Did you know they had over twenty injuries at their other park last year? Someone lost a hand five years ago. What if there's an accident?"

"Not your problem, Gabe, if you're not the owner. You've always hated that place, ever since...you know. Won't it be a relief not to have to worry about it?"

Gabe hadn't been able to look at the hills and loops of the coasters since his parents' deaths. What would it be like to be free of it, to go about his life without his stomach clenched, bracing for news of some accident? Not to have to worry about how to pay for the safety mechanisms he insisted on? Not to have to fight the Armstrongs for every improved restraint?

But he'd never stop worrying about Beach Island, even if it wasn't his responsibility anymore.

"The park is our legacy," Gabe said at last. "Those people are our family. I'm not ready to let it go. I'd like to talk to the other board members about it. I'll be back for the vote on Saturday."

"Gabe, I—" Brandon sounded like his cousin, then. Not like the city dude who flashed a fancy watch and designer ties whenever he came down from Chicago to visit. Like the seventeen-year-old kid he'd gone to high school with, flirted with girls at football games with, ridden in the rear car of Twister of Terror with, hands up and shouting with excitement. But his next words ground the broken pieces of Gabe's heart into dust.

"If I can't count on your support on Saturday, I'm going to call a vote to relieve you of your responsibilities. Considering this new information about your lack of a blood connection to the Armstrong family. You know the bylaws require a unanimous vote for the CEO position. I'm not sure how Mom and Uncle Bobby and Grandpa would vote, given this new information."

Gabe gripped the phone so tight the case popped.

"It's just business, Gabe," Brandon said. A beep told him the call had disconnected.

Business. Not family. Because his favorite cousin didn't consider him one of them anymore.

Chapter Twenty-Seven

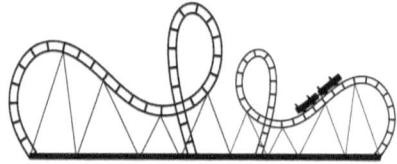

R idiculous. She was being ridiculous.

Sunny swiped a tear from under her right eye. Her thumb was blackened with mascara. Shit, she was going to show up with red eyes and rivers of eye makeup on her cheeks.

Her car was stopped on the highway in Las Vegas morning rush hour. Why'd she have to pick up Gabe's phone? If she'd ignored the call, she and Gabe could be sitting out the traffic in the hotel restaurant. She could've soaked up a little more of his kindness, his strength, his loyalty, plus a few more of his hot kisses, to fortify her for her return home.

But she'd picked it up, stuck her nose into his business. Again. Tried to fix him. Failed. Gabe was wonderful just the way he was. He didn't need fixing.

Unlike her parents. They needed her. She had the increasingly urgent texts from her mother to prove it.

> Mom: When do you plan to get here?
>
> Mom: Argus, the showrunner, is asking about you. When will you be here?

Mom: Susan, please call me. This is an
important opportunity for you, and I need you
here.

She tightened her grip on the wheel. Finally, her mother needed
her. Gabe didn't. He had Michael, Mary, and Rafe. He was better
off without her.

She needed to learn how to be better off without him.

Chapter Twenty-Eight

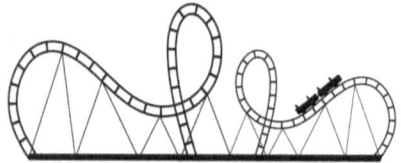

"So, ah, where am I taking you?" Michael kept one hand on the wheel of his truck and rubbed the back of his neck with the other. Carefully, he navigated the exit onto I-15, which would take them south toward the Strip, Gabe's former hotel, and Forza Elite Motors.

"I...I don't know." Gabe's gaze was still on the paper in his hand. His birth certificate. His real one. With the names Joseph and Theresa Forza listed as his parents. When he'd gotten his driver's license at sixteen, his mother had handed over another one, with Luke and Lucille Armstrong's names on the *Mother* and *Father* lines. Focused on passing the driving test in a few minutes, he hadn't bothered to examine it. Had it also been stamped by the state of Nevada?

"Gabe." Michael's voice was louder this time. "Am I dropping you back at the Bellagio?"

"No," Gabe said quickly. Michael had to be wondering what the hell was going on. He'd been clutching his suitcase handle in one hand and a stolen pillowcase in the other, one that still smelled like orange blossoms, when Michael drove up in front of the hotel that morning. Between the argument, Sunny's walking out on him, and his conversation with Brandon, Gabe had forgotten he'd agreed to go with his brother to the records office. Forgotten anything but getting away from the room that reminded him of all he'd lost.

Michael had asked no questions, not about the suitcase Gabe had heaved into the back seat of the crew cab, not about Gabe's wilted silence. They'd exchanged a minimum of words in the complicated process to get a birth certificate for Gabriel Forza, someone who hadn't existed for thirty years.

Now, apparently, Michael was done waiting.

A glance in the rear-view mirror at Gabe's suitcase. "Something happen?"

An understatement. "Yeah." Out the left window, the spires of the New York New York Hotel loomed. Gabe didn't know if the coaster was visible from the highway, but he averted his eyes anyway, staring at the other cars on the road.

"Why didn't they tell me?" he burst out. "Why didn't I ask? It seems obvious now." Gabe stared at Michael's profile. Same sturdy jaw, same olive coloring, same dark hair. Like Gabe's, his head almost brushed the ceiling of the cab. "I don't look like them at all. Never liked the cold. Was better with a socket wrench than a spreadsheet."

Michael tightened that massive jaw. "I'm not good with the touchy-feely stuff. That's Mary. But." He chewed on his words for a while. "Family's a funny thing. They're always yours. The good and the bad. But it's not because of the blood in your veins or even the DNA. It's because of the...the love."

Michael winced when he said it, and his fingers twitched on the wheel. He probably wanted a mallet in his hand as much as Gabe did.

"And I bet your family in Ohio loves you. Whatever they say about blood and water, it's true about love, too. Love's thicker than water."

Gabe squinted at him. "Huh?"

Michael flipped on his turn signal and took the exit, less gently this time. "Fuck! You know what I mean. Love! It's important."

Then he mumbled, almost too softly for Gabe to hear, "Like what you've got with Sunny."

The air conditioning was off, but cold washed over Gabe, freezing him to the seat. He couldn't get enough breath in his lungs to make the words louder than a whisper. "She doesn't love me."

Michael snorted. At the stoplight, he turned to look at Gabe. "Bullshit."

"She *doesn't* love me." He said it louder this time. "She left me."

Michael shook his head, but then he glanced into the back at the suitcase. "You fucked up, man."

"Yeah, I did." He glanced out the window at a palm tree. She had to be home by now. At least he hoped so. He'd wanted to give Cinderella a tune-up before she left. Change the oil. It was a long drive to do alone. But that had been her plan since the beginning. "She was always going to leave."

"Was she?" Michael's words were heavy. "Seems to me she stayed longer than she needed to. Think she would've gone out with Mary last night if she didn't care?"

The white tiger sign came into view. "I don't know."

"I've known our sister for over thirty years. Believe me, I know. She's a lot. The answer is no."

"Doesn't matter now, does it?" Gabe's voice was sulkier than he'd planned. Mulish. "She's gone now."

Michael pulled into the parking lot and pulled around the back of the building. "Maybe," he said. He turned off the engine and got out of the car.

Gabe got out, too. "What now?"

Michael rounded the hood and clamped a heavy hand on his shoulder. "I like you, Gabe." The stern lines of his face softened enough for one corner of his mouth to turn up. "But you're Mary's problem now."

Michael turned on his heel and, whistling, strode through the shop door.

Gabe bumped his suitcase over the threshold to the office at Forza Elite Motors.

Mary, wearing her black logo polo, raised her head from her screen. "Gabe! I wasn't expecting you today." She eyed him. His luggage. The pillowcase that stuck out of his jacket pocket. "You staying or going?"

And that was the question. Gabe froze next to the wedding display table filled with champagne flutes, pink sashes, and tiaras. He could stay with the Forzas. Work and get to know his new family. He'd be closer to Sunny in Las Vegas. Even if she didn't want to see him, the thought of being in the same time zone eased the chill around his heart. He could build a new life and leave Brandon and the Armstrongs behind.

But that thought—of leaving the family who'd raised him, treated him like one of their own for thirty years—twisted his gut. His parents, too. They'd left their legacy to him. Could he let Brandon take all that away? Darlene? Ramirez? All the people who depended on him? No. Not without a fight.

"Going," he said. "Home. There's some business I have to take care of. I came to say goodbye." He gripped the suitcase handle to stop his hands from trembling. The flight was going to suck.

"Where's Sunny?"

"Not with me anymore." Had it always been this over-airconditioned in here?

"Oh, Gabe." She came around the counter, arms out.

He shook his head. "I don't deserve a hug for that. I said things. And then I didn't even ask her not to leave." It wouldn't have stopped her. Still—

"Even a pig-headed Forza deserves a hug." She folded him into her crushing embrace. "The name means power. Force. We go in, guns blazing, and we think later. You're thinking now, right? You regret what you did?"

"Yeah." His arms fit just right around his sister's back.

She drew back to look him in the eye. "She was already standing at the starting line, ready to go."

How did Mary know so much?

"I'm surprised, though, she didn't come say goodbye." Mary tightened her lips. "You sure she left?"

"She took her suitcase."

"She take her car?"

"I—I don't know. It was with the valet."

She patted Gabe's arm. "I'll call her. And if she doesn't answer, I'll call the hotel. You go on out and see Rafe. He's in the garage. There's a container of Italian wedding cookies. Have a few."

He left his bags next to Mary's desk and walked through the door into the garage. A stretch town car was parked diagonally across the floor. No Prince played this time. It was Def Leppard's "Bringin' on the Heartbreak."

Rafe spotted him first. Powdered sugar spotted the corner of his mouth, and his coverall sleeve held a streak of it. "Hey." He approached, extended his hand as if to shake Gabe's, but then reconsidered and flung his arms out wide for a hug. At the last second, he hesitated and ended with an awkward clap of Gabe's shoulders.

Michael poked his head out of the limo's engine compartment, grunted, and turned back to the engine.

Rafe frowned at Michael and then gave Gabe a lopsided smile. "You come to do some real work?"

"Not today," Gabe said. "I'm leaving."

"With Sunny?" Rafe asked. "Mary said she had to get to LA soon."

"No."

"You going home, then?" He stared at his steel-toed boot as he scuffed it along the floor.

Gabe's stomach flopped. He hadn't yet figured out how to talk about one part of his family with the other. "Yeah, there's a thing with the family business. My Ohio family."

"A thing?" Michael peered out from behind the limo's hood.

"A vote. I don't think it's good for the employees or for the guests. But if I don't support it, they're going to move to vote me out. Of the business." Maybe out of the family, too.

"Family doesn't do that to each other," Michael growled.

Rafe leveled his older brother with a narrow-eyed stare.

"Okay, okay." Michael raised his hands in surrender. "I'm not one to talk. I had to work through some shit."

"Are they my family, though?" The question burst out of him, and Gabe didn't know if he was asking his brothers, himself, or the universe.

Rafe stepped closer, so close Gabe could smell the engine oil baked into his coveralls. "You may not have much choice about who raises you when you're a kid, but by the time you're grown, you get to choose. The people you surround yourself with, they're your family. Whether or not they're related by blood. They're connected through love." It was the most words Gabe had ever heard him speak.

"See?" Michael waved his screwdriver. "Love's thicker than water. Just like I said." He nodded at Rafe and turned his attention back to the engine.

Maybe Michael had sniffed too much degreaser. He still didn't make any sense.

But Rafe did.

Love.

His parents—his adoptive ones—had loved him. They'd wanted him. Whatever reason they'd had not to tell him, or anyone, he was adopted, he'd never had a reason to doubt that he was an Armstrong. Not even when his darker hair and complexion made him stick out in family photos, not when he'd surpassed their heights by almost a foot. Until he'd gotten the DNA results, he'd never questioned his place in the Armstrong family. Always accepted that Beach Island was his legacy. That was how his parents had shown they loved him.

Here, he had the love of his siblings. It showed in Rafe's heavy hands on his shoulders. In Michael's trip during work hours to the records office. In Mary's boa-constrictor hug and homemade cookies. It was still new, and they were finding their way together, but standing there with his brothers, Gabe felt their connection.

It was a lot like the connection he felt with Sunny. He couldn't deny that he loved her, too. He'd whispered the words to her last night while she slept. Like a coward. If she'd heard them, if she'd known how he felt, would she still have left him?

Mary eased through the door behind him. "She's not answering her phone, and her car's not at the hotel. But I can't imagine she would've left for California without telling me."

A tiny flame of hope ignited in Gabe's chest. "Where do you think she could have gone?"

Mary came around to stand beside him so they made a ring of Forza siblings. Even Michael circled around the town car's hood, wiping his hands on a rag.

Mary licked her thumb and rubbed the sugar off Rafe's face. "Did she say anything before she left?"

She said a lot of things. About Gabe's living in the past and Sunny's living in the future. Not only did half a country divide their homes, but time itself stood between them. "No, she just packed her suitcase and left. I thought she was going to LA."

"She didn't mention any unfinished business here?"

He had to flip through the images of her pale face, shocked and hurt at his accusation. Her guilty *I'm sorrys*. To the time before Brandon's phone call. She'd still been packing to go, but—

"When we first got here, she mentioned riding the roller coaster before she left."

"Which one?" Mary asked.

"New York, New York."

She winced. "I may have mentioned it to her last night. Sounds like you ought to go look. Rafe'll drive you."

"But I—" Rafe protested. "Yeah, okay." He went to the rack of coveralls and stripped out of his.

Mary gripped Gabe's hand. "You can do it. She might not be

ready to commit, but you're a Forza, and Forzas are persistent. Show her you're not going anywhere, that you're a forever kind of guy."

He nodded, mute. Sunny wasn't a forever kind of woman. She'd told him that.

Michael clapped him on the other shoulder. "Call and tell Mary how it goes. And we want a proper goodbye before you go anywhere. Dinner. With Rafe's gravy. I'll even make salsiccia Napoli. Sausage." When Gabe stared at him, open-mouthed, he said, "What? So I know how to cook. Doesn't make me less of a bad-ass."

Gabe shook his head and, avoiding the grease spots on Michael's coveralls, hugged him around the shoulders. "Thanks. I'll let you know."

Mary tugged him into her arms, almost liquefying him. "You've got this."

Rafe scuffed over, clacking a ring of key fobs. Grabbing the cookie container from the top of the rolling tool chest, he jerked his head toward the garage door. He must've used up all his words on that speech earlier.

Gabe followed his brother past the vintage Mustangs, a pair of sweet Ferraris, a couple Rolls Royces, and Mary's red Corvette to a shiny black SUV. Rafe clicked to unlock it, and Gabe levered himself up into the passenger seat. It was already pushed back to accommodate his long legs.

"This is the Tank. It's safe," Rafe said. "Have a cookie."

Gabe shook his head. His stomach clenched too tight to hold anything but regret.

"One cookie. They're amazing." Rafe waited, the engine idling.

He needed to find Sunny, so he carefully pulled one from the tin and popped it into his mouth. When he crunched it between his teeth, nutty sweetness burst onto his tongue. He licked the powdered sugar from his lower lip.

Rafe put the Tank into reverse and raised his eyebrows.

"Delicious," Gabe mumbled. The cookie tasted like welcome. Like love.

They rode high above most of the other cars. Rafe was right about the confidence the steel beast inspired with its silent cabin and its view over the surrounding vehicles. He probably would've felt the same in Michael's truck if he hadn't been too focused on Sunny to look out the windows. Without a word, Rafe eased the Tank toward the Strip, and soon, the marquee of the New York New York hotel loomed ahead. The lift hill of the roller coaster rose beyond it.

Gabe swallowed. "Rafe, I—I don't know how to get her back."

"Sure, you do. Like in the movies. A grand gesture. Some romantic shit." He pulled the SUV to the curb.

The casino entrance was still a few blocks away. "Guess I'll walk from here."

"No." When Rafe turned to him, it was like looking into a mirror. He didn't think he'd ever get used to it. Though this reflection told Gabe he was being an idiot. Rafe tilted his chin at something behind Gabe. "You need something from in there."

Gabe turned. A jewelry shop. He whipped his head back to his brother. "You don't mean—"

He rolled his eyes. "You know what to do."

He did. And he knew what not to do. He pushed open the car door and jogged straight past the jewelry store, dodging pedestrians. Keeping his gaze straight ahead and off the coaster's loops above, he marched under the glittering neon of the casino's marquee and through the doors.

Chapter Twenty-Nine

R ight up to the moment he walked onto the ride platform, Gabe knew she'd be there.

But one glance inside the mostly empty queuing area made it clear she wasn't.

He'd hoped to find her waiting for him in the ticketing area. He'd pictured it: she'd be sitting on a bench, legs crossed, bouncing her foot while she texted with Cata or Leena. Humming a showtune, she'd light up the darkened room.

No. Only the lights from the neon signs lit the empty space.

He bought a ticket so he could check the platform. The ride loaded indoors in a windowless room. Surely, she'd be waiting there, the lights glinting golden on her hair. She'd be perched up on the bars of the cattle pen, swinging her leg, flirting with the ride operators so they wouldn't make her get off.

Nope.

The only people there looked to be part of a family. A middle-aged couple, a teenage boy and girl, a preteen boy, his mouth flashing with braces, and the youngest, another boy, maybe eight or nine. Just tall enough to ride. Bouncing with excitement, or possibly nervousness. They stood in a clump at the front of the cattle pen. Gabe's gaze darted to the exit on the other side of the platform.

Where he needed to go now that he'd missed Sunny. Damn, he shouldn't have gone with Michael to get his birth certificate. He knew who he was. He didn't need proof. Why hadn't he come straight here?

Scanning the area one more time, just in case he'd somehow missed her, he wiped his palms on his jeans. Even looking at the car, painted yellow to look like a taxicab, made him sweat. Dual restraints—shoulder and lap—were raised to welcome the riders in.

He breathed slowly. In. Out. Sunny wasn't there, tempting him yet again to burst out of his comfort zone, challenging him in a way no one else dared. He didn't have to ride. All he had to do was walk across the car to the other side of the platform to reach the safety of the exit. He'd conquered plenty of fears on the trip. Riding in a car? Check, did it for two thousand miles. Driving a car? Yep, even in a snowstorm. And if he didn't find Sunny—hell, even if he did— he'd be getting into an airplane to fly home. No time to road-trip it now.

He didn't need to overcome this particular fear. Not without Sunny. She was his talisman, his courage. With her, he could've done it.

Without her, he was just tragic Gabe. Someone you lowered your voice around, someone you excused, someone so broken you could push him around and make him do almost anything you wanted.

He shot one last defiant glare at the train, ready and waiting at the loading platform. He had nothing to prove.

The gates swung open, and the teenagers leaped ahead to the front car. The adolescent boy was just behind, and he beckoned to his brother. The parents started toward the middle of the train.

The littlest boy stood, frozen, behind the caution strip. Behind him, Gabe couldn't see his face, but his rigid posture told him all he needed to know.

He was just as scared as Gabe was.

His family was about to abandon him.

No.

"Hey, kid." The words burst out of Gabe before he could stop them. "Want to ride in the last car with me?"

The kid's head whipped around, his mouth open, eyes wide. Gabe stood up as tall as he could. "In the back, you'll be able to laugh at your siblings when they scream." The boy understood what Gabe didn't say: that if he rode behind them, none of his siblings could see him scream or cry or whatever he was afraid he'd do.

Slowly, the kid nodded, then walked toward the last car. Gabe clambered in first, the space too small, the restraints too close. The boy followed. Gabe met his gaze and tugged the lap bar toward himself. The boy copied him. Taking a deep breath, Gabe reached up and lowered the shoulder harness until the boy could grab hold and pull it into place. Then he lowered his own. Gabe hadn't been as bulky the last time he'd ridden a coaster, and he felt squeezed, confined. His breathing quickened.

Still, he smiled the best he could when he turned to the kid. "You like coasters?"

"Dunno. I haven't ridden too many. Last time we were at Disneyland, I was too short for the big ones. I had to ride stupid Dumbo."

"We'll be fine," Gabe assured the both of them. "It'll be fun."

"You think so?" The way he squinched his mouth told Gabe the kid knew he was lying.

He shrugged, or tried to, in the restraints. "If not, at least you can say you rode it. And you don't have to do it again."

The kid nodded and turned his face to the front. A few cars ahead, his mother turned in her seat and waved. The kid set his mouth like he was marching to the firing squad.

The hand that tugged his restraint was pale and freckled, not dark brown, and a red ponytail, not Sid's black curls, bounced into his vision. They were indoors, where they couldn't see the blue sky. Still, chills raced along the back of Gabe's neck, like if he looked fast enough, he could've seen his own mom and dad bending around to flash him their delighted grins.

The attendant finished her checks and gave them a thumbs-up.

Gabe considered mirroring the gesture—when he'd been a ride operator, he'd loved seeing the guests' eager faces before the ride began—but he couldn't. Instead, he gripped the handle on the restraint until his knuckles turned white.

A second later, the car lurched forward.

It was all wrong. The car emerged from the platform between a pair of buildings, not onto a track suspended over green space. Yet the clack-clack-clack of the lift hill, the afternoon sunshine warming his shoulders, the soft breeze lifting his hair off his sweaty brow, the heaviness of his own body tugging him against the seat back toward the earth where he belonged, shot him back to that day, the day his youth had ended.

That day, he'd been the kid, adrenaline coursing through his system. He'd ridden Fright or Flight hundreds of times, maybe thousands. On sunny days, on cloudy days, once with the rain pounding on his face in a sudden squall. In the early mornings next to Brandon before the park opened. Late at night, holding a girl's hand high above their heads. And that day, that last day, empty cars separating him from his parents before the scream of metal against metal and a cloud of dust separated them from life, from his life, forever.

"How high do you think it goes?" the kid's voice squeaked.

Gabe blinked back to the present. They were still climbing, maybe another thirty slow feet to go. "Not much more. You can see the top of the hill from here. And that's the highest point on the ride." No need to explain to the kid how potential energy and gravity fueled the ride.

Next to him, the kid nodded. "We won't fall out, will we?"

"No." As the track flattened at the top of the hill, Gabe tapped his restraints. Again, no need to get into the physics of inertia. "These keep us safe."

They hadn't kept his parents safe. But he couldn't tell the kid that, either.

The car crept to the end of the flat and tipped forward. "Hold on!" Gabe shouted into the roaring wind. But holding on wouldn't help. Even if his parents hadn't been waving their arms in the air, their car still would have jumped the track when the axle snapped. Holding on wouldn't have done anything when the ground rushed up to meet them, when the metal buckled around them.

Maybe if they'd all made different decisions that day, he could have held on to them. Kept them around a little longer. Or a lot longer. He'd wished for it every day since. He'd wish for it every day for the rest of his life.

But wishing wouldn't bring them back. Neither would holding on to his fear.

He had to trust the physics, the ride operators, the mechanics.

He had to let go.

The way his parents had let go. The way they'd lived their lives in the present, wringing the pleasure out of every day, trusting there'd be a tomorrow.

Because holding onto fear was like staying on the dark, dingy ride platform, never experiencing the joy of a vertical loop, of a diving twist, of the wind in your hair and a delighted shout in your throat.

Like his life before Sunny had burst into it and spun him around like a quadruple heartline roll.

"Hey, mister. You okay?" The kid's voice came from around Gabe's shoulder. He opened his eyes, blinking away the tears the wind had torn from his eyes, just as they rolled back onto the boarding platform. The car stopped suddenly, jerking them forward against the restraints. Then they lifted, and Gabe finally freed his hand to wipe the moisture off his face.

"Yeah, I'm good. You?"

The kid grinned, showing his too-big front teeth and gaps behind. His chest heaved. "Yeah! It was awesome. And Blake and Devin screamed the whole time. I'm gonna make so much fun of them."

Gabe extended his hand to shake the kid's tiny one. "Good job. Thanks for riding with me."

Lurching out of his seat, Gabe wobbled on shaky legs to the

unloading platform. His neck was sore from the jolting, and he bet he was going to have a bruise on his shoulder from hitting the side of the car. The boy skipped past him with a "See ya" to rejoin his family.

Gabe stumbled to the exit and eased himself down the stairs, finally regaining his equilibrium at the bottom. But she wasn't waiting for him there, either. Nausea, not from the ride, churned his stomach as he walked to where Rafe waited in the car, checking out the passers-by from behind a pair of aviator sunglasses, another dusting of sugar on his chin.

"No luck?" he asked when Gabe opened the door of the SUV.

"She wasn't there." He leaned back in the seat, trying to slow his pulse. "She's gone."

"Shit. You made your grand gesture, and she wasn't even around. That never happens in the movies."

The car speakers rang out. Gabe scrambled for his phone, hope filling the empty place where his stomach had been before the ride. Sunny was calling him at last!

Rafe pressed a button on the steering wheel. "Hey, Mary."

It wasn't even Gabe's phone that had rung. He looked at its home screen, innocently taunting him.

"Gabe still with you?" she asked.

"Yeah."

Gabe couldn't muster the energy to greet his sister.

"Good news is I heard from Sunny. She's fine."

"And the bad news?" Gabe asked. Rafe shot him a concerned look.

"She's on her way to LA. She called from a truck stop just over the state line."

Gabe's vision tunneled to a speck of powdered sugar on the black leather seat. She was gone. She was the balloon, aching to soar away. He was the string, tethering her to the earth. Now she'd loosened that string. She'd left him to pursue dreams that didn't—couldn't—include him.

"Head back to the garage." Mary's voice came from far away. "We'll figure out what to do."

"Take me to the airport."

"Car would get you to LA faster." Rafe checked his mirrors and pulled out onto the street. "We'll lend you one. This one, if you like."

"You're following her to LA?" Mary's voice rose to her upper register. "That's so—"

"No." Gabe stared out the window at the neon lights of the Strip. "I'm going back to Ohio to save my business."

Chapter Thirty

S unny handed the keys to her Mercedes to a valet standing in front of her parents' Bel Air mansion. Cars lined the long driveway, and a few vans parked on the side lawn. "Is there a party?"

"Nah, just setting up for tomorrow's filming." The kid winked at her and slid into the driver's seat.

"Filming?" She handed him the last couple of bucks from her wallet and snatched her suitcase out of the back seat before he drove off, leaving a cloud of desert dust behind on the pristine circle drive.

She trudged past the tinkling three-tiered fountain and up the steps. Without knocking, she pushed open the heavy carved-wood door, bumping a guy in a black T-shirt and jeans standing just inside, unspooling cable.

"Sorry—"

"Susan! There you are." The cloud of Chanel No. 5 reached her a second before her mother's gym-sculpted arms encircled her shoulders.

"Mom, what's going on?" She dropped her suitcase on the marble tile in the foyer.

"It's for the show," her mother said, raising her eyebrows like it wasn't odd that strangers traipsed through the house with camera bags, lighting kits, and miles of cable.

"Our house is one of the sets?"

"Our house *is* the set, silly. Where else would a show about the Lafortunes take place?" She stepped back and pursed her lips. "You look terrible, Susan."

Sunny wiped under her eyes to clear away the flaked-off mascara. "Sorry, I—driving into the sun, you know." She wasn't about to unburden her broken heart in front of all these people.

Her mother pinched Sunny's chin between two manicured fingernails and tilted her head to the left, then the right. "You look older than twenty-three."

"Twenty-three? I'm twenty-seven!"

"That can't be right." Gwen Lafortune released her chin. "I'm only forty-five."

"You're—" Sunny clamped her mouth shut. Growing up, it had been a joke that her mother was perpetually thirty-five. Had she actually lost track of her own age?

"Rey!" Mom raised her hand in an elegant wave, and a young woman with a perfect cat eye and a makeup train case scurried up. "Make her look eighteen."

"Eighteen?" Sunny and Rey gasped it at the same time.

Gwen Lafortune flounced off, her perfume lingering behind.

"Come on," Rey said, her sharply lined lips set in a grim line. "I need better light for this."

Half an hour later, Sunny emerged from the first-floor powder room, her face stiff from the layers of foundation and makeup Rey had applied to make her look dewy.

"There you are, Susan." This time, it was her dad. A spray-tanned man with a thick shock of white hair stood next to him. "Meet Argus Sanderson, the showrunner."

Showtime. Sunny drew herself up and stuck out her hand. "Nice to meet you, Mr. Sanderson. Please, call me Sunny."

"Hello, Sunny. Call me Argus. Rey!"

Rey emerged from the bathroom, her train case repacked. Her head snapped up at the showrunner's summons. "Yes, Argus?"

"She needs more dramatic makeup. Vampy. Sunny is playing the bad girl."

"About that. What, exactly, am I auditioning for?" Did Argus mean she'd already gotten the part?

Her father patted her shoulder. "We'll see you when you're out of makeup." He and Argus turned, stepped over a snaking cable, and walked toward the kitchen.

"Vampy." Sunny shrugged.

"More eyeliner and a dark-red lip," Rey said.

Twenty minutes later, Sunny reemerged from the bathroom. Rey had teased her hair into a cloud around her head. Her eyelids were heavy from the layers of mascara, and her eyes burned.

Her mother scurried toward her. She'd changed into a white pantsuit with a black bustier underneath. Sunny tried not to hunch her shoulders. She wished her boobs looked as good as her mother's.

"What's all this?" Mom pointed a French-tipped nail at Sunny's face. "Now you look thirty. At least. Scrub all that—"

"No time, Gwen." Gene Lafortune threw an arm over Sunny's shoulder, and she breathed in her father's familiar cedar cologne. "Argus needs to brief us."

Finally, Sunny could get off the merry-go-round of confusion and figure out what was going on. She slipped an arm around her dad's waist. "It's good to see you, Dad."

Her father didn't break stride. "I'm glad you made it. We were worried."

Happy fizzes filled her chest. No matter what Gabe and Cata said, she'd been right to trek across the country to answer her parents' call. They'd worried about her. And now all three Lafortunes were together again. They'd be a real family.

"Remember," her father said, "this is a fantastic opportunity for you to rebrand yourself. Make people forget what you did in New York."

Her stomach dropped with the reminder. "I'm really sorry about that. I hope you didn't get any blowback from it."

He chuckled, but it sounded forced. "Don't worry about me. My reputation can handle it."

Sunny's reputation couldn't. She needed this project.

She let her father guide her past the busy living room, through the main wing, where a few techs were setting up lights in her mother's bedroom, and finally into the housekeeper's suite.

Sunny had spent so many evenings in that room while her parents had been on various sets. When Nadia had been their housekeeper, she'd come in here after school to do her homework, to run lines from her latest play, or just to talk. But Nadia had left them when Sunny went off to college. Maybe she'd been lonely, too.

It didn't smell like the orange-scented furniture polish Nadia used anymore. The room was barren, containing only a bed with a navy comforter and a pair of coordinated plaid wing chairs. No photos lined the dresser.

Most important, there were no cameras in this room.

Her father released her and stepped back. "This is a great opportunity for you and for all of us to refresh the Lafortune family brand. Remember this."

"Okay." Sunny scrunched her eyebrows, then relaxed them. Had she creased her makeup? "Can you tell me more about the project? What's my role?"

Argus paraded into the room with her mother. "Just waiting on Kai and Bryce," he said.

"Who are they?" Producers, perhaps?

"The rest of the cast." Argus turned to survey the pair of techs outside the window as they wrestled with a massive lighting reflector.

Sunny turned to Gene. "While we wait—"

"Yeah, yeah. Gotta go. Love you." An impossibly tall, impossibly broad guy with sun-kissed skin, wavy dark hair, and dark, soulful eyes shoved his phone into the back pocket of jeans so worn, frayed, and tight they were in danger of exploding off his muscular thighs.

"Kai." Argus nudged Sunny forward. "Meet Sunny."

"Hey." He held out his hand, and Sunny let it envelop hers. He was built like Gabe, though with more muscles. And she bet Gabe's skin tanned as well in the summer. His eyes were the same rich brown color. But he was all wrong. He smelled like cologne and not fresh air and motor oil. He winked. Something Gabe would never do. "Looking forward to working with you."

She had to stop thinking about Gabe. In the end, he'd rejected her, too. That part of her life was over. "What role are you playing?"

He grinned, showing blindingly white, straight teeth. "I'm your boyfriend."

"My...what?"

Argus clasped her shoulder and one of Kai's. His thin hand didn't go all the way around Kai's massive deltoid. "Market research said your character would be more popular in a relationship. At least at first."

Right. Her character. "Maybe you can tell me a little more about the project." Like, did she already have the part? She hadn't auditioned yet, and even her family name had never gotten her past that hurdle.

Argus rubbed his hands together. "As soon as Bryce gets here."

Sunny hoped Bryce had some answers.

Her father had settled into one of the wing chairs, and her mother fluttered nearby like a well-toned moth in her white suit.

Sunny remained next to Kai. He seemed to know what was going on. "Mom, Dad, maybe you could prep me a little."

"This will be good for all our careers," Mom said. "Though, Gene, really, who's going to believe her as my daughter? She looks so *old.*"

"But I am your daughter." Was Sunny dreaming? Had she fallen asleep at the wheel and drifted into a ditch, and this was one of those coma dreams? Or maybe she was still snuggled warm in bed with Gabe, and they hadn't fought, and she hadn't stormed out of their hotel room.

No, from the ache in her heart, that had been all too real.

"Here's Bryce."

Sunny turned and saw a blond guy who couldn't have been older than eighteen. His light-blue T-shirt matched his eyes and skimmed rangy muscle tapering down to a vee at his hips. His jeans weren't as tight as Kai's, and his thighs weren't as muscular, but he looked like a centerfold in a teen magazine. Fifteen years ago, Sunny and her friends would have drooled over him.

"Okay." Argus clapped his hands. "Now that we're all here, let's set the stage. Gwen, please." He indicated the second wing chair.

Pursing her lips, Sunny's mother perched at the edge. Sunny could tell she was trying to minimize creases in her white suit pants.

"You two are the loving, doting parents. Obviously, Gene will be in and out due to his filming schedule. But, Gwen, you are the matriarch. You'll hold everything together at the center."

Matriarch? Sunny almost snorted. Did a family of three have a matriarch?

"Sunny," Argus barked, "you're the bad girl. Do you know how to drive a motorcycle?"

"Um. No?"

"You have a sports car? Or a convertible, at least?"

"I drive my grandma's old Mercedes. But what does that have to do with anything?"

"The production can rent something appropriate," her father said.

"Dad, I still don't follow."

Argus frowned at her father. "Gene, didn't you explain all this to her?"

"I must have. Didn't I?" His rugged brow lowered when he looked at Sunny.

She cringed. She'd screw this up if she made him look bad in front of Argus. "I'm sure you did, but maybe explain it to me again?"

His lips pursed before he let out a humorless chuckle. "That's our Susan. Beautiful, but not the brightest bulb in the box."

Heat washed up from her chest and set her face on fire. Tittering, she fell into the tired, old role. "That's me. So what's going on?"

Argus rubbed his chin and squinted one eye at her. "Maybe we should go for a Jessica Simpson vibe instead of Kim Kardashian."

Her father said, "Your mother's been on a bit of a...hiatus from acting. So when Argus approached us about doing a reality television show, we agreed. It'll get her name back out there. *The Lafortunes* will create demand for more Gwen Lafortune films."

"A...reality show?" Her parents were film stars, not television. And they'd always sneered about people who let TV crews poke around in their private lives. Their marriage would never hold up under the glare of the TV lights.

"It worked for the Kardashians. And the Osbornes," her mother said.

"So my role is just acting like myself?" She blinked hard to unstick her left eyelashes.

"Think of it as a persona. A heightened version of yourself." Argus raised jazz hands into the air.

The pieces snapped into place. "The heightened Sunny Lafortune is a bad girl. With a boyfriend." She gestured at Kai. "Can I still go to auditions?"

Argus scratched his jaw. "We were planning to spend a few episodes establishing the characters and their lives at home. But I think mid-season, we could plan an arc where you decide to follow in your parents' footsteps and go to an audition."

"Decide to follow...? But I'm already an actress."

"Susan." Her father stood and stepped in close, laying a manicured hand on her shoulder. "This show is a vehicle for your mother. We're all side characters here. We can figure out a way to get you an audition off camera, if that's what you decide to do."

"Of course, of course." Argus's voice boomed through the small room. "We can worry about that later. Now, let's all sit down and talk through the script."

Her father waited until Sunny met his gaze. He gave her a slight nod, and she knew what it meant. This show was important to him and her mother. She was a Lafortune, and she needed to go along. They were family. She returned his nod.

Sunny squeezed onto the edge of the bed between Kai and Bryce.

When everyone had taken a seat, Argus said, "The first episode will center on Gene and Gwen's reaction to Susan's return from New York." He chuckled. "I wish someone had thought to film your outburst on *New York Bomb Squad*. But we have a few eyewitness accounts that will help set the scene."

"You—what?" If they made public what Sunny had done, she'd never get another audition, not in Los Angeles, not in Toronto, not in flipping Timbuktu. Heat rushed again to her cheeks.

"All part of your persona. We can fit in a redemption arc if we get a second season." Argus flipped his hand like her reputation was nothing.

Her father gave her an almost imperceptible headshake like he knew how much she wanted to resist. To stand up for herself this time. She clenched her fists next to her thighs.

"So am I her New York boyfriend or her LA boyfriend?" Kai scrunched his brow.

"You dated in New York, and now you've come back to LA with her. It'll give you an excuse to move in here."

"Move in?" Sunny's voice went squeaky. "Like, with me? Into my room?"

"Exactly." Argus smiled at her for the first time, like he was proud of her for finally catching on.

"But I'm...but we're..." Sunny's throat closed. She'd left Gabe's bed only that morning. And now they expected her to jump into bed with Kai.

"It's just a role, Susan," her mother's voice was thin, waspish. "What am I doing while we're centered on her?"

Argus turned his back on her to reassure her mother, and thoughts crowded into Sunny's head. What would Gabe think when he saw it? And what about Mary? They'd think it was real. Perhaps even that she'd been dating Kai all along. That she'd led Gabe on. They'd hate her.

She unfisted her hand and stared at her palm like she could see the invisible marks of Gabe's kisses. They might not be together any longer, but part of her—hell, maybe all of her—still belonged to him.

She looked up to say something, she didn't know what, and found her father watching her. He nodded at her again.

Right. She was an actress. Her father had kissed dozens of women who weren't her mother in his various roles. Her mother had kissed dozens of men. It meant nothing. They were still together. In name, anyway, if not in spirit.

Though she'd never seen her father look at her mother or any of his on-screen love interests the way Gabe had looked at her.

"Right." Argus clapped his hands again like there were more than six people in the room. "We'll start with Sunny and Kai walking up the front steps and through into the living room, where Gene, Gwen, and Bryce will already be seated—"

"Wait. Who's Bryce?"

Argus's nostrils flared with impatience. "He's your brother."

Now she knew she was dreaming. "My brother."

"The focus groups preferred a show with two children. And Bryce appeals to the 18 to 24 age bracket, particularly among females," Argus said.

"But he's not a Lafortune. Don't people know how many of us there are?"

"We have a backstory prepared if it's needed. But Gene and Gwen's private lives have been out of the spotlight for a few years. If we present him as part of the family, viewers will accept him."

"Mom, Dad." Sunny couldn't be the only one who thought this was insane. "Did you know about this?"

"I approved it. The viewers want what they want. Besides, I always wanted a boy." Her mother smiled fondly at Bryce, the way she hadn't smiled at Sunny since she'd come home. The way she couldn't remember her mother ever smiling at her.

He blew Gwen a kiss.

"No." The word burst out of Sunny.

"Hey." Kai rubbed a circle on her back. "It's okay. We're all just playing our parts here."

"No!" Sunny jumped up. "I came all this way. For you. I left Gabe in Vegas so I could come here."

Gene stood and flashed a smile at the three other men. "Excuse us, gentlemen. We need a few minutes with Susan." He took Gwen's hand, then guided her and Sunny into the housekeeper's bathroom. He flicked on the light and shut the door. The room wasn't much bigger than the interior of Sunny's Mercedes. Her mother leaned a hip on the vanity. Gene stood in front of the door, hands on his hips. Sunny took the remaining spot on the bathmat in front of the tub.

He crossed his arms. "Who's Gabe?"

Sunny rubbed the flare of pain in her chest. "It doesn't matter now. I gave him up. I thought you needed me. That I could finally win your affection."

"Our affection?" Her father's eyebrows tried to rise. Failed. "We love you."

"Do you know I spent more time in here than I ever did in either of your rooms?"

"In the housekeeper's bathroom?" Gwen asked. Her forehead couldn't frown anymore, but her lips pursed.

"In her room. Nadia cared about me."

"We care about you." Her father put his hands on his hips. "We all went skiing together last Christmas."

"I spent last Christmas with my friend Cata in Columbus. I haven't been skiing with you since I was in college." Even then, her parents had stayed inside the lodge, signing autographs and being worshiped by their fans, while Sunny had hit the slopes. She'd made some friends, and it hadn't been awful, but it hadn't been the family vacation they'd promised.

Did her parents know what a family was? What Gabe had with his adoptive parents and what he'd already started to build with the Forzas? Or did they only know how to play one on film?

"Oh." Gene drummed his fingers over his mouth. "Who did we take skiing over Christmas?"

"Your costar from *I'll Die Tomorrow*. She's about Susan's age." Gwen stared into the mirror and smoothed a line beside her mouth.

"Ah. Right."

"It doesn't matter, Dad. It wasn't me. I was never part of your lives. I was only ever a—a prop." Her voice broke on the last word. She cleared her throat. "Like Bryce and Kai."

"That's ridiculous. You're our daughter."

"But I was never a priority for you. Not like your work."

"Our work made all this possible." Gene gestured at the tiny, outdated bathroom. "Well, not all *this*, but the house. The vacations. That big party on your sixteenth birthday."

"That party was full of studio executives and actors. It wasn't for me. And it wasn't what I wanted. All I wanted was time with you."

"You know our lifestyles make it difficult—" her mother began.

"I know. But I never felt important to you. Never good enough."

Her parents' expressions were blank. Did they not understand, or was it the Botox?

Gwen smiled, the bright one she used to use on her love interests in her movies. "But here we all are, together, now. You can have all the time you want."

"In front of cameras?"

"The cameras won't be here every day." Gwen tilted her head.

Disappointment settled onto her shoulders like the winter coat she didn't need in LA. "And neither will you."

"Susan, I think you have an overly romantic notion of what families are like. This is your family. We spend time together when we can. We care about each other."

"Do we, though?" Her lip trembled. The Forzas would have

been hugging by now. Lafortunes didn't hug. When they were together on the red carpet, sometimes her father would put a hand on her mother's lower back. They rarely held hands. She couldn't remember ever seeing them kiss other than a peck on the cheek for the cameras.

None of it was real. And she wanted real.

"I want more." She mumbled it the first time, and then she repeated it, louder and more clearly. "I want more."

"But you never asked for anything," her father said. "You've always been so self-sufficient."

Sunny tried to smile, but her face felt too heavy. "I had to be. I think you gave me everything you could. I mean, I want more from my life."

"Argus said you could go on auditions," her mother said. "And you should. You should take advantage of your youth. Your good looks." She frowned into the mirror and plucked at a silvery hair at her temple.

Suddenly, she felt like she was on one of those rotor amusement park rides and the floor had just dropped out. Nothing she'd thought she cared about—success, recognition from her family, even getting her next role—seemed important. She'd give it all up for one more of Gabe's hugs. To hold his hand across her Mercedes's console again.

"That's not what I want."

"What do you want, Sunny?" Her father leaned back against the door.

The answer was at the tip of her tongue like a line from a play she'd performed every night for a month. "I want to go home."

Her mother turned from the mirror. "But you are home."

"No. I'm not." Cata's apartment with its shabby velveteen sofa and the pipes that banged in the winter seemed more like home than the giant mansion. She'd had more fun singing with the high-school kids at Beach Island than she'd ever had on the set of *New York Bomb Squad*. And safe in Gabe's embrace, she'd felt more love than she'd ever felt growing up.

She hoped he could forgive her for failing to see it. For failing to accept everything he'd offered. For thinking there was anything else she could want as much.

"I need some cash. I'm going back to Ohio." She had the money she'd saved for the car repairs, but last-minute airfare for a cross-country flight was expensive.

"You can't leave now. What about the show?" Gwen flung out her arms.

"You can manage the show without me. I imagine Argus has a Plan B based on his focus groups."

Gene stepped forward and put a hand on her arm. "You'll be all right?"

Sunny smiled. "I think so." She'd done a lot of things on her own before, but this time felt different. Like a kite with a cut string. But the string had been her own creation. Now she was free to do what she wanted. And she wanted Gabe.

As she stepped outside the mansion to meet the crewmember assigned to drive her to the airport, a one-way ticket to Columbus saved on her phone, and cash from her father's wallet in her purse, a white convertible screeched to a stop on the driveway.

A tall blonde a few years younger than Sunny flipped her hair over her shoulder and tossed her keys to the valet. She tugged down her tight miniskirt and strode up the steps on tanned, svelte legs. Her eye makeup was almost as perfect as Rey's.

She stuck out her hand. "You must be a production assistant. Can you take me to Argus? I'm his new Susan."

Sunny laughed. Argus must have called her as soon as Sunny had stepped into the mansion earlier. "Nice to meet you, New Susan. I'm sure you'll be perfect for the role. One of the PAs inside can take you to Argus. I'm on my way home."

Chapter Thirty-One

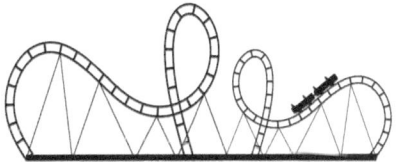

G abe held the résumé at a forty-five-degree angle to his desk, appearing to anyone who looked into his office—Darlene, mainly—to be evaluating yet another candidate for the park's entertainment director. But the type blurred in his vision. What was Sunny doing right now? It was early on the West Coast, so she was probably still in bed, her red-gold hair fanned out over her pillow the way he'd seen it those days in Vegas.

After today, he'd know the board's decision, whether he'd be staying to run the park or leaving. Whether he'd be shackled to Beach Island for the rest of his working life or they'd sell, and the freedom he'd tasted during the road trip would be his forever.

Whether he'd get the chance to find Sunny, ask her to give him another chance, or be stuck at his desk, two thousand miles separating him from his own heart.

A knock on the doorframe startled him. Darlene's eyebrows hovered low over her eyes, her smile turning over. "Are you okay?"

He set down the résumé. "Of course. Why wouldn't I be?" Besides the fact that the woman he loved was three time zones away, and if things went well today, he'd never see her again.

"Because you miss her."

"Miss...her?" He hadn't told Darlene about Sunny. She'd have told him to do something reckless, like get on another airplane—he suppressed a shudder—and track her down. Beg her to give him another chance. Even calling her would be reckless. What would he say? He couldn't make any promises until he knew the outcome of the board meeting. Gabe Armstrong was steady, dependable, predictable. He'd already used up his quota of reckless acts, if not for his entire life, at least for this fiscal quarter.

She folded her arms and leaned a hip against the doorframe. "Riley. It's Valentine's Day, and you're not with anyone. Holidays can make you miss people, even if they're not right for you."

Was that what was happening? He supposed in the back of his mind he knew it was Valentine's Day as he'd glanced at the giant bouquet of blood-red roses that had appeared on Darlene's desk sometime that morning. Maybe that's what had dredged up all these distracting thoughts of Sunny.

No. He'd been thinking about Sunny since the moment she'd slammed the hotel door in his face, through that pointless roller coaster ride, through the white-knuckling airplane ride, and the three days since. He'd snugged the stolen hotel pillowcase over his pillow to recapture her scent, the feeling of being with her, the calm that'd let him sleep so well in Vegas. It had only reminded him of what he'd lost.

Darlene's phone rang, and with one last, concerned look at him, she walked back to her desk. Gabe returned his attention to the résumé. The candidate worked in a high school theater program like the one Sunny had told him about. Had she reconnected with old friends? Had they helped her through the reunion with her parents? He was sure it had been fraught.

"Gabe?" Darlene was back at his door. "There's been a security issue. Someone climbed the employee entrance gate."

Kids did that at least once a week in summer. The only unusual thing about the incident was that it was February. Security usually escorted the kid out with a warning that they'd press charges next time. "And?"

"She asked to see you. Insisted on it, actually. Her name's Sunny—"

Gabe bolted upright, sending his chair spinning behind him to crash into the credenza. "Sunny's here?"

Darlene's eyes narrowed. "You know her?"

"Bring her in. Please." What did it mean? She was supposed to be in Los Angeles. Going to that audition. Getting her career back on track. Why was she in Ohio?

Darlene returned to her desk. Gabe glanced behind him at the chair and considered sitting down. They could be calm, civilized. She'd sit in the guest chair on the other side of his desk. They'd start with small talk, and then he'd ask her why she'd come.

No.

Gabe paced around his desk, glanced through the open door, and paced to the window. He repeated the circuit like a lion at a zoo, pausing each time he passed the door to gaze out. Darlene remained in her chair, watching him as if he made one more out-of-character move, she'd call 911. He must look like he'd been body-snatched. He ran his fingers through his hair, tugging at the roots.

Four minutes later, the office building's door clanged shut. Gabe strode to the doorway but froze like it had a yellow caution line painted in front of it.

Two uniformed Beach Island guards flanked Sunny. Her long hair was pulled back into a ponytail, and she wore her puffy pink coat over dark jeans and sneakers.

She took in Darlene at her desk before her gaze arrowed to him. "Gabe." Her eyes lit up in radiant blue.

Gabe didn't realize he'd moved until she was folded in his arms, the familiar scent of orange blossoms surrounding him. He breathed in, and his eyes nearly rolled back in his head. Sunny had come to him. She hadn't abandoned him, after all.

He nodded at the guards. "Thank you." He grasped Sunny's hand and pulled her into his office, shutting the door behind them.

She stood before him, her cheeks pink, but her smile faded. "I'm sorry I caused a commotion. I didn't think anyone would watch the gate in the off-season."

"Why—" Why had she come? Why hadn't she called? Why had she tried to sneak in instead of walking up to the guard at the front gate? The questions blocked his throat like too many people trying to crowd through a narrow doorway.

"I wanted to see you. Not just hear your voice on the phone. Be with you today if you needed me." She gazed down at the carpet, at the tip of her pink sneaker. "I'm sorry. Sorry I told Brandon your secret. Sorry I ran away from you. Sorry I didn't tell you I—I—"

He stepped closer. "What didn't you tell me?"

"That you're the only person I regret leaving. That I wish I'd stayed and we'd talked. But I was scared. Scared of what I felt for you. Scared that we'd turn into my parents." Her eyes burned into his. "I'm still a little afraid I'll be like them. But I have confidence in you, that you'll stop me. That you'll remind me what's important. Do you think you can do that?"

His chest clenched. Love and family were important. And Sunny knew that deep inside, or she wouldn't have raced across the country when her parents called. She wouldn't have stayed in Vegas until he'd reconciled with his siblings. And she wouldn't have come back to Ohio to be with him.

"I can. Sunny, I—" He stopped himself. He couldn't tell her he loved her. She'd feel obligated to, if not reciprocate, say more, do more, than she wanted. He couldn't put that on her.

She swallowed, the long column of her throat clenching. "I'm sorry I left you stranded in Vegas. How'd you get back to Ohio?"

"Mary gave me some nice drugs, and Rafe put me on a plane. It wasn't terrible." Except the taking-off part. And the landing part, especially when he was groggy and disoriented. "And I rode the roller coaster before I left. I thought you—" No. He wouldn't tell her about his pathetic search for her. "Maybe I can ride that one this summer." He nodded out the window toward Twister of Terror.

"You're the strongest man I know. You can do anything you set your mind to." An expression flitted over her face. Regret? Disappointment? Had she only come to apologize again, and this was the moment she told him goodbye?

No. He'd stall. "What happened with your mother's project?"

Her lips twisted. "Funny story, that. They're doing a reality show. Except none of it was real. They had a fake boyfriend for me. And a fake"—she gulped—"a fake brother."

He closed his eyes to shut out the pain on her face. "Maybe that was fake, but I'm sure their love for you is real."

"Not as real as what you feel—felt—for me. Or what I feel for you."

"What do you feel for me?" He held his breath.

Her gaze flicked to the window. "Life is short. Precarious. And I want to fill mine with joy and with love. Like your parents did. I love you. I want you in my life. I don't really know how to do this, and I can't promise I won't screw it up. I might hurt you again. I'll probably hurt myself. Still, I want to try. Can you trust that I'll try? That I love you?"

She'd closed the distance between them, and she picked up his hand, twining her fingers with his. Gabe was sandwiched between her and the door. His chest heaved. She loved him. He didn't know what it all meant, what she was offering. But he knew he couldn't take it.

"I can't." His heart ripped when he eased around her. Gently, he untangled his fingers from hers. He set his palms on his desk and leaned on it, his back toward her.

"You can't?" Her voice trembled. He was glad he couldn't see her face.

He'd been here before. Right here, in his dad's office. Mere days after his parents' deaths, his heart had been broken—like it was now —and the family had asked him to step into Luke Armstrong's role as CEO. He'd put others' needs ahead of his own. And today, he was doing it again.

"At the board meeting today, I'm going to try my hardest to

keep Beach Island independent and to remain as the CEO. Maybe they'll vote me down, but if not, I'm going to protect my parents' legacy. Do what they tasked me to do. Make Beach Island a safe place where families can come and make memories together. Our employees and guests need me."

He sucked in a deep breath. "You said you needed love and joy. And acting gives you joy. You have to go back to California. And I can't go with you."

Gabe's back was a slab of navy wool gabardine. Only his heaving breaths gave away the fact that there was a living human inside that suit coat.

Sunny had come all this way, risked falling and spraining something or else being arrested for climbing that gate, laid her heart out there on the faded office carpet, and he'd rejected her.

She deserved it. She'd broken his heart, and now he was breaking hers. He'd said, "I can't," and it was like that time she'd played Juliet and they'd put her inside the shroud. Her hearing was muffled, and although her eyes were open, her vision was limited to Gabe's back when he turned away from her.

This was why she ran. She'd never wanted to feel the rip in her chest, the sawing of her breath, the ringing in her ears. Had those guys she'd left felt this way? Had tears burned in Cade's eyes when she'd hurled his ugly necklace into the ocean? If so, it served her right.

"Sunny?" Her name came to her like a candle through fog. "Sunny?"

Gabe had turned so her unfocused eyes hit the buttoned front of his suit coat. "Did you hear me?"

"I heard you. You don't love me back." Maybe he hadn't meant it that night she'd pretended to be asleep. Or maybe he had, and now he couldn't get past the pain she'd caused.

"No." He laid his hands on the sleeves of her coat. She wished it wasn't so thick and that she could feel the warmth from his palms. "I do love you. But we can't be together. Not if the board sides with me and lets me stay. Not unless you'd be open to long-distance?" Hope shone in his brown eyes.

"No." She was nervous enough about starting a relationship without a three-month expiration date. She'd be sure to screw it up if she saw him only a couple weekends a month.

His broad shoulders drooped. "No?"

"No, I mean, I'll move here. I'll figure something out. Find a way to act and still wake up next to you every morning. I missed you, Gabe. I don't want to miss you anymore."

"You'd give up your dreams for me?"

"No, but I'll change them. For me. All I want is to perform, to make people happy for a couple hours. You were right. Mary, too. I was happiest singing karaoke with you. Singing at that piano bar made me feel more alive than I ever did on *New York Bomb Squad*.

"I need to be where you are. I can figure out the rest. As long as you're okay with having a girlfriend who *isn't* on TV."

"I'm very okay with that." His lips descended on hers, soft and strong, like Gabe himself. It was a closed-mouth kiss, yet it was infused with two days' worth of longing. And love. Every brush of his lips told her he loved her, and he'd love her as long as his heart continued to beat.

Her heart gave an answering thud. She wasn't sure about forever, but she was exactly where she wanted to be.

Still, she pulled back. "Hey, I believe you have some business to attend to."

"Yes. I do." He nuzzled under her ear at the spot that made shivers race across her skin.

With a laugh, she pushed him away. She'd do nothing but laugh with Gabe now that they were together. "Not that kind of business. You're supposed to be protecting your family's legacy."

"Right." His smile dimmed.

She knew exactly what he needed. She twined her fingers with his. "Remember how I told you family was important?"

"Yeah. The day you knocked on my door like a lunatic." But his mouth crept up at the corners.

"We're family now. And we're doing this. Together." Like she'd been doing since they met, she led him out the door and nudged him toward his future.

Epilogue

THANKSGIVING, LAS VEGAS

Sunny carried three bakery loaves of Italian bread under her arm —she'd checked with Mary to find the most authentic one in Vegas—and rang the doorbell. Gabe's bulk landed on the doorstep beside her. Perfume from the yellow roses he clutched filled the space between them.

"Don't be nervous. It's just—"

"Family," he murmured just as the door flung open.

"Why'd you ring the bell? You're family. Come in." Mary's apron crinkled when she crushed Sunny into a hug.

Rafe hulked into view. His apron had a splash of tomato sauce across the front. Sunny's mouth watered. He must be making one of his pasta dishes. He was the best cook of any of the Forzas, though he always denied it.

When Mary moved to hug Gabe, Rafe hugged Sunny. "Glad you came," he said. "Both of you."

"We wouldn't have missed it, would we, Gabe?" They'd seen the Forzas on opening weekend and again on Labor Day weekend, but they hadn't been back to Vegas. The park stayed open weekends through Halloween, and on weekdays they'd been busy preparing for the annual Holly Days. But Thanksgiving was for family, and Gabe had agreed to spend it with the Forzas.

"Wouldn't have missed it," he echoed. Despite the air travel that still made him nervous, he'd stepped up like the hero she knew him to be.

"How's everyone back in Ohio?" Mary asked. "Especially that cute cousin of yours, Brandon?"

"He's working," Gabe grumbled. "Besides, Brandon's off-limits to you. He's family."

"Hey now," Sunny said, smoothing a hand over his button-down. "He's *your* family, but he's not exactly Mary's. He's a catch." She hadn't thought so at first, when he'd threatened to vote Gabe out of the park's board. As it turned out, he only wanted what was best for Gabe, which, he thought, was taking the heavy responsibility of the park from his shoulders. But Gabe's shoulders were broad and strong, and when he'd reassured the family he wanted to stay and lead, Brandon had apologized and backed down. He'd felt terrible about the way he'd acted and begged Gabe for a way to make up for the hurtful things he'd said. So when Gabe asked, Brandon moved down from Chicago to accept a position as vice president of marketing. She winked at Mary. "Since Gabe brought him on, park attendance is up twenty percent."

"Because of you." He tucked an arm around her waist. "People are coming just to watch you in the shows."

She had a love-hate relationship with the heavy brocade Sunshine Queen gown she'd worn three shows a day all summer at the Beach Island Court of the Summer Sun Extravaganza. Sure, it'd been her idea to belt out hits from *Into the Woods, Camelot,* various other fairy tale–themed musicals, and of course, the band Queen. The gown may have been gorgeous, but in Ohio's summer heat, Sunny felt like a hot dog left too long on the roller.

For Gabe, the gown was an aphrodisiac. Countless times, he'd been waiting for her after the last show, his pupils blown in his dark eyes. After locking her dressing-room door, he'd hummed "We Will Rock You" as he went to work under her rustling, voluminous skirt.

Her cheeks burned, and she swatted his arm. "That's just you. Everyone else enjoys the rides, too."

"I ride the rides. Sometimes."

She smiled at the memory of Gabe squeezed into the new Mile of Mayhem ride next to Brandon. The on-ride camera had captured Gabe with his eyes shut while Brandon raised his arms, whooping. Sunny had framed the photo and set it on Gabe's desk. She sometimes caught him grinning at it.

A voice cleared behind them. Michael. Secure in his place in the family, he hadn't rung the bell. "Gabe, Sunny," he growled.

Gabe stiffened. But then Michael tugged him into a tight hug, and his shoulders eased down. Michael clapped him on the back and then, more gently, bent to hug Sunny.

When Sunny lowered to her heels in the small foyer of Mary's house, squeezed in among the Forzas, she knew she'd been right to make the trek with Gabe the winter before. In the end, it had all been worth it. Both Gabe and she had learned how they fit in with their respective families. His grandfather had explained that he'd known all along about Gabe's adoption, but he hadn't wanted Gabe to question his place in the Armstrong family.

Sunny had bumbled into his life and made him question it anyway. But in the end, her meddling had done something good: Gabe was a part of two families, the Armstrongs and the Forzas. And although she was still a Lafortune, she was part of Gabe's families, too.

And in that moment of clarity, she knew what she wanted. Beyond everything she already had, which included her job as Beach Island's entertainment director and the star of its shows.

It wasn't Hollywood or Broadway, but Sunny was the queen of Beach Island's small entertainment venue. And while many of the guests were only looking for an air-conditioned respite from the thrill rides and the scorching summer sun, most of them gave her cast of choir and theater kids a standing ovation at the end. Sunny was entertaining people the way she loved, working with a man she adored. She couldn't ask for more out of life.

And she wanted to hold on to that life forever.

"Where should we put our coats?" she asked. It wasn't Ohio-cold, but the temperature would drop by the time they left that night.

"In the guest room. Second door on the left." Mary pointed.

"I'll take them," Rafe said.

"No," Sunny said. "We'll do it. Pour us a glass of wine? Or champagne, if you have it?"

"Champagne? What are we celebrating?"

"I'll tell you in a minute." She handed the bread and flowers to Mary, then took Gabe's hand, towing him toward the guest room. She closed the door and leaned on it.

"Come here."

Gabe didn't hesitate. One arm out of his coat, he turned and stepped in front of her. She tunneled her hands into the thick, dark hair behind his ears and pulled his face down for a long, lingering kiss.

When she broke the kiss to drag in a breath, he grinned. "What was that for?"

"For you, Gabe. I love you and the life we've made together. The family we've become. Marry me," she whispered, the words just audible because her lungs wouldn't pull in enough air.

His eyes opened wide, and he released her hands. "What?"

She sucked in a breath like she was about to step out on stage. "Marry me." This time, her words came out loud and strong. This wasn't anything from a movie. Heroines didn't propose to their love interests inside a shoebox-sized guest room. But this felt real. And right.

"But I thought you didn't—"

She rested a finger on his lips. "I didn't. But, with you, I do. Our love is forever. And I want everyone to know it. You're mine, Gabe Armstrong."

He stood, proud and tall. "I'm yours. I'll marry you, Sunny Lafortune."

She threw her arms around his neck. "Tomorrow?"

He pulled back, frowning. "On Thanksgiving weekend? Holidays are about friends and family and togetherness."

"Who said that?"

"You did, the first time we spoke. Besides, we promised Mary we'd help her decorate the shop for Christmas."

She tightened her grip on him. "The next day, then."

"You really want a Vegas wedding?" His frown deepened.

"I want to be married as soon as possible. We're here." She shrugged. "It's perfect."

"You don't want bridesmaids? A white dress? Rings? Cake?"

She saw it, then. Those were things that Gabe wanted. His big, romantic heart wanted it all. Her own heart swelled, and she landed a gentle kiss on his lips. "Half of your family is here. I'll call my parents and invite them to come out. We can buy rings at one of the shops, and I'll even wear white if you want. I bet Mary knows someone who'll make us a cake. But what's most important is right here. Just you and me." She gazed at him, willing him to understand that she didn't have any romantic hopes and dreams to give up. That all she wanted was him. For the rest of their lives.

When one side of his mouth kicked up in a half-smile, she knew. He got it.

"No Elvis impersonators, okay? This is for real."

She tried to keep her expression serious, but her lips twitched. "Absolutely. And we can have a party or reception or whatever you want to call it when we get back home to Ohio. With more cake."

The other side of his mouth lifted. "I'd love that. And I love you."

"I love you, too." She pressed her cheek to his chest, feeling the low, slow thrum of his big, soft heart.

"Though Rafe does a pretty good Elvis impression," she joked. "What if he—"

"No. He's wearing a suit. No sequins or tassels." He gripped her tighter. "Our life is full of entertainment. We don't need more on our wedding day."

Our life. His and hers. Entwined together. Forever.

"Okay," she said. She shrugged out of her coat and laid it on the bed. Gabe laid his beside it.

"Take a deep breath, Gabe Armstrong. Everyone's about to flip out."

"They'll be happy for us." He paused. "Okay, maybe Mary will flip out a little."

"You know she will. But the important thing is that we're happy. Are you happy, Gabe?"

He crushed her to him again, and his heart beat loud in her ear. Still, she heard his next words clearly as a movie voiceover and remembered them for the rest of her life. "With you by my side? Always."

Thank you for reading! Did you enjoy? Please add your review because nothing helps an author more and encourages readers to take a chance on a book than a review.

And don't miss the next book of the *Forza Family* series, 4 WEDDINGS AND A FEUD available now. Turn the page for a sneak peek!

You can also sign up for the City Owl Press newsletter to receive notice of all book releases!

Sneak Peek of 4 Weddings and a Feud

It's not a bachelorette party until the woo-ing starts.

"Wooooooooo!"

Mary smiled when her passengers' yells penetrated the partition to the driver's compartment. But when the motor whirred to retract the convertible top and the sleek limousine started to sound like a human-powered ambulance, she knew the bachelorette party had taken a turn for the worse.

Not necessarily for the ladies partying in the back, but for the upholstery.

She glanced in the rearview mirror as she slowed to stop at a red light on the Las Vegas Strip.

Yep, the bridal party was standing on the leather seats, the petite blond maid of honor still wearing her stiletto heels.

Mary winced. Her brother was going to be *pissed* if she brought back Nick Cage with punctured leather.

The privacy screen was still up, so she couldn't simply holler back, "No shoes on the seats!" like her brother would've done. She put on the flashers. Ignoring the middle finger of the driver who zoomed around her, she got out of the driver's side, circled the front of the Escalade's hood, and stopped on the sidewalk next to the rear passenger door.

"Hey, ladies." She scanned each of the seven bridesmaids to identify the least-drunk one.

"Girl, I told you to keep the top on," a curvy Black woman said.

"I did! Look!" The blond bride, Bristol, glanced down at her shirt, which had "I'm the Bride" printed on it, not the most original slogan Mary had seen in many years of sending out bachelorette parties in the family's limousines. "No one's throwing beads anyway, not like Mardi Gras at home."

"Not *your* top," her friend said. "The limo's top."

"But I wanted to see the lights." Bristol pointed her champagne flute—Mary had stocked the limo with plastic, never glass for these types of parties—at the glowing Paris Las Vegas hotel. "I couldn't see the tippy top of the Eiffel Tower through the roof," she pouted.

"Ladies," Mary repeated, "it's not a good idea to stand while the limo is moving, but if you do, I need you to take off your shoes."

Finally noticing her, Bristol shouted, "Hey, Mar-eee!" She threw out her arms, knocking into her maid of honor, who toppled from the seat.

"Ooh, is she okay?" Mary leaned over the side of the limousine. The woman on the floor was the bride's sister, Mary recalled. Normally, she'd have memorized the names of all the party guests, but she'd had to step in for Rafe at the last minute, unprepared. All night she'd mentally called the maid of honor "Bristol's sister," which her exhausted brain had finally shortened into "Sistol." Sitting on the carpeted floor, Sistol swayed.

"Oh, hey, let's get you some fresh air." Vomit in the vehicles was the worst, and Mary couldn't spend hours cleaning and deodorizing the carpet tonight. She needed a good night's sleep for her big event tomorrow. She opened the side door, reached inside, and tugged Sistol onto the sidewalk. Her uncooperative pinky finger twinged, and she shook out her hand.

Perspiration glittered on the woman's pale forehead. "I don't feel so good."

"That's okay," Mary said. "I've got you." Gripping her upper arm, she shoved through the crowd of tourists and partiers on the sidewalk toward a trash can. When Sistol belched, Mary grasped her blond hair in one hand and pressed the other into her back, bending her over the opening just in time.

After emptying the contents of her stomach, too much booze

and hardly any food, into the bin, Sistol straightened, still pale. "Sorry, I..."

"Don't worry about it, honey." Mary rubbed a circle on her back, the way her mother used to do when she was sick. "It happens all the time. Drink some water, and you'll be better in no time." It might even be true. She couldn't be older than twenty-five. Alcohol treated Mary better when she was in her twenties. Now thirty-six, she'd have a two-day headache if she drank as much as these ladies had.

But why come to Vegas for a bachelorette party if you weren't going to get drunk off your ass, dance in the limousine, and scream until your throat hurt? It was all part of the package Forza Elite Motors offered, with a fully stocked bar inside the limousine for cruising the Strip until two A.M.

Someday, Mary hoped to get a larger cut of the wedding action, beyond transportation. Then she'd be able to focus on the party planning she loved and leave the driving to someone else. Plus, with the extra money coming in, her brothers wouldn't have to work such long hours. None of them were as young as they used to be. Fatigue led to injuries like Rafe's.

She glanced at her watch. Ten minutes until two. Time to wrap it up so she could snag a few hours of sleep before she had to set up her brand-new booth at the wedding expo.

Snugging an arm around Sistol's waist, Mary led her back to the group of women, who'd attracted a crowd of equally drunk men. Bristol leaned over the side of the limo and huffed at the short veil clipped to her rhinestone tiara.

Gently, Mary pushed herself between the men and the car and opened the door to let the still-pale Sistol inside. "Sorry, guys, can't you see she's taken?" She shut the door.

"Not yet, she ain't." The cowboy hat–wearing guy closest to the limo sucked on the straw of his glowing yard-long cocktail.

The drunken douche would've never talked back to either of her brothers. It was one benefit of their tank-like builds. "Afraid so,"

Mary said. "And her fiancé's a lot bigger than you. Think Jason Momoa."

"Whoa." The guy stumbled back.

The bride protested, "No, he's—"

"In fact," Mary interrupted, "it's time to get you back to him. Night, guys. Ladies, shoes off if you're going to stand on the seats." She checked that the women followed her instructions, then circled around to the driver's seat and punched the ignition. The engine purred to life like her brother Michael's cars always did.

Michael had offered to drive the party tonight. But he'd spent the day repainting his pet project, a '71 Mustang Mach 1, and the paint fumes always gave him a headache. Her other brother Rafe, who was scheduled to drive tonight, had broken his finger in the shop when a car hood had unexpectedly crashed down.

Rafe had argued that he could still drive with his splint, but years later, she remembered the agony of a broken finger. She'd been only eleven and all too aware of her family's precarious finances when she'd hidden her hand in the pocket of her school uniform skirt. It was only later, when the side of her hand swelled and she couldn't hold a pencil, that she finally told her dad what had happened and he took her to the ER. By then it was too late, and her pinky was permanently crooked.

She'd taken better care of her baby brother than that, driving him to the ER herself and putting the enormous deductible on her credit card. He couldn't drive tonight's bachelorette party with the pain meds, and none of their part-time employees were available that night. That left her, the co-owner of Forza Elite Motors, to do it.

Someday, if her plans worked out, they'd have full-time employees who weren't named Forza to pick up the slack. But until she'd achieved her dream of branching out into event planning, she was stuck as the backup chauffeur.

Signaling, she pulled the limo into the porte-cochère of La Villa. The hotel's location toward the end of the Strip meant it wasn't quite as crowded as the larger ones in the prime locations, but Mary was glad to see people entering the revolving door. She hoped it would be even busier when she came back in a few hours for the wedding expo.

She heaved her tired body from the driver's side, circled the hood, and opened the rear passenger door. The fresh air had done its job, putting color back in Sistol's cheeks. She leaned on a friend as she shuffled toward the door.

Bristol waved exuberantly. "Greg!"

The groom, a slender man no taller than Mary and certainly no Jason Momoa, scurried toward the limo.

Bristol bounded to him and all but fell into his arms. "Why aren't you at your bachelor party?"

"They're still in the suite watching...uh, a movie. But I missed you." He pushed his glasses up his nose. "Did you have fun?"

"The best time. Thanks to Mary."

Mary realized only then that she'd been watching the couple like a creeper. She busied herself by scanning the interior for forgotten shoes and handbags. She picked up a tiara, which had "MOH" spelled out in rhinestones.

"Can you give this to Sis—to your sister?" She held it out to Bristol, but Bristol was lip-locked with her groom.

Mary sighed. She'd seen some couples too caught up in strippers and porn to remember what they were celebrating during their weekend in Vegas. But Bristol and Greg were adorable. He'd left his bachelor party to check on his bride, and now they'd spend the night together.

Would she ever find a love like that?

She shook it off. She didn't have time for romantic love. Besides, she had all the love she needed from her brothers. Her family. And tomorrow at the wedding expo, she'd find customers for her new side hustle, enough to pay off Rafe's medical bill and maybe even enough to find the security they all craved.

Don't stop now. Keep reading with your copy of 4 WEDDINGS AND A FEUD.

And sign up for Michelle's newsletter to get all the news, giveaways, excerpts, and more at linktr.ee/michellemccraw.

Don't miss the next book of the *Forza Family* series, 4 WEDDINGS AND A FEUD available now, and discover all of her books at www.michellemccraw.com

LOVE IS A GAMBLE...

Her dream business. His Sin City empire. A reunion that could change everything.

Mary's got big dreams—starting her own event planning business, proving her brothers wrong, and escaping the rut of the family business. But when Alex Villa, the man who humiliated her on prom night, resurfaces in her life, those dreams might just be about to go up in smoke.

When Mary lands the high-profile wedding of the year in Las Vegas, it could be the career-making opportunity she needs. But there's one catch: the bride demands Alex's exclusive luxury hotel as the venue. Saying no would cost Mary a fortune—and possibly her reputation. Ignoring the unresolved tension between her and Alex? Not so easy.

Gone is the cocky teenager who broke her heart. Now, Alex is a powerful, enigmatic Vegas mogul whose presence still sends shivers down Mary's spine. The heat between them is undeniable, but so is the painful history that lies between them—one her brothers would love to settle... with a punch.

Working together is a gamble, but what if the stakes are higher than they ever imagined? When old feelings resurface, will Mary take a chance on love again, or is the man who shattered her heart still the biggest risk of all?

Please sign up for the City Owl Press newsletter for chances to win special subscriber-only contests and giveaways as well as receiving information on upcoming releases and special excerpts.

All reviews are **welcome** and **appreciated**. Please consider leaving one on your favorite social media and book buying sites.

Escape Your World. Get Lost in Ours! City Owl Press at www.cityowlpress.com.

Acknowledgments

This book is about family, and something they say about families is also true of books: it takes a village.

Thank you, Tina Moss and Tee Tate of City Owl Press for believing in this story. Thank you to Tee and Yelena Casale for polishing it into the version that's in your hands today. Thank you also to the designers, formatters, and other folks who I haven't met, but I know you also put your heart and hard work into this book.

Thank you to my agent, Amy Brewer, who had faith in me and my career. Thanks for your wise advice and for listening when I needed to talk so I could understand what I wanted for my publishing journey. Thanks for your support always, whether I'm self-publishing or working with a publisher. You are awesome!

Thank you to everyone who gave me feedback during the writing of this book. So many people helped me: Meka James, Lauren Accardo, Bella Ellwood-Clayton, and Maureen Moretti. Thanks also to Kristen, Dawn, Deb, and Laura for your feedback. Thanks, Michelle Rascon, who donated her time through the Romancing the Runoff auction to perfect my query package.

Finally, thanks to my friends at Central Ohio Fiction Writers, Georgia Romance Writers, and Contemporary Romance Writers for your encouragement and friendship. I appreciate you all!

About the Author

MICHELLE McCRAW writes swoony, steamy contemporary romance that just might make you laugh. Her stories center on characters passionate about science, engineering, and technology. A native Texan, she now lives in Georgia and enjoys reading, travel, drinking bourbon, and spoiling her extraordinarily ill-behaved but adorable dogs.

Follow Michelle on social media and get her VIP love notes for writing updates (and, not gonna lie, TONS of puppy pics) at linktr. ee/michellemccraw.

facebook.com/MichelleMcCrawAuthor

instagram.com/mmowriter

goodreads.com/michellemccraw

bookbub.com/authors/michelle-mccraw

About the Publisher

City Owl Press is a cutting edge indie publishing company, bringing the world of romance and speculative fiction to discerning readers.

Escape Your World. Get Lost in Ours!

www.cityowlpress.com

facebook.com/CityOwlPress
x.com/cityowlpress
instagram.com/cityowlbooks
pinterest.com/cityowlpress
tiktok.com/@cityowlpress